THE
BERLIN
WIFE'S
RESISTANCE

BOOKS BY MARION KUMMEROW

MARGARETE'S JOURNEY
A Light in the Window
From the Dark We Rise
The Girl in the Shadows
Daughter of the Dawn

GERMAN WIVES
The Berlin Wife
The Berlin Wife's Choice

Not Without My Sister
The Orphan's Mother

LOVE AND RESISTANCE TRILOGY
Unrelenting
Unyielding
Unwavering

WAR GIRLS SERIES
War Girl Ursula
War Girl Lotte
War Girl Anna
Reluctant Informer
Trouble Brewing
Fatal Encounter

THE
BERLIN
WIFE'S
RESISTANCE

MARION KUMMEROW

bookouture

Published by Bookouture in 2024

An imprint of Storyfire Ltd.
Carmelite House
50 Victoria Embankment
London EC4Y 0DZ

www.bookouture.com

ISBN: 978-1-83790-279-8
eBook ISBN: 978-1-83790-287-3

1

BERLIN, GERMANY, OCTOBER 1941

Edith Falkenstein was finally on the way to the destination she'd dreamt of. After begging her husband Julius for years to leave Berlin, at long last they were sitting together on the hard wooden bench of a third-class passenger wagon. An amused smile curled her lips. Even five years ago she wouldn't have considered traveling anything less than first class, or preferably in their own private limousine.

Alas, her formerly rich and powerful husband, one of the most influential bank owners in Germany, had come a long way —downward. For the mortal sin of being born a Jew, he had first lost his citizenship, then his bank and his beautiful mansion right next to Goebbels', and ultimately almost his life.

Alongside her husband, Edith, a pure-blooded Aryan woman with a brother in the SS, had been tumbling down the social ladder at speed, which had given her no time to process events.

She leaned back against the unpadded backrest, scrutinizing the other passengers in the crowded compartment. There was a mother with three small children, possibly being evacuated from the capital to the relative safety of the countryside.

Opposite her sat a dark-haired man in his forties in Wehrmacht uniform, no doubt on leave to visit his family.

A shudder raced down Edith's spine as she thought about her brother Knut, also a soldier, who had just turned forty. Obviously, Julius and she hadn't been invited to the celebration, despite Knut being the only family member with whom she was still on speaking terms.

The rest of her family had broken ties with her, or more precisely she with them, following her refusal to divorce her Jewish husband. Knut had driven them to the train station today, but he would never go up against their parents and risk a scandal by inviting Edith to a family gathering.

Please stay safe! She sent a silent plea to her brother and continued with her perusal of the other passengers. Next to Julius sat a man in a worn suit who continuously wiped his forehead with a damp handkerchief, in spite of the cold temperature in the compartment.

Edith cocked her head to better observe him, making sure he didn't notice her interest. Was he a smuggler? Or an illegal, someone making an attempt to flee Germany, like them?

At least Julius had managed to get the coveted permission to emigrate and all that it entailed. Even with his connections and the money they'd kept hidden, it had taken the better part of a year to secure an affidavit from his sister in London, a tourist visa to Switzerland, the approval for a visa to England, issuable in Bern, and proof of payment for the *Reichsfluchtsteuer*, a malicious tax destined to punish those who finally broke under the Nazi yoke and ran for their lives.

Edith had no doubt that every Jew left in Germany would soon be fighting for his life. Subsisting on food rations not even a withered old woman could live on, they were pressed into hard and dangerous labor, beaten up for sheer amusement, or refused medical treatment. Yet even harder times were coming. The elation she felt at finally being able to flee mixed with sadness over her friend Helga, whom she'd left behind.

"Why are you looking so forlorn?" Julius asked.

"It's just... I'm thinking about Helga." The Goldmann family—an interracial couple like Edith and Julius, plus their two half-Jewish children—did not have the means to pursue emigration.

"As soon as we've settled down, we'll write her a letter."

"Letters are not—" *carried between England and Germany*, Edith wanted to protest, but Julius muted her with a curt shake of his head.

She bit on her lips, scolding herself for being so indiscreet. One never knew who was listening in. Even though they were legally leaving the country, it wouldn't do to have blabbering mouths reporting an alleged crime to the Gestapo.

Or a real one, she thought bitterly as her gaze fell on Julius' chest, where no yellow star was visible. To counter the risk of trouble with their fellow passengers, they had decided he should carry his star-blemished coat carefully folded over his arm, only showing the proof of his "sub-humanity" when a patrol asked for it.

"We'll do as you suggest," she answered, closing her eyes for a moment to gather her thoughts and vowing to work on getting her friend out of Germany as soon as possible. Then she looked out the window, seeing how slowly at first, then ever faster, the skyline of Berlin disappeared behind them.

It would be a long ride, almost one thousand kilometers crossing the country from Berlin in the northeast to the Swiss border in the south. Thinking ahead, Edith had packed a basket with food and bottles of water, since she didn't know whether they would have time or opportunity to buy something along the way.

According to the ticket, they had to change trains three times in different cities with little time to spare. In any case,

Julius couldn't buy anything while wearing his star-stained coat and she didn't want to leave him alone, either.

The train stopped several times, resulting in more and more people crowding into the compartment until not only the seats but the entire standing space in between was packed. Soon the air became barely breathable, the people standing near the door leading to the aisle demanding to open the window. As soon as one of the passengers close to the window took pity on them, a piercing gust of wind blew in, causing goosebumps to break out on Edith's arms.

She wrapped her shawl tighter around herself, at once grateful and resentful of the cold air. Next to her, Julius moved as if wanting to put his arms around her shoulder, but for lack of space stopped midway.

Nonetheless, she cast him a grateful smile. This journey wouldn't last forever and, if it got them across the border into Switzerland, the discomfort and aggravation would have been worth it. She dreamed of a hot bath in the luxurious hotel Julius' sister Adriana had booked them into, paid for with money stashed away from the Nazis' greed years ago.

In Hitler's nation the Falkensteins might have fallen beneath the lowest criminal—as long as that criminal was a pure-blooded German—but elsewhere in the world, Julius was still a respected, wealthy businessman.

The train came to a screeching halt and Edith craned her neck to look outside, but her view was obstructed by people.

"Where are we?" someone asked.

"Difficult to say. Not in a station anyway."

They waited for at least half an hour before word got round that the train had been shunted into a siding to give right of way to trains transporting Wehrmacht soldiers to wherever the nation needed them most.

Edith looked at her wristwatch. Almost four hours had gone by, they should have reached Leipzig by now, where they were supposed to change trains. She didn't delude herself into believing the carefully planned connection would wait for them. A rush of anxiety raised the hair on her neck at the prospect of having to venture to the information counter and ask for another connecting train. She would have to do it without Julius in tow, since the self-righteous Reichsbahn employees would surely refuse to offer assistance to a Jew.

Biting her lip, she turned her head toward him, casting him a plea for help. It was such a peculiar situation she found herself in: during their twenty-plus years of marriage, he'd been the one to take care of their needs and organize their travels. How was she supposed to cope with the many issues liable to arise on such a long journey through a country at war.

Julius, despite having suffered ever-growing harassment during the past decade, gave her a slight shrug and mouthed, "We'll get there somehow."

Sometimes she admired his unshakable belief in law and order, at other times she loathed his tendency to shrug away all adversities. He didn't seem to fear the hassle of a conductor asking for their ticket or passport and taking offense at a Jew traveling on this train. Luckily, it was so crowded, the inspector would have severe difficulties pushing his way through.

Finally the train jerked into motion again and she let out a sigh. Every meter toward Switzerland brought them nearer to freedom. When they finally arrived in Leipzig, hundreds of passengers beleaguered the information booth, wanting to know about the next train going to wherever their destination was.

Glimpsing at Julius, Edith realized the long journey had taken its toll on him. Fast approaching sixty years and with deteriorated health due to the hard forced labor, his face was a pained grimace.

"I'd love to drink a strong, black coffee and perhaps smoke a Cuban cigar before squeezing these old bones into the next sardine can." Edith cast him an unbelieving stare, since these were unknown luxuries in a nation at war, until she recognized the black humor in his words.

"That would be nice, wouldn't it? For now we'll have to make do with a sip of water and some bread." She handed him a sandwich from her purse.

Carefully chewing the bread, she looked at the long queue in front of the information desk. "That'll take hours."

"There aren't that many directions for us to go from here. We could simply ask any person who leaves the counter until we find someone with the same destination," Julius suggested.

In awe of his clever idea, Edith was about to walk toward a man in a suit who had just left the information desk when Julius held her back. "Wait. Best err on the side of caution: don't ask for a train going to Switzerland."

"So, where are we supposedly going?" Edith didn't think it was necessary to hide their destination; after all, they possessed the necessary papers.

"Let me think. There are two routes we might take. Our original plan was to travel via Frankfurt, because it's the fastest. Since we missed that connection, we might as well travel via Munich and visit some old friends there. I for one would welcome a change of clothes the way this is going."

"You still have friends in Munich?" Edith asked, her eyes widening.

"Of course I do, we used to live there." Julius pursed his lips.

"But will our former acquaintances welcome us when they see your badge?" She never publicly mentioned the yellow star for fear of attracting unwanted attention.

Julius' chin fell to his chest, a picture of dejection and misery. "I guess some might."

"We can't afford to lose time finding out who's still with us and who isn't." Edith gave a sad shake of her head, then got up and approached the next person leaving the information desk.

The third one she asked told her there was a train going to Nuremberg within the hour.

When she relayed the information to Julius, he decided they should hop aboard. As long as the train went southward it would bring them nearer to the Swiss border and thus their freedom.

2

Knut remained on the platform long after the train with Edith and Julius on board had disappeared from sight, leaving an empty hole in his soul. He and Edith had been close, in spite of the wedge the Nazis had tried to push between them.

After what seemed an eternity, he turned to walk away, his heart numb with fear that he would never see his sister again. His mood worsened when he exited the station into a slight drizzle falling from the gray sky.

You should be happy for her, he scolded himself, knowing full well that she and especially Julius had no future in Germany while the Nazis were in power. A sense of guilt chilled him to the bones, for he was a Wehrmacht officer working for the Abwehr, the military intelligence service. His own complicity in the persecution of Jews weighed heavily on him.

The regime would have him despise his own sister for the crime of staying married to her husband. With a queasy stomach he remembered the gathering at the home of his other sister, Carsta, where their oldest brother Joseph, an SS-Sturmbannführer, had urged Edith to divorce Julius for the sake of family and Fatherland.

Even years later, shame for not speaking out on Edith's behalf burned its way to his ears, which must be flaming red by now. He hunched his shoulders, raising the collar of his Wehrmacht greatcoat against both the cold drizzle and the searing shame. Hands deep inside his pockets, he entered his car. As he settled behind the wheel, his gaze fell on the empty passenger seat where his scarf should be.

"I must have forgotten it at Edith's place," he murmured, retracing his steps in his mind until he was certain that was the most likely place. Giving a shrug, he set the vehicle in motion.

After being kicked out of their luxurious mansion on Schwanenwerder Island, the Falkensteins had moved into their city apartment two years ago. Not long after that they'd been forced to sublet rooms to two more families—the Goldmanns and the Gerbers—plus their former maid Delia, bringing the total number of occupants to eleven. He was banking on someone being at home to let him in.

Knut reached the correct floor just as a young man climbed down from the attic. The stranger turned and, noticing his uniform, stopped in his tracks, the guilt of being caught red-handed clearly visible in his face.

"Oh…" he said.

Knut slightly bowed his head in greeting to let the man know he wasn't there to cause trouble. "*Guten Tag.*"

Moments later a second young man climbed down. Knut recognized the newcomer as David Goldmann, the son of Edith's tenants. It took him only a split second to recognize that neither David nor the other stranger wore the obligatory yellow star.

"Has something happened?" David asked.

Knut had to give him credit for acting with such nonchalance. Maybe the best way forward was to ignore the compromising situation. "No. Everything went just fine. I delivered the Falkensteins to the train, but driving home I realized that I must have left my scarf here."

The other two men exchanged glances and David gave a nod.

"I'd better get going," the stranger said, racing down the stairs.

"Come in." David unlocked the door to the now empty apartment where earlier around twenty people had gathered to say goodbye.

"There it is." Knut pointed at his scarf hanging on the rack next to the door, where two jackets hung, the Star of David sewn onto them. Another pang of guilt hit him, because as a Wehrmacht officer, he was supposed to report all suspicious incidents. But how could he report twenty-two-year-old David, who had impressed him with his chutzpah coupled with friendliness?

David looked at him with caution in his eyes. Though he concealed his nerves well, Knut sensed the tension rolling off of him. David knew that he knew the two men had been doing something illegal up there in the attic.

"About what you saw just now—" David started, but Knut waved him off.

"Don't mention it." He looked down at the floor and then back to David. "I wear this uniform, but I don't agree with many things, especially the hate toward your kind."

David's set jaws visibly relaxed. "It's just... I'd appreciate if you would forget anything you saw in the stairwell. Not that it's anything criminal or so... just..." Judging by David's stutter, it was definitely criminal. If Knut were to make a guess, he'd say the stranger was an illegal in hiding.

A surge of compassion welled up inside Knut. Still reeling from shame for not standing up for his sister, he vowed to do better this time. "Listen, we've met each other only today and there's no reason why you should trust me. But for the sake of my sister, I want you to know that if you need help, anything at all, I'll do what I can."

"Thank you," David said. "I appreciate that more than you know."

Knut took a business card from his pocket and handed it to the young man. "Call this safe number if you're in need. Tell the telephonist that you have news for Herr Hesse from his sister. Don't mention who you are. I'll come here to find you."

"Not here." David cocked his head. "If I ever need your help, I'll wait the next day at noon in the Berlin Zoo in front of the elephant enclosure."

A smile spread across Knut's face. "I haven't been to the zoo for ages. Would be a nice change of scenery." Then he extended his hand. "Good luck, you'll need it."

"Good luck to you too."

By the time Knut returned to his own apartment, he had the distinct feeling that something had changed today. Edith and Julius had finally been able to leave Germany for a safer country, but something more subtle had happened too.

Something that was in close connection to David and whatever he and the other man had been doing in the attic. It was strangely exhilarating, yet very frightening. To distract himself, he put on a kettle of water to brew coffee. A good friend had connections to merchants in the Netherlands with limited access to real coffee beans. Soon, the enticing smell of freshly brewed coffee wafted through the room, calming his nerves as well as the whirlwind of thoughts in his mind.

3

Julius muttered a curse beneath his breath. That damn Hitler had ruined everything. He couldn't even take a train from Berlin to Basel without obstacles. After changing trains in Leipzig, it had taken them an entire week to finally arrive at the Swiss border.

Time and again the train had stopped and waited... for what, nobody knew. Rumor had it they needed to give priority to military trains transporting soldiers or freight trains sending much-needed equipment to the frontline, which was rapidly approaching Moscow.

Nobody in their right mind, least of all Julius, had believed Hitler would turn against his strongest ally, Stalin. Once again the Führer had defied reason and tumbled headfirst into a fight that he could not win.

Much to Julius' surprise, the Wehrmacht had advanced deep into Soviet territory, using the Blitzkrieg tactics honed during the invasions of Poland, France, the Low Countries and others. He shook his head. The Swiss border finally in sight, he did not have to worry any longer about Hitler's newest folly.

Once they'd arrived at their final destination in London,

he'd investigate whether there was anything he could do to help hasten Hitler's defeat. For now, he needed to put Edith and himself first.

"I can already smell the scent of freedom," he said to Edith as they disembarked the train in Basel.

She cast him a warning look, side-glancing at the other people around him. He didn't care. It was only a short walk from the platform to customs and passport control; on the other side they would board a train to Bern, where their English visas were waiting for them in the embassy—along with a heap of money in different Swiss bank accounts.

It wasn't only the smell of freedom that delighted him, but also the prospect of leaving years of poverty behind. The Nazis might have seized all his German possessions, but fortunately their arm didn't reach into the fortress of the Swiss banking system. Finally, Julius could live in style again.

"Passports please," the border guard in SS uniform asked.

"We have a tourist visa for Switzerland, as well as the proper paperwork to leave Germany, including the receipt for the *Reichsfluchtsteuer*." Julius handed him his and Edith's passport.

The border guard opened first Edith's passport, while scrutinizing her from head to toe, apparently making sure she was actually herself, before he stamped it and then proceeded to open Julius' passport.

In the exact moment the border guard's eye caught sight of the ugly red "J" for Jew on the first page, his entire posture changed. Where he'd been guarded, yet friendly, as he inspected Edith, his jaw tightened and his shoulders drew backward as he looked up at Julius. Following the nod of his head, another soldier stepped out of the sentry box. According to his shoulder flaps, the newcomer was a senior officer.

"A problem?" he asked, hovering his right hand above the weapon in its hip holster.

Edith's distraught gaze caught Julius' eye and he signaled her to keep calm.

"This man. He's a Jew," the guard explained, handing Julius' passport to his superior.

"What does he want?" the superior asked, much to Julius' surprise, because what could someone with passport and exit visa possibly want at the Swiss border? Especially a Jew, suffering from harassment in Germany. Certainly not chit-chat.

His tongue itched to deliver a witty remark, something he would have done years ago, when he had been a respected, wealthy businessman. Having been reduced to a supplicant for so many years, he suppressed his indignation and answered in his most pleasant voice.

"We wish to emigrate. As you can see, we have obtained an exit visa, the tax exemption and an entry visa to Switzerland."

The officer scoffed. "Yadda, yadda, yadda. None of this is valid."

"Excuse me?" Julius swallowed the lump forming in his throat, refusing to believe his own ears.

"She can pass." The officer pointed at Edith. "But not you."

"Excuse me, sir, this must be a misunderstanding. This woman is my wife, we are traveling together."

"Her bad luck."

Now Edith entered the discussion, giving Julius' hand a quick squeeze to warn him not to risk an altercation. "Officer, please, would you tell us what exactly is wrong with our papers?"

"Nothing wrong with them." He shrugged. "The day before yesterday, a new directive was issued, forbidding Jewish subjects to leave the country."

"But... we have the exit permission..." Shudders rippled down Julius' back, making him shake.

"All permits ceased to be valid the minute the new decree went into effect at midnight, which was"—the officer checked his wristwatch—"exactly seventeen hours and thirty-four minutes ago."

"But..." The officer seemed to be swaying, or was it just Julius' vision swimming? Breathing became difficult as the two SS men suddenly seemed to multiply, surrounding them. He blinked several times until they returned to their previous locations, yet their faces appeared bizarrely distorted. A swooshing sound caught his attention, getting louder until it morphed into an ugly cackling laughter. Finally, Edith's clear voice cut through the noise.

"Officer, can't you make an exception? Please."

"I'm sorry, *gnädige Frau*, my hands are bound. A law is a law."

Unable to utter a word or form a coherent thought, Julius witnessed with an open mouth how Edith pleaded with the border guard.

"We acquired all the necessary paperwork, paid the taxes due, endured a harrowing train ride across Germany just for you to tell us it was all for naught?"

"I'm really sorry. You should have traveled earlier. Your tax exemption was signed ten days ago, which gave you plenty of time to cross the border before the new law came into existence."

"Nobody told us about the new law." She groaned.

"Where would we be if the government had to alert each and every citizen—or non citizen," he added, with a side-glance at Julius, "about every new law."

Edith tried again. "We left Berlin on the very next day after receiving the permit. It isn't our fault that we arrived at the border a couple of hours late."

"Almost eighteen hours late," he insisted.

"We've endured a journey from hell, which took us more than week, having to change trains endless times, delays, diversions, everything. We even suffered several air-raid alarms, during which all passengers had to leave the wagons and find cover in the woods." Her pleading tone could have melted steel.

The officer, though, was unmoved. "It's not my fault that the Allied air pirates are threatening our population. You shouldn't visit the enemy, it's not right."

Julius found his sangfroid again and came to Edith's help. "Officer, you're right, we wouldn't normally—"

"I'm not talking to you." The officer cut him short, his expression indicating how much he loathed being in the presence of a Jew.

It hurt twofold: first, because the officer considered him a subhuman unworthy of breathing the same air, and second because Edith, a woman, was considered his superior.

"Please, officer, I beg you, our family is waiting for us just across the border. If we could at least let them know." Edith lied without batting an eye. Despite the grave situation, Julius had to hide a smile of admiration for his wife.

"As I said, you are free to cross the border, just not the Jew."

"I can pay," Julius offered, thinking of the diamond necklace and the matching earrings hidden in their suitcase. The earrings alone were worth more than what this man would earn in his entire life. It would sadden Julius to give them away, because the jewelry had belonged to his beloved mother, but if it paid for his escape he was willing to give everything away.

"Are you offering me a bribe?" the officer asked.

Measuring up the SS man, Julius opted for the careful approach. "Certainly not, officer. I was merely inquiring whether there is an additional permit that might require a fee."

The officer glared daggers at him, causing Julius to involuntarily hunch his shoulders. "Devious scum! I should arrest you for corruption!"

"Please, officer, my husband didn't intend anything malign." Edith put on a honeysweet smile. "We'd be indebted to you for the rest of our lives if you could find it in the goodness of your heart to let us pass, despite being eighteen hours late."

"I would rather gnaw off my right hand than be indebted to a Jew." The officer sneered at Julius, then turned to face Edith. "If you want my advice: cross the border to reunite with your family and leave your lout of a husband here. Our government will take care of him."

Violent shudders rushed down Julius' spine at the thinly veiled threat. He had suffered enough at the Nazis' hands not to know what kind of care the officer meant.

"When I married, in a *protestant* ceremony, I vowed to honor the insolubility of matrimony and stick with my husband through good times and bad." She smiled sweetly. "Therefore I cannot in good conscience heed your advice."

"In that case, unfortunately, you cannot leave the country either. And now, I must urge you to leave, as there are other travelers waiting." With these words he waved forward the person standing next in line.

Dumbstruck, Julius stood motionless until he felt Edith's small hand grabbing his arm and pulling him away. In that moment, he sensed a rumble beneath his feet, a foreboding of terrible, terrible things to come. Deprived of his hope to escape the country, all energy seemed to vanish from his body, trickling away into the earth like blood seeping from an oozing wound.

He followed Edith's lead like an automaton, devoid of the spark of life. Only when she nudged him to sit on a bench on the same platform where they had arrived a short time ago, his heart bursting with elation, did he fully realize that this might well be his end.

He buried his head in his hands and wept for the first time in almost sixty years of life.

4

In a rare moment of idleness Helga stared out the window, watching the raindrops slide down the glass. She'd never considered herself to be weather-sensitive, but recently the gray and gloomy sky affected her already subdued mood.

Over the last years her life had been on a downward spiral, getting more challenging by the week. A pang of nostalgia hit her as she remembered the happier times, before Hitler came to power and destroyed everything. Before the violence, the fear, the harassment, the ostracization. Before Jews had ceased to be citizens of the Reich and Helga's interracial marriage had become illegal with one stroke of a pen.

A deep groan escaped her throat. She should get up to wash the dishes. She'd always been a tidy housewife, but she now questioned whether it mattered. Who cared if the dishes stayed dirty? The floor smudged? What did all of these mundane issues matter when she constantly worried about the very lives of her husband Heinrich and their children David and Amelie?

At least their friends Edith and Julius Falkenstein had finally been able to escape this hell on earth. A tiny smile tugged at the corners of her lips. Two weeks ago they had thrown a farewell party and sent them off to a safer place. Helga wondered how long it would take them to arrive at their final destination in London. Any day now she hoped to receive a sign of life from them and, hopefully soon, the affidavit Edith had promised.

With that precious paper in her hands, the Goldmann family would finally be able to leave all of this behind. Helga had secretly bought an English textbook at a thrift store and had begun learning the basics of the language.

If she was to emigrate, she needed to make herself understood, because under no circumstances would she depend on the charity of the Falkensteins. Again, she thought fondly of Edith, who'd become a good friend and trusted confidante, welded together by fate even as they belonged to vastly different social classes.

Perhaps that was the one good thing Hitler had achieved: doing away with traditional social divides and making Jews equal—admittedly on the lowest possible step, barely considered human at all.

Helga sighed and turned away from the window. She didn't have the luxury to idle more than a few minutes; without her continued strength, her family had no chance to survive. Shuffling her feet, she walked into the kitchen, which had lost all of its former splendor, to finally wash the dishes. When that was done, she'd brave the awful weather and go hunting for groceries.

She was drying her hands on a threadbare kitchen towel when she heard a knock at the door. Instantly she froze. These days an unannounced visit was never a good thing. Her heart hammering against her ribs, she frantically searched for a way out.

Another knock, more forceful this time, roused her from her stupor and set her feet into motion. Halfway through the living room, she noticed that she was still holding the towel in her hands and tossed it into the kitchen, racking her brain as to who might be waiting on the other side of the door.

"Please, don't let it be the Gestapo," she whispered. Hers wouldn't be the first Jewish household to be searched.

"I'll be right there," she called out, suddenly afraid the visitor might otherwise smash the door down. Steeling herself for the worst, she looked through the peephole. "Oh my dear heavens!"

Barely able to comprehend what she was seeing, she turned the knob with a trembling hand. The door creaked open to reveal two dreadful figures, their fine clothes crinkled and dirty, their eyes bloodshot for lack of sleep, their faces a grimace of lost hope.

"Oh my dear heavens!" Helga repeated. "What are you doing here?"

"It's a long story," Edith answered. "May we come in?"

"Of course, how inconsiderate of me." Helga had a million questions on the tip of her tongue, but after one glimpse into her friend's exhausted face, she offered instead, "Please, sit on the couch, I'll brew coffee for you."

"Thank you." Herr Falkenstein limped to the couch and laboriously settled down.

Helga escaped into the kitchen, in need of a few minutes to process the shock. What on earth had prompted the Falkensteins to return to Berlin? Brewing the Ersatzkaffee, she cut two slices of bread, coating them with plum jam her sister Felicitas had gifted her.

Felicitas lived alone in the nearby town of Oranienburg, in a huge mansion surrounded by gardens with fruit trees. Notwithstanding belonging to the NSDAP party and being a fervent Hitler supporter, she loved Heinrich and the children as much as she loved her sister. If not for her generous support, the Goldmanns would have starved a long time ago.

"Here you go," Helga said, as she sat a tray with a plate and three cups of hot Ersatzkaffee on the coffee table. Curiously she inspected Herr Falkenstein, who was a mere shell of his former self. His once robust frame had wasted away, his piercing eyes had lost their liveliness. It was hard to believe that a human being could decline this much in a matter of two weeks.

She watched as he reached for the cup, bringing it to his lips with a trembling hand, seemingly costing him a lot of effort. Then she gazed at Edith, her old school friend, who had so graciously offered to sublet a room in her posh apartment to them when the Nazis had ruled that Jews must live in Jewish-only buildings.

For a while, they sat sipping their coffee, until Helga couldn't bear the silence any longer. "Why on earth did you come back?"

"It wasn't by choice. They guards wouldn't let us cross the border," Edith said, astonishingly calm for someone who'd just been denied a future.

"But... you had all the papers?" Helga's mind raced as she tried to process the gravity of the situation.

"Apparently a new law came into effect the day we finally arrived at the border, stipulating that Jews aren't allowed to leave Germany."

"What?" Helga doubled over as if someone had punched her in the stomach. Within a split second all her hopes of leaving this hellhole had evaporated forever.

Edith nodded solemnly. "Yes. We were turned away, along with many others. God only knows why the Nazis want to keep us trapped here, when all they're doing is making our lives miserable."

"I can't believe this is happening," Helga muttered, her voice choked with emotion. "What are you going to do now?"

"It looks like we're stuck here." Herr Falkenstein shrugged.

Edith cast a long gaze toward her friend, then said, "We came to you because we have nowhere else to go. If you haven't sublet the room already, we'd like to ask if we can move back in."

"Of course, it's your apartment—" Helga interrupted herself, since that wasn't true any longer. Herr Falkenstein had transferred the apartment to his sister Silvana Lemberg before leaving. The room they had vacated was supposed to be used as temporary shelter for Jews in need. "We had guests for a few days, but currently your room is empty. You might want to visit Frau Lemberg and inform her, so she doesn't send more guests."

Herr Falkenstein let out a groan. Giving her husband a sympathetic gaze, Edith said, "You stay here and rest. I'll go."

"Thank you, dear, but I can't expect you to make the trip all on your own."

"Don't be silly. I'll take the bus. When I'm alone, nobody harasses me on public transport."

Pragmatic as always, Helga's mind leapt to the next problem. "You need to register and apply for ration cards as soon as possible."

"I'll do that too, first thing in the morning," Edith sighed.

Moved by her friend's desolation, Helga put a hand on her arm. "For what it's worth, I missed you very much. Don't misunderstand me: I didn't begrudge you the chance to leave all of this behind, yet I'm happy to have you around again."

"That is the silver lining, to know we're not alone but have friends to help one another," Edith replied.

5

DECEMBER 1942

Chanukah, Christmas, New Year's Eve... the holidays passed without giving Edith much respite in the bleary situation. Reluctantly she had accepted that they wouldn't be able to escape the horrors Hitler inflicted on the Jews and had thrown herself into housework.

The same day she had registered them for ration cards, Julius had been pressed into work at a munitions factory, earning next to nothing. The money they'd stashed was running out fast, so she had decided to look for a job herself for the first time in her life—much to Julius' chagrin; he still thought a husband had to provide for his wife.

She shook her head in disgust. Thanks to the "mean little man"—the term she used to describe the Führer in private— nothing was the way it had been. Herr Dreyer, who had bought the Falkenstein bank and knew about Edith's organizational skills, had helped her to find a comparatively well-paid position with one of the bank's affluent clients.

Her new boss Daniel Kahn was a kind man in his sixties, who sorely needed someone to organize his social life after his wife had died from a stroke several months ago. He employed

Edith as housekeeper and somehow "mixed up" her paperwork so it referred only to her birth name, Frau Hesse.

"You can't possibly work as a servant," Julius protested.

"Why not? I have been cooking, cleaning and doing the laundry since Delia was forced to work in a munitions factory."

"Just because you know how to do these tasks doesn't mean it's appropriate. You're a Falkenstein—"

"According to Herr Kahn, I've reverted to being Frau Hesse."

Julius' eyes sparked with anger. "How dare he be so disrespectful!"

"You're doing him an injustice. In the current situation he wouldn't be allowed to employ me if it were known that I'm married to a Jew."

Julius clamped his jaw, his genealogy being a sore spot. "Still, you are a lady and shouldn't be treated as if you were less than one."

"We need the money." Edith didn't want to engage in the same discussion they'd had so many times about propriety. Ever since they'd been turned back at the Swiss border, Julius had retreated into himself, pretending the Nazis didn't exist. It was a constant sorrow for her to see him so desolate.

"We never used to need money," he mumbled under his breath. Edith's heart squeezed, recognizing how much psychological pain he was in. This situation was so much harder on him than it was on her. At least she was still—somehow—a part of society, whereas he'd lost everything, including his human dignity.

Fortunately, their argument was cut short when the door crashed open and the three Gerber children trampled inside. In contrast to the Goldmanns with their adult children, the Gerbers were much more demanding sub-tenants. Herr and Frau Gerber worked long shifts in a munitions factory on the other side of Berlin, which left the two boys and one girl, aged eleven, nine, and six, unsupervised most of the time.

They returned from school after lunchtime and spent the afternoons either shouting, fighting, trampling or dirtying something. Furthermore they seemed to be constantly hungry, gobbling up whatever little edibles they could find. Despite being malnourished, they grew much too fast, which was a dire problem, for the fully Jewish Gerber family didn't receive clothing cards.

"Look what we got!" Holger, the oldest, said, beaming from ear to ear as he stretched out his hands toward Edith.

It was refreshing to see the children happy for a change, yet Edith took a step backwards, raising her hands in defense. "What is this?"

The little furball in his hands squeaked, thrashing about with all four legs as it tried to escape from the hand holding it.

"A rabbit." Holger said.

"Aren't they cute?" Hertha, the youngest, added, fondling the furball in her arms.

Edith's eyes wandered from one child to the next, counting a total of three animals. "Where did you get them?"

"We didn't steal them," Hans, the middle child, assured much too quickly, giving Edith the impression this was exactly what they had done.

"You can't keep them. This apartment is no place for rabbits," Edith protested, sending a pleading look to Julius. She counted on him to raise his voice to the authoritative tone that always ensured he got what he wanted. He merely shrugged his shoulders, completely disinterested. It was another cause of worry for Edith; in the meantime, she had to attend to the more pressing issue of three rabbits possibly roaming free in the crowded apartment.

"They can live in the yard. We already built a cage for them," Hans explained.

"The yard?" Edith asked incredulously. "You mean our backyard? The tiny concrete space behind the building?"

"The rabbits won't mind."

"What are you going to feed them?" Edith desperately tried to reason with the children. Food was scarce enough, they certainly couldn't afford to give valuable vegetables to pets.

Hertha pushed forward her second hand, exposing a bunch of grass. The rabbit on her arm seized the opportunity and jumped down, escaping with a loud squeak and hiding beneath the heavy wardrobe.

"Oh dear." Edith had never owned a pet, thus she was at a complete loss as to how to recapture the little refugee.

The door opened and David, Helga's adult son, came in, his huge frame blocking the path. He assessed the situation in a split second and slammed the door shut before the panicked animal could escape outside.

The remaining two rabbits, clutched in the children's arms and apparently in uproar over the distress of their comrade, squeaked pitifully, scratching and scrambling to free themselves. David took them by the scruff of their necks and confined them in a hastily emptied drawer. Then he ordered Holger to bring the cage from the yard while luring the escaped rabbit from beneath the wardrobe with a piece of apple.

Once all three were safely stored in the cage, he asked the Gerber children, "What the hell were you thinking?"

"We just wanted to help." Hertha cast her eyes downward to avoid meeting his gaze. "At school there's this girl whose family raise angora rabbits. Her mother shears them every few months and makes wool from their hair, which she sells on the market."

Edith stared perplexed at the six-year-old. It was a brilliant idea. Back in the day, she had owned the finest angora underwear, which was both warm and fluffy, and commanded premium prices. Selling the wool would definitely make a difference to the Gerbers' income, especially if they exchanged it on the black market for children's clothes.

If they still lived in their Schwanenwerder mansion with the vast gardens, Edith would have agreed wholeheartedly to the endeavor. But here, in the center of Berlin? With only a tiny concrete yard?

"In theory, it is a good idea." She tried to sound as friendly as possible. "Unfortunately, we have neither the space nor the food for these little ones."

"I love Cuddly so much. I can't give her away." Big, fat tears streamed down Hertha's dirty face and her older brothers looked as if they'd join in any moment.

Since Edith didn't have children of her own, she was way out of her depth. Once again it was David who answered her silent plea for help and took charge. "No need to cry. We'll find a way. I suggest"—he looked to Edith for her consent—"for now we put the rabbits in the yard. When your parents return home from work, we can discuss a solution."

Instantaneously, Hertha's tears stopped and a smile stole onto her face. "Holger said we could go to the park every day to pluck grass and weeds."

"Tell this to your parents, will you? For now, let's take the rabbits down to the yard." David grabbed the cage the children had built from wood billets and cardboard, and carried it down the stairs, followed by Holger, Hans, and Hertha.

It reminded Edith of the fairy tale about the Pied Piper of Hamelin, and for a moment she wondered whether any of them would return. She shrugged off the ridiculous thought, since David was a wonderful young man who'd never harm the children.

Several minutes later he returned—alone.

"What happened?" Edith asked, alarmed.

"Nothing. The children decided to stay with their new friends and brush the fur so it will achieve a better price."

"It would be nice if they could keep the animals, God knows these children don't have much joy in their lives."

"We might make it work. Next to my workshop there's a vacant plot overgrown with dandelions, stinging nettles and other weeds. I can show Holger the way."

Edith nodded pensively. "Their parents will have to make the decision."

When Herr and Frau Gerber returned home from work late at night it was decided that the rabbits could stay—on probation. If it worked out, fine. If not, the animals had to be sold.

6

Knut was at home, having dinner with a dear friend, when the doorbell rang. Instantly the two of them sat up straight, their ears pricking at the sound.

"Are you expecting anyone?" Bernd asked, his mouth pressed into a thin line.

"No. Perhaps it's the *Blockwart* leader again." Knut swiftly brushed Bernd's shoulder, standing up to get the door. Every building had a *Blockwart*, whose duty it was to be a primary link between the population and the authorities.

"That woman is much too nosy. Last week she told you there was an air-raid alarm. Does she think you're deaf?"

Knut chuckled. "Or she's desperately in love with me?"

Bernd let this go without comment. When Knut opened the door, his jaw fell to the floor. This was the last person he'd expected to find knocking on his door.

"What on earth are you doing here?" Thunderstruck, he forgot his manners and stared openly at the petite woman in front of him.

"May I come in?" Edith asked.

"What? Oh, sure. Please." Still flabbergasted, he stepped aside to let her through.

She stopped, eyeing Bernd, who was still sitting at the table. "I'm so sorry to drop in like this, I'm Edith Falkenstein, Knut's sister." And turning toward Knut, she asked, "Is this a bad time, should I return another day?"

"No. Of course not. I thought, you were... Why did you come back?" Knut was finding it difficult to grasp the situation.

"I'd rather talk to you alone, if possible." Edith looked as composed as ever, yet beneath her impeccable exterior, he sensed her torment.

Bernd knew about Edith being married to a Jew and was sensitive enough to bid his goodbyes. "I was about to leave anyway, Frau Falkenstein."

"Wait... I'm..." Knut said lamely, not wanting his friend to leave. They spent little enough time with each other, since they could never be seen together in public.

"Don't worry. Family comes first. Give me a phone call." Bernd put on his uniform jacket and left the apartment.

"Who was that?" Edith asked.

"Just a friend." Knut wasn't going to burden his sister with his problems; she had enough of her own. Slowly he regained his composure. "Why on earth did you come back?"

In a very unladylike manner, reminiscent of their childhood, she flopped on the sofa with a mammoth sigh. "They didn't allow us to cross the border."

"But why not? You had all the papers."

"On the day we arrived, a new law came into effect, forbidding Jews to emigrate. So we had to come back." Her voice was dangerously near to breaking.

Knut had no answer to this.

"I don't know what to do," she whispered.

"I'm so sorry." Her terrible desperation hit him like a punch in the guts. He took a seat next to her on the sofa and drew her into his arms. Slipping out of her shoes, she leaned against him with her knees drawn up.

"What will become of us?" Her voice trembled treacherously.

"I don't know." In that very moment the fog of ignorance lifted and Knut saw with terrifying clarity the bleakness of her future. Julius and, by association, Edith were doomed. In Germany neither of them would be safe.

Though he wasn't privy to Hitler's plans for the Jews, Knut was certain they weren't pretty. Anyone who believed the current situation was bad would soon learn that it could become a lot worse.

He rubbed his hand across her back, at a loss for uplifting words. There was no point in trying to spare her the truth. Edith knew. He knew. Soon, every single person in Germany would know.

Hitler's Reich was no place for Jews. They weren't wanted here, yet now it seemed they weren't permitted to leave. What was going to happen to them? Looking at Edith's terrified face, his own brain closed down, refusing to think this through to the end.

"I have done everything I could to protect Julius. When he finally realized the danger and arranged for our emigration it was too late." A sob erupted from deep within her chest. "I don't know how I can carry on."

"Of course you can. You're strong."

"No, I'm not. All my energy has been used up, there's nothing left." With this she threw herself into his arms, bawling like a baby.

"Please don't cry, Edith," Knut repeated over and over, stroking her back. With every passing minute her sobs became more desperate until at long last she stopped. Knut offered her his handkerchief. "Here, take this."

After blowing her nose, she looked up at him, her desolation piercing Knut to the marrow. "We're done for."

"Don't say that," he pleaded, wondering how to instill some hope into her.

"You know we are. It's only a matter of time." Strangely enough, the realization of the utter hopelessness of her situation seemed to infuse her with renewed energy.

"Then make the best of your time." Knut felt compelled to say something wise. "None of us know how long we're going to be on this earth, especially now, with the war raging. So we must live every day to the fullest, enjoying what little or much time we're given."

"Since when have you become a philosopher?" Finally, a small smile appeared on Edith's lips.

"Since my friends started dying like flies." Knut had to bite his lip, remembering the many comrades missing or killed in action. He vowed to follow his own advice and enjoy life as much as possible, despite the circumstances.

"Thank you for listening." Edith dabbed at her eyes. "I needed this."

"You're always welcome to visit and I'll help however I can." Though there wasn't much he could do, given that he wasn't in a position to grant Julius status as protected Jew or otherwise guarantee his safety.

"I appreciate it." Edith unfolded her legs. "Where is the bathroom?"

"Over there." He pointed at the door to the left. It was the first time she'd come to visit his new apartment. When she returned several minutes later, only a keen eye could detect the traces of her tears.

"I'd better return home."

"Keep in touch." He handed her the card with his office phone number. "There's always someone there who can pass along a message to me."

"Let's hope I won't need it." Her hand on the doorknob, she

turned to look at him. "Would you please not tell anyone about my nervous breakdown?"

Knut couldn't help but grin. "Sure. My lips are sealed. Not even the Gestapo will pry your meltdown out of me."

"Don't joke about these things." She glared at him, then her expression softened. "I love you, brother."

"I love you too."

7

An icy wind swept up the dust, swirling a piece of paper through the air. Moments later, driving sleet hit David's cheek as he hurried across the street to seek shelter under the roof of the bus station. Pushing his hands deep into the pockets of his warm sheepskin coat, he waited with hunched shoulders for the bus to arrive.

When the bus approached, it drove through a puddle, splashing water onto the sidewalk. David would have been drenched if he hadn't taken a quick jump backward. As he boarded the bus, he quickly scanned the passengers for anyone who might recognize and denounce him for not wearing the obligatory yellow star.

When he disembarked two stations prior to his home, a particularly strong gust unbalanced him and he stepped into a puddle. Muttering a curse, he hurried into a side alley, where he put on his old dilapidated jacket over the sheepskin coat. Not because it would keep him warm—it wouldn't—but because this was the one his sister Amelie had sewn the yellow star onto. Then he stepped out onto the main street again, happy for the warm coat he'd inherited from Uncle Ernst. It was a fantastic piece of clothing, which he'd never have been able to afford on his meager salary.

Once, David had complained to the personnel department that even the untrained workers received higher pay than he did. Every time he reflected upon the answer, his blood boiled.

"Since you're only half-Aryan, you receive a half-salary," the manager had said with a smirk. Even David's boss, Baumann, hadn't been able to budge the vile man's opinion.

David arrived at the apartment. Despite the inconvenience of sharing one kitchen, bathroom and sitting room between three families, it was a luxury compared to how most other Jews lived, which David was thankful for.

As he opened the door, he found Frau Gerber in a terrible state. The usually composed woman who rarely raised her voice and strictly forbade her children to use cuss words, was waving a piece of paper and screaming, "That bloody bastard! Hasn't he caused enough suffering already? Now he wants us to freeze to death!"

Having spotted the imperial eagle on the announcement, David knew without asking who she was cursing. "What's it this time?"

Frau Gerber looked up, apparently unaware that he'd entered. "Oh, it's you, David." Suddenly all the angry energy flushed out of her and she seemed to shrink several inches.

"He wants our coats," she answered, handing David the sheet of paper.

"Our coats?" The poor woman must have gone mad; her statement made no sense at all.

David quickly read the text under the heading: "Collection Campaign for the Eastern Front". In a supposedly patriotic effort to help the Wehrmacht through the harsh Russian winter, all Jews had to turn in their fur and wool clothing, as well as skis, ski and hiking boots. No compensation would be offered.

"Patriotic, my ass!' David snorted. 'We're not even citizens of this oh-so-great nation anymore. Why doesn't he ask the Nazi scumbags to provide their coats for the good cause?"

For once, Frau Gerber ignored his cussing. "My children are freezing as it is, how will they cope walking to school without their woolen hats and jackets?"

"I'm not going to surrender my coat. They will have to pry it from my cold, dead hands."

"Who's robbing corpses of what?" asked Amelie, who'd just returned from work in a beautiful and warm fur coat—courtesy of Aunt Felicitas.

"Hitler." David glanced across at his sister. "He wants your fur."

"What?" Accustomed to playful banter from her brother, she jumped backwards, pulling the coat tighter around herself. "It won't suit him. He's much too big, and, if I may say so, unfashionable, for such a wonderful garment."

"It's not for him but for one of our heroic soldiers on the eastern front, who'd look absolutely stunning in a woman's coat." David grinned. Living in such misery, he found amusement in the smallest things. It helped him not to lose his joie de vivre.

Amelie furrowed her brows with suspicion. "If that's meant to be a joke, it's not very funny."

"It's no joke," Frau Gerber had recouped her aplomb. "There's a new regulation which obliges all Jews to surrender their winter clothing."

"That can't be true." Amelie shook her head. "Are we supposed to freeze to death on our way to work?"

David cocked his head. "I assume that would be a welcome side effect."

"Don't be silly," Frau Gerber scolded him. "The Nazis hate us Jews for whatever unknown reason, but they certainly don't want to kill us."

David had his doubts. Except for a few rogue SS men, the

government might not actively murder Jewish people, but they certainly wouldn't mind if all of them suddenly died—perhaps of hypothermia or starvation due to the minimal rations. To avoid an argument, he kept his thoughts to himself and shrugged. "It says fur and wool clothing, which means my sheepskin doesn't fall under the rule."

Amelie rolled her eyes. "It totally does, you know that."

"I'm not giving it away. Nobody will notice, since I don't wear—" Amelie, a good seamstress, had altered their jackets to be reversible, one side with the derogatory symbol, the other one free of it.

His sister hushed him with a quick nudge. Frau Gerber wouldn't approve of the siblings not abiding by the law.

By no stretch of his imagination could David fathom why Frau Gerber, along with the other adults in their household, adhered to the Nazi rules meant to ridicule and ostracize the Jewish population. If it were for him, he'd be up in arms, fighting against the unjust government. Alas, he seemed to be the sole warrior in an ocean of sheep doing as they were told, however demeaning, unjust or damaging it might be.

When the others returned home, the new atrocity was discussed and in the end it was decided to comply with the new rule, for the simple reason that they were afraid of the consequences.

David didn't admit it, but he, too, was afraid. Not for himself, because he knew how to find his way to and from work without running into a control, but for his father, whose health had been on the decline following his imprisonment at the Sachsenhausen camp after the Night of Broken Glass three years ago.

Due to their Aryan heritage, David's mother and Frau Falkenstein were allowed to keep their winter clothing. Therefore Amelie traded her precious fur coat for her mother's worn-out cotton jacket. Everyone else—except for David—piled their warm garments onto the table and it was decided that David and Frau Gerber would deliver them to the police station the next morning.

For the occasion he dressed not in his lambskin but a shabby jacket which offered little protection against the icy gusts of wind, even after stuffing sheets of newspaper between jacket and shirt.

Along the way, Frau Gerber bemoaned this latest measure, carefully omitting any mention of Hitler's name in case someone overheard them. "What will my little ones wear against the cold? Does this man have no shame?"

"Apparently not." David's answer earned him a horrified gaze.

"How can you say that? He's a human being, there must be some kindness in his heart. At least where children are concerned." Frau Gerber looked as if she wanted to break out in tears, which David found very discomfiting.

He himself had long ago given up trying to find rhyme or reason in the Nazis' actions—because the one time he'd stopped to question their motives, he'd recognized how sinister the trajectory was. If things didn't change very soon, the unlucky Jewish compatriots who hadn't had the fortune to emigrate would freeze to death or die of starvation or untreated sickness.

What he didn't understand was why, if it hated them so much, the government had forbidden Jewish people from emigrating. And that had been the exact point at which his brain had frozen, refusing to finish the train of thought.

"I sometimes wonder whether these people do have a soul or if they perhaps sold it to the devil for earthly riches and are now reduced to empty shells doing his bidding."

"You really should know better. While Satan is mentioned in the"—Frau Gerber lowered her voice to a barely audible whisper—"Talmud, he's not an actual being. In fact, *yetzer hara* is the sinful impulse every human is subjected to, tempting us to do wrong."

David pursed his lips. He'd been raised on secular virtues like honesty, empathy and kindness, and had attended synagogue or church exclusively during the high holidays of the respective religion. Before attending the Lemberg school for Jewish children he had never read the Talmud or spoken a word of Hebrew.

A lump formed in his throat as he remembered his year-long *hachshara* at the Zionist farm, where he'd learned farm work as well as Jewish culture and traditions, including a passable mastery of Hebrew. The *hachshara* was a training course to prepare young people for emigration to Palestine, but that ship had literally sailed without him. No sooner had he been given the coveted ticket than he'd fallen sick; another lucky man had taken up his passage.

He swallowed down the devastation he still felt every time he remembered the missed opportunity. If only... he'd be safe now, merrily working in a kibbutz. In the Promised Land he wouldn't have to worry about freezing to death without a winter coat or all the other antisemitic rules the Nazis issued.

He let out a deep sigh. Frau Gerber looked at him with kindness in her eyes. "The winter will soon be over and by next year things might have changed."

"I'm sure they will," David answered, expecting them to change for the worse. The only saving grace was, thanks to Baumann, he'd gotten his old job at the workshop back at the end of his convalescence. It was the best outcome possible, since Baumann knew he was a mixed breed but feigned ignorance and made sure none of the other workers found out. The factory owner and the accountant knew too, but neither ever stepped down into the areas where the actual work was done.

In front of the police station they joined the queue of wretched people waiting to give up their warm clothes. Once more, David wondered what would happen if the persecuted men and women banded together to oppose Nazi rule. Would the SS openly mow down thousands of protestors?

Alas, there was no way to find out, because the vast majority of Germans, not only the Jews, had been cowed into submission through years of brutal conditioning. The Gestapo had their eyes and ears everywhere, ready to pounce upon anyone who stepped out of line with the ruling party—or so the population thought.

After years of observation, David had come to the conclusion that the Gestapo was much too busy to pursue small fish. They relied heavily on the population to denounce their neighbors, colleagues, friends and even family members. Without the willing collaboration of the many informers, the oppressive government could not function.

Now, looking at the crowd of old, haggard, exhausted people, he discarded the idea of an organized protest. It was nothing but a dream. Not everyone was young and strong like him.

"We'd better get it over with," he said to Frau Gerber when it was their turn. He pushed the coats, hats, gloves, and scarves across the counter, where a policeman inventoried them and dutifully issued a receipt, the items listed in a neat handwriting.

David was about to shove the paper into his pocket when his gaze fell on the sentence written beneath the stolen goods: *Thank you for your contribution to the Fatherland!*

It took all his self-control not to go back and drive his fist into the policeman's jaw.

8

January drew to an end when Joseph finally returned to Berlin after extensive travels to former Poland, now called General Government district. He'd been sent by his boss, Reinhard Heydrich, to scout suitable locations for the huge concentration camps that would be needed to receive the mass of Jews being relocated from all over Europe.

They would be gigantic cesspools soaking up the subhuman waste thrown into them—far from German settlements so the population wouldn't have to endure the stench, or to look upon the inmates lest they should elicit uncalled-for sympathy. Hitler, with his usual genius, was going to kill two birds with one stone: he'd rid the nation of the Jewish pest, while exploiting their working power mercilessly to their last breath.

The locations had to be easily accessible by train. Not only to transport the subjects cheaply and quickly to their destination, but also, more importantly, to deliver the goods they produced to wherever they were needed.

"How was your trip?" his second wife Liesl greeted him as she opened the door of their beautiful home in Charlottenburg.

"Exhausting, my love." He kissed Liesl and proudly patted her huge stomach. "How is my child doing?"

"Growing." She smiled sweetly at him. "You must be so tired. Take a seat and let me brew you some coffee."

As she vanished into the kitchen, he settled on the couch. Liesl had been the perfect choice after he'd had to divorce his first wife Sandra, due to a Jewish great-great-great-grandmother in her lineage. Liesl had come highly recommended by a friend. Barely nineteen, she'd graduated from the Faith and Beauty Society with honors and had passed the rigorous tests required for the wife of a leading SS man with flying colors.

Mere weeks after their wedding night, she'd fallen pregnant with their first child, which was due to be born any time. Like all fathers, Joseph hoped for a son. Forgoing family tradition to name him after the paternal grandfather, he'd decided to name him Adolf in honor of the Führer.

If it turned out to be a girl, he'd honor Hitler's good taste in literature and give her a name from the Nibelungen Saga, a story the Führer adored and often called a national epos. The name he'd finally settled on was Sieglinde, the hero Siegfried's mother. The old Germanic name meant victorious, gentle woman; very befitting the daughter of an SS officer.

"Here's your coffee." Liesl approached him lead-footed. In contrast to Sandra, who'd flourished during her pregnancies, she seemed to have had a difficult time throughout.

Joseph wrinkled his brow, hoping she'd cope better the next time, because he intended to make his Führer proud and gift him a dozen pure Aryan children.

"Thank you. Would you like to sit with me?"

"I should prepare dinner," she answered, always putting her duties first.

"That can wait. I shall take you out tonight to celebrate my return," he offered, and patted the seat next to him. He was eager to tell her about all the great things he'd seen and done during his extended travels, obviously leaving out the gory details not appropriate for a delicate woman.

"By the way, your brother Knut has telephoned twice. He wouldn't tell me the reason, but he seemed eager to talk to you," Liesl said after raptly listening to his adventures for almost an hour.

Glancing at his wristwatch, he calculated Knut was most likely still at work. If Knut hadn't told Liesl the reason for his telephone call, it must be work-related. "I'll give him a call now. Will you change into something beautiful so we can leave for dinner as soon as I'm done?"

"Of course, darling." She heaved herself up the stairs, leaving Joseph with the hope the child would come soon, so she'd return to her normal, energetic self. Then he walked into his office, where he had a second landline, specifically for work-related calls.

"It's me, Joseph. Liesl said you needed to talk to me?" he greeted his brother as soon as Knut answered the phone.

"Yes, can I return your call in five minutes?"

"Sure—" Before Joseph could ask the reason, he heard the distinctive click in the line. He wondered why Knut was so uncharacteristically terse.

While he sat waiting, his mind wandered to the upcoming Wannsee Conference. He, along with Obersturmführer Reiner Huber, a delegate from another department, had been invited to attend the momentous conference as Reinhard Heydrich's personal assistants. No one outside the select circle of invitees knew the purpose of this conference: to deal with the Jewish problem once and for all.

Despite knowing Huber as an intelligent, upright man, Joseph had carefully expressed doubts on the man's suitability when Heydrich informed him. The Obersturmführer had recently lost his mother and father, the highly respected Standartenführer Wolfgang Huber, during a vicious attack on Berlin by the Allied air pirates. Joseph feared Huber might regard the Wannsee Conference as an opportunity to pursue a personal vendetta, rather than a forum dedicated to achieving an outcome in the best interests of the nation.

Proudly he reminisced about scouting locations for the huge work camps in Polish territory. Belzec, Sobibor and Treblinka would soon be known across the Reich as places where the cosmic order was restored. Each of them able to host tens of thousands of prisoners at any given time, they were going to cope with the hordes of Jews arriving from all over Europe.

He'd also visited Chelmno and left the place extremely impressed with the ingenuity of the department responsible for the Jewish solution. It was a widely known, if inconvenient, fact that even the most hardened SS men could only kill so many people at point-blank range without succumbing to mental problems.

Since a solution was sorely needed, the camp administration had been instructed to find more elegant ways to get rid of the vermin. They'd started a fascinating experiment: the subjects were squeezed into trucks and driven around. But not just any trucks: a clever engineer had sealed them air-tight and modified the exhaust pipes so that carbon monoxide was introduced directly into the sealed space behind the vehicle cab.

Inevitably after twenty to thirty minutes of driving, all the subjects in the back were dead. Joseph had had the honor to witness one of those tours. Expecting a nice and clean operation, he shuddered at the memory of the carnage once the back doors had been opened.

It was a sight he'd never forget, and weaker men than him had vomited right next to the truck. Despite the unsavory sight, the experiment was a success. To cap it all off, the prisoners themselves had been forced to dig their mass graves before being shoved into the truck. A select few prisoners had been granted preferential treatment in return for the gory task of throwing the corpses into the graves—after extracting their gold teeth.

Joseph's mind was spinning, trying to come up with an even more elegant solution that would eliminate the need for SS men to witness such ghastly scenes, when the telephone rang.

For a few seconds he stared at the black apparatus, trying to remember where he was. Then he took the receiver and spoke. "Sturmbannführer Joseph Hesse on the line."

"Sorry, but I couldn't speak in the office," Knut said.

"You sneaked out to call me from a public phone? What's so sensitive it can't be discussed over a government line?" Incredulity registered in his voice.

"Edith."

Joseph appreciated Knut's discretion. He'd been forced to disavow all ties with her, due to her stubborn determination to cling to that Jewish husband of hers. Her unwillingness to get a divorce for the wellbeing of the German nation was not only utterly selfish, it also put Joseph in a bad light. It might be the reason why he'd not yet been promoted to Obersturmbannführer.

Fortunately, that problem was solved. At long last his sister had emigrated and would never bother him again.

"Did she contact you from her final destination?" He refused to pronounce the name of an enemy country.

"She's back."

"Back where?"

"In Berlin."

Joseph needed a few seconds to absorb his brother's words. Her returning home could only mean one thing. "So, she finally left that husband of hers?"

"No, they're both back."

He muttered a curse beneath his breath. "Why on earth would they do such a stupid thing?"

"When they arrived at the Swiss border, they were turned

away by the border guards because of the new law forbidding... you know."

"I know full well! I was part of the group who drew up the rule! That's the reason why—" he yelled into the phone, only to stop himself mid-sentence. Not even Knut needed to know that Joseph had taken a huge risk and visited Edith last autumn to implore her to urgently leave Germany if she wanted to keep Julius safe.

"It seems they arrived the day after the law went into effect. Despite them having all the necessary papers, the guards wouldn't allow them to pass."

"Don't tell me you're still in contact with her."

"I am. She came to see me on her return. That's the reason I needed to talk to you, but your wife said you were traveling. How is she, by the way?"

"Fine. The baby is due to be born any day now. I returned early from my trip to be here when it happens."

"She didn't know how to contact you. Where have you been?" Knut asked casually.

Joseph wasn't about to be caught unawares. "Wanting to pry top secret information from me? You really should know better." It was an old game between them, to try and find out what the other department was planning.

"Can't blame me for trying." Knut snickered into the telephone.

"Seriously, you should disavow her. As long as she stays with Julius, the connection might harm your career."

"I don't give a shit about my career. She's my sister and if she needs my help, I'll be there for her," Knut protested.

As the oldest of four, Joseph was used to looking out for his younger siblings. He didn't care to remember how often he'd had to coax them onto the right path. "Look, I know you love her, I do too. But she's old enough to make her own decisions. Unfortunately, she has decided to stay with that husband of hers, to the detriment not only of herself, but her family, friends, Führer and Fatherland."

"You're exaggerating," Knut mumbled.

"I've done what I could to protect her for the longest time. I even bailed out Julius after his arrest. But enough is enough. Since she refuses to see sense, it is high time for some tough love. Let her sink to the bottom and then, when she finally repents, we can elevate her again into the midst of the German Volksgemeinschaft." While Joseph secretly feared it would soon be too late for her to escape the just punishment of enablers for the Jewish pest, he would never give up hope. She was his sister, after all.

"If you say so." Knut sounded unconvinced.

"Sorry, Knut, but I need to get changed. I want to take Liesl out to dinner to celebrate my return from the General Government district."

"Thanks for the info," Knut snickered, making Joseph aware of his lapse.

He shrugged. Knut couldn't begin to imagine the real purpose of his trip.

9

It had been the coldest winter in decades and Julius sighed with relief when finally the days grew longer and the sunshine returned. If winter had really been exceptionally cold, or if it was a subjective experience due to not owning a warm coat, he did not know and didn't care.

He had always been proud of his keen ability to assess a situation and take appropriate preventative measures to counter a major crisis. He'd weathered the First World War, the great depression, the short time of upswing, but never in his wildest dreams—or rather nightmares—could he have foreseen the atrocities Hitler had unleashed on the Jews.

After the unsuccessful attempt to emigrate, he'd completely lost his will to live. As far as he was concerned, Edith should have left him at the border to rot and escaped alone. Inexplicably that stubborn woman had refused the chance to live a comfortable life with his sister Adriana in London, or in a chalet in the Swiss mountains, or wherever her heart desired. Instead, she had chosen to return to misery by his side in Berlin.

Often at night he woke up screaming. The nightmares he'd

experienced after his time in the Sachsenhausen concentration camp tormented him once more, but this time they were of a different nature.

Over and over he saw Edith being beaten or drowned, and all the while she had a millstone round her neck. When Julius tried to disentangle her from it, he saw his own face engraved on the millstone. Then he woke up and screamed.

"Shush. You had a nightmare." Edith sat up straight in the bed beside him, grabbing the thermos with a hot infusion she always kept on her nightstand. "Here, drink this."

He groaned with desperation. If anything happened to her, it would be his fault, and his fault alone. This certainty weighed so heavily on his conscience, he struggled to breathe. "You should leave the country, it's not too late. They'll let you go."

"Nonsense," Edith protested. "Without me, who knows what they'll do to you."

Throughout the past months, the Nazis had issued a succession of new rules to denigrate the Jews: they had to mark their houses with a yellow star, they weren't allowed to use public transport except with special permission to travel to work. And then came the ominous orders to assemble for relocation to the East.

Knowing the Nazis, there was a sinister reason behind it, yet many, especially young people, had welcomed the opportunity to eke out a better living on farmland deep in what used to be Poland. Where exactly, nobody knew, despite postcards arriving from the departed.

Stilted, and formal, yet glowing in their praise for the wonderful places further east, most of these missives spoke of hard, but rewarding work. The senders urged their relatives to join them, since there was enough space and food for everyone.

Julius had been shown some of these postcards by acquaintances. The wording struck him as eerily similar. But then, how much could one write about a piece of land that had to be cultivated?

He slept fitfully for a couple more hours, then got up to eat breakfast with Edith.

"Julius, are you sure you want to accompany me?" Edith asked, as she readied herself to go to the State Library, where she was going to borrow a book for Silvana.

"I do. She's my sister, after all, and there's a book I need for myself. I've been mulling over a financial problem for weeks without finding a solution."

If Edith was surprised at his upbeat tone, she didn't show it. "I'm afraid they won't let you enter the library."

"I know." He clamped his jaw. Another humiliating rule. Considered subhumans, Jews apparently had no need for literature. "I'll tell you exactly what I'm looking for and wait for you outside." Rather than meet Edith's gaze, he stared intently at his shoes. The humiliation was worse than when he'd been a small boy and the librarian had told him that a coveted accounting book was too advanced for a child of his age. These days every book was considered out of his league.

"Then let's go, we don't know how long we're going to need for the trip."

Julius had a permit to use public transport, but only to and from work. Thus, they had to walk to the library. For a moment he considered asking David if he might borrow his bicycle.

Secretly he admired the young man's bravado in defying the Nazis whenever he could. Everyone in the household knew that David and his sister Amelie used reversible jackets to hide their yellow stars when they were out and about. It was no secret either that their mother almost died of grief every time one of them returned home even a minute later than the agreed time. Being caught without the star was punishable with prison time, or a ticket on the increasingly frequent transports to the East. It was debatable which was worse.

David, as was to be expected, had chafed at the prohibition on using public transport. Unlike other household members, he had not been issued with a special permit because his place of work was less than the required seven kilometers from his home.

To circumvent the nuisance, the ingenious lad had procured and repaired an old bicycle which he now used to get to work.

"It'll do us good to promenade in the sunshine," Julius said a bit too cheerfully. Under normal circumstances the distance to library was negligible and would take less than twenty minutes of leisurely walk. But thanks to another abhorrent law, Jews were forbidden to enter parks, and several major thoroughfares, including the main shopping street Kurfürstendamm, were out of bounds. Julius shrugged the thought away; even if he were to be issued ration cards for clothing, there was nothing to buy.

Last night he'd sweated over a map of Berlin, working out a feasible route from the apartment to the library. In the end they were forced to circumvent the enormous Tiergarten park, turning several times to avoid the prohibited streets and finally arrived, bathed in sweat, in front of the state library after a two-hour journey with numerous senseless detours.

Julius craved to sit down on a bench at the sidewalk, while waiting for Edith. Alas, for those brandished with the yellow star, even that wasn't allowed. Taking a handkerchief from his pocket to wipe the sweat from his forehead, he feigned nonchalance. "You go and get the books. I'll stay here and wait."

"Are you sure?" Edith's face was full of worry.

"I'm fine, now hurry up." As soon as she was gone, he turned the corner and settled on a bench that was out of sight from the street. Breathing a deep sigh of relief, he stretched out his sore legs.

A rebellious feeling made him smile. He was patently able to defy the Nazi regime, if only in such a small measure. Unfortunately, his luck didn't last longer than a couple of minutes.

"I'm so very sorry, but you're not allowed to sit here," an approaching policeman said in a surprisingly kind tone.

With as much dignity as he could muster, Julius rose to his feet. "Thank you for letting me know."

"It's a shame they do this to you," the policeman mumbled, and quickly disappeared.

Julius stared after him. If the policeman didn't agree with the harassment, why did he partake? A second later, shame burned its way up his neck, since he himself had never questioned a rule, however absurd or vile it was. Until recently, he had dutifully complied with every new atrocity the Nazis had thrown at him.

In hindsight, he realized the breaking point had come when the border guard had turned them away. Then, he'd finally stopped believing in law and order. Waiting for Edith to return with the books, he vowed henceforth to be more like David and less like a lamb being led to slaughter.

About twenty minutes later, Edith emerged from the library with an armful of books. "Is this what you needed?"

He scrutinized the three books she held out. "Yes, those are exactly the ones I need." Despite being anxious about the long return journey, he was in a hurry to get moving, eager to settle down into his armchair and prop up his legs.

As soon as they arrived at their apartment building, Edith set off on another errand. Without him in tow, she was allowed to use public transport to take her to Silvana's house. He would have loved to visit with his sister, but just thinking of a ten-kilometer walk made his calves cramp.

"I'll visit her another day," he said, knowing that he'd never manage to walk there and back in a single day. "Give my best wishes to Silvana and Markus."

"I will. Go and get some rest, I'll be home in time for dinner."

Enviously he watched as she boarded the bus—something

he'd never thought possible a few years ago. He well remembered how upset he'd been when the Nazis had forbidden him to use his own car and he'd had to use a tram for the first time in his life.

What he would give now to still be allowed to use public transport.

10

Amelie found Hertha in the backyard, cuddling one of the rabbits. They had grown dear to everyone in the household, providing a happy distraction from their dreary lives. But nobody had taken to them like the youngest Gerber child. Hertha had given each rabbit a name and spent hours in the yard, feeding them, brushing their fur and talking to them as if they understood.

Sometimes she staged plays, where the rabbits were the students and Hertha was the teacher. Other times Amelie found her taking one of the rabbits to a piece of greenery, which was strictly forbidden for Jews. She even used a home-made leash to take the rabbits on walks the way other people did with their dogs.

"Here you are! Your mother has been searching for you everywhere!" Amelie called out.

The little girl reluctantly put the fluffy animal back into the cage. "When is it time to shear their fur?"

"Soon, I should think."

"Won't they be cold?" Hertha's eyes were full of concern.

Amelie had to suppress a laugh. "On the contrary, I'm sure

they'll love to get rid of their thick fur now that summer is approaching."

"The nights can get chilly. Maybe I should make a blanket for them?"

"You do that," Amelie agreed. "But now be quick and rush upstairs to your mother or you'll get into trouble."

"On my way." Hertha raced away, leaving Amelie to watch her small figure disappear into the house.

How she wished to be as carefree as the little girl. Hertha seemed to live in her own world, devoid of hate or evil, just love and cuddles. Tears pricked Amelie's eyes at the memory of how happy she'd been at Hertha's age, before Hitler came to power. Back then, her world had been perfect. Her father had a well-paid job, and they'd often visited Aunt Felicitas in Oranienburg or taken weekend family trips to one of Berlin's beautiful lakes.

Never in her most horrible nightmares would she have dreamed up the horrors she currently faced. Absorbed in her reflections, she stroked the tame rabbits through the mesh of the cage. Her fingers caressed the soft fur, inducing a delightful sense of calm. At least for a few minutes the cute animals granted her the gift of returning to the carefree time of her childhood.

The rhythmic motion of her hand soothed both her and the animal, which relaxed in response to the touch, letting out a soft purr. Just like that, reality disappeared. Amelie lifted one rabbit out of the cage and cuddled it against her breast, burying her nose in its fluffy, soft fur. A smile at the simple pleasure appeared on her face and wouldn't leave her, even as she returned the animal to its cage.

Still smiling, she entered the apartment to find an inconsolably bawling Hertha. Both Frau Gerber and Amelie's mother stood next to her, looking worried.

"What has happened?" An icy fear crushed Amelie's soul, sensing that something terrible was going on.

Frau Gerber, usually not prone to emotion, and always eager to utter a fitting phrase from the Talmud, shrugged her shoulders, apparently unable to voice a word.

It was Helga who spoke up. "It's the rabbits."

"What have they done?" The affection shared with the animal still lingering, Amelie furrowed her brows.

"Nothing. It's just... we can't keep them." Helga was unusually evasive.

"These monsters want to kill Fluffy, Cuddly and Gizmo!" Hertha screamed at the top of her lungs.

"Who wants to kill our rabbits?" Amelie's eyes wandered between the sobbing girl and the two helpless women.

"Here, read for yourself." Helga handed her an issue of the newspaper *Jüdisches Nachrichtenblatt*.

Amelie never read that garbage, because it printed nothing but new antisemitic rules. Squinting her eyes, she skimmed the article, which announced that effective immediately the keeping of domestic animals like dogs, cats, or birds was forbidden to anyone obliged to wear the yellow star and to persons living in close proximity to them.

A shudder ran down her spine. "It doesn't say anything about rabbits."

Frau Gerber gave a tortured glance. "That's what I told the Jewish Cultural Association. They insisted that, while not explicitly stated on the announcement, rabbits definitely are pets and thus are to be surrendered to state-appointed veterinarians to be put down."

Hertha's bone-chilling scream threatened to shatter the windows. Amelie racked her brain for a solution, not only because she'd grown fond of the rabbits herself, but also because she couldn't withstand the girl's inconsolable grief. "We could give them away, perhaps?"

Helga shook her head. "As always, the Nazis have meticulously closed all loopholes for us. "Paragraph four says: a different accommodation of the pets, especially with third parties, is not allowed."

"How long do we have?" Amelie wasn't going to let the Nazis kill innocent animals.

"I was told to bring the animals to the Jewish administration next Wednesday. By then they will have nominated the veterinarians."

Another banshee-like wail came from Hertha's direction and Amelie walked over to console her. Crouching, she stroked her back and whispered into her ear, "We'll save the rabbits. I promise."

A hopeful light glittered in Hertha's eyes. "Really?"

"Yes, but you can't tell anyone, especially not your mother."

A knowing nod was the answer. Frau Gerber was honest to a fault and would never condone breaking a government rule, however unjust, stupid or cruel it was.

Later, when the adults were busy, Amelie and the three Gerber children thought about ways to rescue the rabbits.

"We could set them free in the woods," Holger suggested.

Amelie shook her head. "A fox might get them."

"Then in the Tierpark," Hans chimed in.

"That's not a good idea either, since they're not used to living in the wild." Amelie doubted the animals, which had been born and raised in captivity, would last more than a few days on their own.

Hertha was near to tears. "We can take them to the zoo. They care for animals there."

"I don't think they will accept rabbits." Amelie discarded the idea with a heavy heart.

After a long silence, Hans suggested, "What if we found someone to take them in."

"That's not allowed." Holger objected.

"That's correct, but"—Amelie cocked her head—"we don't have to tell anyone."

"You mean we give Fluffy, Cuddly and Gizmo to a kind person and don't say what we did?" Hertha's eyes shimmered with hope.

"Exactly. And I already know the person to ask."

"Who?"

"I can't tell you. But I promise your little fur babies will be perfectly happy there." Amelie silently prayed Aunt Feli would indeed shelter the rabbits, knowing it was illegal. She furrowed her brows in thought, then said, "So, here's the plan. Tomorrow morning, each of you will take one rabbit to school."

"To school?" Hans all but shrieked.

"Let me explain: I'll meet you halfway and take them. When you return home, you can tell your mother that you set them free so they wouldn't have to be killed."

"That's brilliant," Holger was impressed. "She needs to explain to the Jewish council why the rabbits are gone."

"You might get grounded, because you disobeyed a rule," Amelie warned them.

"I don't care, as long as Cuddly is safe." Hertha's voice was but a quiver. "Will you let us know once they are safe?"

"I will. And perhaps, a few weeks from now, we can go and visit them."

"That would be nice."

The next morning Amelie collected the three rabbits and put them into a covered basket. Having changed her jacket to wear the starless side out, she then took the train to Oranienburg to visit her aunt.

"Amelie darling, how are you doing?" Aunt Felicitas greeted her. After a disapproving gaze at her niece's chest, she added. "You really shouldn't do this. What if you get caught?"

"Ach, Aunt Feli, you know full well that I'm not allowed to use the train otherwise."

"You should have called me, I would have met you in Berlin. Anyhow, come in—and make it quick in case someone recognizes you." Feli ushered her into the huge mansion surrounded by lush gardens, which were in full blossom this time of the year.

Amelie's mouth watered as she imagined the delicious fruits and berries that would soon be hanging on the trees and shrubs. "I actually came her to ask you for a favor."

"I thought as much. But first, let's have breakfast." Felicitas called to her maid, "Laura, will you prepare a big, fat breakfast for my niece and serve it in the dining room."

After pondering how to best broach the topic, Amelie simply blurted out, "Our tenant's children have three rabbits that are destined to be killed if I don't find a good home for them."

"You want me to care for pets?" Felicitas Ritter had many qualities, love of animals was not one of them.

"Please, the children are heartbroken!"

"Is that what's rumbling in your basket?"

"Yes, do you want to have a look?"

"That won't be necessary." Felicitas raised her hands in defense as Amelie opened the basket and took out the beautiful light-gray Cuddly.

"*Gnädige Frau*, would you like coffee, too?" The maid stopped in her tracks when she saw Amelie holding the animal. "What a beautiful little rabbit."

"Not just any rabbit—an angora." Amelie seized the opportunity to bring the maid onto her side. "Would you like to cuddle her? You can't imagine how soft the fur is."

"If I may? I love rabbits." The young woman's eyes lit up as she patted the animal.

Out of the corner of her eye, Amelie saw her aunt's resolve weaken and decided to strike while the iron was hot. "Her name's Cuddly. She is super tame and, as her name implies, she loves to cuddle. Take her if you want."

Felicitas sighed. "Can they stay outside in the garden?"

"Thank you so much, Aunt Feli." Amelie flew around her aunt's neck.

"I didn't agree to anything, yet."

"But you would, if Laura took care of them, wouldn't you?" Turning toward the maid, Amelie pleaded, "These three babies need a new home. Their upkeep is minimal, basically all they need is a cage and grass to eat."

"I would love to care for your animals, provided"—Laura cast a side-glance at her mistress—"Frau Ritter allows. I would do it in my spare time."

Felicitas clapped her hands. "Well then. If you promise I won't have to lift a finger, they can live in the garden for as long as necessary."

Upon her return home, Amelie was waylaid by three children eagerly awaiting news about their furry friends.

"They're in good hands." She described the huge gardens, the soft grass, the comfy cage and the loving care they would receive.

Later that night, when the children had gone to bed, Helga came up to Amelie. "You wouldn't know anything about the disappearance of the rabbits, would you?"

"Me?" Amelie shrugged. "I've been out all day."

Helga scrutinized her with *that* motherly gaze, patently able to see through walls and innocent expressions like an X-ray. "I hope you know whom to trust."

"I do, Mutti, I do."

"I love you, my darling. Please be careful. It would devastate me if something happened to you."

"Don't worry, Mutti. Everything will be fine."

That night, Amelie went to bed smiling.

11

David had owned his bicycle for less than a month when yet another announcement forbade Jews to own or ride bicycles. Gnashing his teeth, he crumpled the paper in his hand and threw the ball against the wall.

"I'm not going to comply," he hissed under his breath.

"Please, David. I don't want you to get into trouble," Helga implored him.

"You can talk, you're still allowed to do everything! Nobody is taking away your rights!" He lashed out at his mother.

"David, darling. I get that you're angry, but you're being unjust. I'm suffering under the Nazi regime, too." The hurt in her eyes made everything worse.

The pent-up fury of several years, added to his shame at making his mother suffer, proved a volatile combination. Unable to contain his anger, David lashed out. "Don't pretend you're the victim here, because you're not! You are allowed to use public transport. You have higher grocery rations. You have clothing cards. You are allowed to enter the Tiergarten and sit on a bench. You aren't pressed into hard labor. It's not your bicycle they're taking away, and you certainly don't have to fear evacuation to God knows where! So don't you dare compare yourself to us!"

Tears shimmered in his mother's eyes, but he couldn't stop himself. "If you think your life is hard, why don't you walk to work with the yellow star on your chest just one time?"

"David, please," she pleaded.

"Oh no." He shook his head, his pulse ratcheting up until the only sound he heard was the blood rushing in his ears. "Not me. I'm not going to walk like a lamb to the slaughter. I'm going to fight. The rest of you can keep groveling to the Nazis and digging your own graves. I'm done!" He turned on his heel to flee the apartment, where the very air had become too oppressive to breathe.

His father blocked the way. "Not so fast, David. You'll apologize to your mother first. This is no way to talk to her."

His blood boiling, David had difficulties to see through the red haze. Years ago he'd overtaken his father in height, weight and strength, yet he would never consider pushing him aside. He balled his hands into fists, digging the fingernails deep into his flesh, taking several long breaths.

The red mist dispersed, but the rushing in his ears continued. He definitely needed to go outside and run off his ire. Yet his father would not tolerate him taking off in such a way, so he turned to face his mother, whose face was pallid from witnessing her son's meltdown.

"I'm sorry, Mutti. I shouldn't have raised my voice against you."

"Apology accepted," she said, giving him a loving smile. "Your agitation is understandable. I'm certainly not subjected to the same harassment you are, but you have no idea how much it pains me to see my family suffer."

Reminded of the reason why he'd become so furious in the first place, David needed more than ever to escape the apartment. "If you will excuse me, I need to take some exercise to burn off my anger."

His father, understanding how he felt, simply opened the door, and stepped out of the way. "Don't do anything stupid."

"I won't."

After walking aimlessly for hours, he returned home to a silent apartment. Not wanting to wake and confront his parents, he decided to sleep on the sofa in the sitting room. The next morning he rose before everyone else, took his bicycle and rode to work. On his way home he hid it behind some bushes a few blocks from the apartment and walked the rest of the way.

This worked well for several weeks, until one evening, after hiding the bicycle in the bushes and changing his reversible jacket to wear the star-marked side out, he found three young men waiting for him on the street.

"There you are, Jew," one of them said, spitting on the ground.

"Leave me alone." David had enough experience with brawls to know he was hopelessly outmatched. He tried to escape by sidestepping them. Unfortunately, a fourth man emerged from the shadows.

"We've been waiting for you, scum." To reinforce his words, the man slapped the baton in his right hand against his left palm.

Frantically searching for a way to escape, David's eyes wandered from the big man in the middle with dark curly hair hanging a bit too low into his forehead, to the blond, tall and slim man to his left, holding the baton in the hands. At that moment a flash of recognition hit him. Gustav had been a class-mate, before David had switched to the Lemberg school.

He swallowed hard, forcefully pushing the distasteful memories aside to concentrate on the present. His gaze fell on the scraggy figure on his right, more a boy than a man. His best chance of escape would be to dodge past the youth and run as fast as he could.

His train of thought must have been obvious, because the scraggy one said with a surprisingly deep voice, "Don't even think about it." Smirking, he directed his gaze toward the knife that had materialized out of nowhere.

An icy shudder ran down David's spine, recognizing that he was completely and utterly screwed. He couldn't even scream for help, because neither civilian nor police would lift a hand to help a Jew. It was much more likely they'd join in the beating—and a beating he'd receive, that much was certain.

"What you hiding there?" Gustav asked.

"Nothing." Still hoping to get out of the dire situation, David took a step back into the bushes until he felt the steel frame of his bicycle blocking the way.

"Aha." The big one smirked, walking toward David, until he'd trapped him between his huge body and the hidden bicycle. In the next instant, David screeched with pain. It happened so fast, he didn't understand how exactly, but his arm was twisted behind his back, leaving him unable to move without aggravating the pain.

The fourth man stepped into the bushes and returned with the bicycle. "If that Jew hasn't been breaking the law!"

David inwardly groaned. There was nothing he could do or say to improve his situation.

"I guess that deserves a punishment, don't ya think so?" another one asked.

"You can have the bicycle," David offered in an effort to save his neck. "It's worth a tidy sum."

"We aren't criminals like you, Jewish swine. We don't want your dirty bicycle, we want justice for the German nation," the small man said, adding with a smirk, "Although I think we'll accept your generous offer and keep the bicycle, so you won't break the law again."

Then they patted him down. David bit his lip, hoping something would distract the man twisting his arm long enough to allow him to squirm free. But he never got the chance.

Suddenly the grip on his arm loosened and David was sent flying to the ground, where he curled up into a ball, putting his arms over his head to protect it from the blows, punches and kicks raining down on him.

He must have passed out, because he found himself alone. Hurting all over, he somehow managed to crawl to the next streetlamp, which he used as support to stagger upright. Luckily it wasn't far from home and by superhuman effort he reached the entrance door, where he fell inside, unable to climb up the stairs. The lift had stopped working months ago.

It was his sister Amelie who found him there, throwing her hands up in horror. "Good heavens, what happened to you?"

"Some thugs stole my bike," he croaked.

"Can you get up?"

"I'd rather die right here."

Amelie put her hands on her hips, giving him a reproachful stare. "Not funny. Get up before Mutti comes home and sees you like this."

The thought of giving his mother the shock of her life pushed a bit of energy into his bones and he pulled himself upright using the banister as support. Amelie half-carried him all the way up to their apartment, where she led him into the communal bathroom and locked the door behind them.

"Except for a split lip and a scratch, your face looks alright," she announced after inspecting him. "Which cannot be said for the rest of you. Can you take off your shirt on your own?"

At the first movement he groaned with pain. "I guess not."

"I should cut it off, but since we don't have clothing coupons, I'd rather not." Amelie scrutinized him. "Sorry, but you'll have to put your arms above your head."

His body ached too much to counter with a quip.

Clenching his teeth, he obeyed, tears forming in his eyes when she ripped the encrusted material from his bloodied wounds.

When Amelie was done, she sucked in a breath. "Oh my dear God! They made mincemeat out of you."

While she rummaged in the mirror cabinet for something to clean and disinfect his wounds, he caught a glimpse at his bloodied torso, where black bruises were forming and red lines criss-crossed his skin.

"I'm going to clean your wounds. Hold still," Amelie warned him as she carefully dabbed a wet cloth against his skin.

It didn't hurt as badly as he'd anticipated and he let out a breath, only to hiss with pain the next moment, when the cloth reached an open wound.

"I'm sorry." Once she was done, she looked at him with sympathy and anguish. "You were lucky."

"Then I'd rather be unlucky I guess."

She cast him a desperate gaze. "Don't talk like that. You could have been killed."

"I wasn't." David refused to contemplate the possibility or he'd break down with fear.

Not giving an answer, his sister turned toward the cabinet to take out a vial of iodine.

"Don't you dare!" David backed off, groaning with pain at the sudden movement.

"It'll hurt just a bit." Amelie waved the iodine-soaked cloth in front of his face. If he weren't in so much pain, he'd shove it into her mouth.

"Like hell would be more accurate." He knew the awful sting from experience.

"I wouldn't use it if it weren't necessary. You don't want the wounds to get gangrenous." Her eyes met his. She might put on a brave face, but she couldn't fool him. It was obvious how worried she was about him. "Want something to bite down on?"

He nodded miserably. "Probably better. I don't want the

Gerber children calling the police because they believe you're slaughtering me."

"Here you go." Amelie handed him a towel and waited until he'd clenched it between his teeth before she went to work on his wounds.

He writhed, moaned, grunted, and gnashed for what seemed an eternity. When she finally stopped, the sweat was dripping from his forehead.

"That's it, you're done." When he didn't move, his sister carefully unclamped his cramped fingers, then helped him into the family's bedroom and dressed him in a fresh shirt. "You'd better get some rest while I wash your clothes."

"Thanks," he croaked.

Sometime later, Amelie returned with a bowl of hot soup and a piece of bread. "How are you feeling?"

"Much better since you stopped trying to kill me with that iodine."

She sat at the foot of the bed, watching him eat. "Do you know who they were?"

"One of them was a former classmate from the public school. I think it was a coincidence. Or perhaps they discovered the bicycle and wanted to find out who it belonged to." He breathed through a wave of pain as he swallowed a spoonful of soup.

"That's bad. Does he know where you live?"

"I don't think so. We moved after switching school, remember?"

"At last, some good news." Amelie furrowed her brows. "We'll have to be especially careful for a while. We should stop going starless."

David shook his head, groaning at the agony the movement prompted. "I'm not giving up. Ever."

"It would only be for a while. To make sure these people

aren't following you. After this beating, the last thing you want is to fall into the Gestapo's hands."

"The Gestapo can just piss off!" David's bravado was mostly show.

"*Ach ja?*" Amelie fell back into their usual teasing. "Shall I remind you of your pitiful wincing over a bit of iodine? What do you think the Gestapo will put on your wounds? Salt, perhaps?"

"I won't stop rebelling against them," he pouted.

"And you can continue to do so, all you want. As long as you promise to be more careful."

David silently ladled his soup into his mouth. When he was done, he handed the bowl to his sister. "Tailor a Wehrmacht uniform for me."

"What?" Amelie all but dropped from the bed.

"You work as seamstress in a uniform factory. Make one for me. It'll be so much easier to be inconspicuous."

"Under no circumstances! It's much too dangerous. For both of us, if we get caught. How do you think the police will react if they find out you're not really a soldier?"

"Thing is, they'll never find out. Have you ever seen a man in uniform being asked for his papers?"

"Yes. On the train. Or entering the Sportpalast."

"True. But they're never subjected to a random inspection on the street." David pleaded with his sister. "We need to fight back."

"That may well be, but not by doing such a foolish thing you're proposing. And that is my final word." She got up. "Get some sleep. I'll tell Mutti and Vater you fell off your bicycle."

12

"David fell from his bicycle?" Helga scrutinized her daughter with pursed lips. "You actually expect me to believe this?"

Amelie shrugged. "That's what he told me."

"From the bicycle he was supposed to turn in months ago?"

Again, Amelie shrugged.

"Did you know about the bicycle?"

"No."

Helga fixed her with an inquisitive gaze intended to remind her daughter how much she abhorred lying. "Really?"

"I might have suspected it."

"And you didn't see fit to tell your father or me?"

"David's old enough to do as he wants." Amelie clearly wanted to cut short the awkward interrogation.

"Not if he endangers all of us with his actions. What do you think will happen if the Gestapo pay us a visit because your brother broke the law?" Helga sighed. On days like this, it was all too much for her.

Whenever she tackled one problem, two new ones sprung up. The last thing she needed was her son engaging in shady activities and her daughter covering up for him. Not for a second did she believe his excuse. Even a cursory glimpse was enough to see that his wounds were the result of a beating.

"The Gestapo can do to us whatever they want, they don't need a reason for it." Amelie pouted.

"One more reason not to attract their attention. David's behavior is dangerous." She stared at her daughter for a full minute. "And yours too."

"Me?" Amelie gave her mother the most innocent gaze. "What have I done?"

"I know all about your shenanigans." Helga was too tired to argue with her daughter. Working a full-time job scrubbing floors at an insurance company, queuing up to buy groceries and doing her share of housework was exhausting, especially since Edith had taken up work and didn't pitch in at home as much as she used to.

The physical exhaustion she endured was nothing compared to the constant worry about her family. She worried about them every minute of every day, until, oftentimes late at night, the last of the three returned home.

She didn't blame her children for wanting to enjoy what little pleasures were left for them. At their age, she'd been dating Heinrich for four years and they'd spent their weekends enjoying picnics beside Berlin's lakes, visiting the zoo and attending dances, until they got married, settled down and had children.

None of these activities were permitted for Amelie and David. It broke her heart to watch her children being deprived of all the happy moments she and Heinrich had spent together or in their friends' company.

"I need to get going or I'll be late for work." Amelie pecked Helga's cheek, wrapping her arms around her longer than usual. "Don't worry so much, Mutti. David can take care of himself."

Despite being moved by Amelie's words, Helga sarcastically remarked, "I can see that."

. . .

When Helga returned from work in the evening, she found the apartment empty, save for Herr Falkenstein, who sat motionless at the table in the living room. She'd always been intimidated by his presence, feeling completely out of her league whenever she talked to him.

Not today. It hit her how much his appearance had deteriorated. Physically, but also mentally. In front of her sat an old and destitute man at odds with his fate.

"Good evening, Herr Falkenstein," she greeted him.

He didn't move or acknowledge her presence. Instead, he continued to slump in the chair, his right hand holding the *Jüdisches Nachrichtenblatt*. A presentiment of doom stabbed her heart. That newspaper never printed positive news. It merely announced the new regulations intended to increase the suffering of the Jewish population.

Torn between leaving Herr Falkenstein alone to wallow in misery and wanting to cheer him up, she carefully approached him. "Herr Falkenstein. What has happened?"

Finally, he looked up, his eyes empty holes in a haggard face, surrounded by unfashionably long hair, due to being forbidden to visit a hairdresser. Completely out of character for the elegant, worldly man he'd once been, he also sported a dark stubble on his chin and cheeks.

"This." He raised his hand as if the newspaper he was holding weighed a hundred pounds.

She took it from him and read the headline aloud: "Jews have to turn in all electrical and optical devices, including radios, cameras and typewriters." Her hand sank and she mumbled more to herself than to Herr Falkenstein, "How will we stay informed without a radio?"

He flinched as if she'd hit him, his head dropping onto the table with a thud.

Scared out of her wits for the old man's well-being, Helga let the paper fall, oblivious to the way it sailed elegantly to the floor. "Are you hurt?"

"No," he croaked.

"Can you sit up?"

"Yes," he said, but didn't move.

Unsure what to do, she ran into the kitchen to get a glass of water and held it out to him. "Here, drink this. It'll help."

"I don't want to," he murmured. "I'm a miserable failure."

"None of this is your fault." Helga settled on the chair next to him, sensing that he needed someone to talk to.

"But it is. I should have known." He gazed at her for a second, the tormented look in his eyes hitting her deep in the guts. "I studied economy and politics. I know everything about crises and how to avoid them. I've managed the Falkenstein bank for decades and yet... I dismissed Hitler as a harmless fool, his ideas as too radical to take root in the German population." He breathed laboriously, patently exhausted from his speech. "I was so blind! Why didn't I listen to Edith? Or to my sister Adriana? Why did I arrogantly believe I knew better than everyone else? I saw the warning signs and dismissed them, feeling myself secure because of my important position in the German elite. And what has become of me? An utter and complete failure!" He shouted the last words.

"Please, Herr Falkenstein. You're certainly not a failure." Helga tried to soothe him.

"Really?" He snorted. "Let's be honest here, Frau Goldmann. I'm a nobody. Less than a nobody. One of the most influential businessmen reduced to a forced worker in a munitions factory. Does that sound like an achievement to you?"

"You'd still be important if it weren't for the Nazis and their intention to eradicate every last Jew from public life."

Her assurance had the opposite effect to what she had intended. He shot up, his face turning beetroot-red, the vein at his temple pulsating violently. "I should have fought against them when it was still possible instead of complying! In addition to being an abject failure I'm also a coward. Hitler is right: I'm subhuman, unworthy to set foot on this earth."

"Herr Falkenstein!" Helga gasped in shock. "That's not true. You are a very valuable human being."

"If that is so, what do I have going for me?"

Helga wished she could find the words to console him. The way she'd done with Heinrich so many times. But Heinrich was her husband, her love, her soulmate, with him it was easy to say: *You have produced and raised two wonderful children, you've made me happy throughout so many years, you have brought smiles on the faces of your friends and you've helped so many of your bookkeeping clients to keep their businesses afloat. You are a wonderful man through and through, and for the lack of you the world would be much poorer.*

Unfortunately she couldn't say the same for Herr Falkenstein. Despite living as a tenant in his apartment, she didn't know him all that well. So she lamely protested, "You gave my husband a job when nobody else would. The Falkenstein bank has helped so many people—"

He interrupted her with a dismissive wave of his hand. "It's not mine anymore."

"You invited us to live in your apartment."

Another dry snort. "Because the Jewish Council forced me to. God knows, I would have preferred to live here alone with my wife and our maid."

That was news to her. It didn't matter. What counted was that he'd offered them a place to live when they'd needed it most, following the horrendous rule forcing all Jews to move into Jewish-only buildings.

"My family is very grateful to you," Helga said, hoping to get through to him.

"I doubt that." He stood up and walked into his room, closing the door firmly behind him.

Helga stood with her shoulders hanging for a long time, full of concern for the man literally trapped behind a closed door. Resolving to talk to Edith about her husband's mental struggles, she picked up the newspaper from the floor.

Another abomination to deal with after David's supposed accident, which had prevented him from going to work for three full days. For a few minutes she stood there, frozen in place with fear. Foremost for her family, but also for Herr Falkenstein and Edith.

13

Julius slumped on the bed, burying his face in his hands and grappling with his own irrelevance. All his life he'd been a powerful man, but now he was nothing. He couldn't even provide for his wife, who'd been forced to find work outside the house like a commoner.

Frau Goldmann's misguided attempt to console him had only reinforced what he knew to be true. To all intents and purposes, the Julius Falkenstein the world had known had ceased to exist. He might as well do the world a service and make it official.

The rest of the day, he moped around, barely enduring dinner with the rest of the household, except for Herr and Frau Gerber, who were working the night shift that week. Their children seemed not to mind, chattering along, grating on his nerves. Yet, no one, including him, admonished them for bad table manners, because the adults were too occupied with their own problems.

It confirmed his opinion that he had no value to offer. The world truly would be better off without him. At least the Nazis would be delighted if he took that unsavory task from their hands.

"I'll retire early," he excused himself and returned to his room, where he retrieved his mother's diamond necklace from the hidden safe to admire the flawless stones, reflecting the rays of electric light in all colors of the rainbow.

He caressed the precious jewelry, remembering better times, when his mother was alive and Hitler had been but a ridiculous Austrian with delusions of grandeur. This was how Edith found him.

"Are you sure you're alright, Julius?" She sat next to him, scrutinizing his face.

"No need to worry," he lied. "I'm just exhausted."

"Who isn't worn out by tribulations these days?" She said it softly, her voice laced with sadness.

In that instant he realized what he must do. If he was no more, Edith would be free.

He put a hand on hers. "If anything should happen to me, I want you to sell the diamond necklace. The proceeds will allow you to retire comfortably in Switzerland or anywhere else you might choose."

Fear crept into her eyes. "Don't talk nonsense. Nothing will happen to you. We'll get through this, just you wait and see."

Julius wondered when their roles had reversed and he'd become the pessimistic voice in their relationship, while Edith had chosen to blind herself to the warning signs and look unduly optimistic into a nonexistent future.

When he didn't answer, she added, "It can't get much worse than it already is."

"From your mouth to God's ears."

Her feigned confidence wasn't going to deter him from his plan to set her free. At breakfast the next morning, he casually mentioned Dr. Petersen. His longtime lawyer had all the necessary powers to deal with the Falkenstein legacy.

Then he tenderly kissed Edith goodbye and left for work. As usual, he ran the gauntlet of insults boarding the tram. Two stops later, two women entered. He recognized them; a week ago, they had been transferred to his factory.

Careful not to seem too friendly, he gave a curt nod. At the factory, fraternizing was strictly forbidden, so he knew nothing about them, not even their names. By their looks and behavior, he assumed them to be mother and daughter.

The older woman was an elegant blonde around Edith's age. Out of the corner of his eye, he scrutinized her appearance. The haircut and dress attested to years of poverty under the Nazi thumb. Imperceptibly he shook his head. Frau Artist, as he secretly called her, definitely possessed the demeanor of a middle-class woman. Her long and slender fingers suggested she might have pursued a career as a musician or an artist. The raw wounds and ugly callouses on her hands were a sure indication that she was unaccustomed to handling rough cloth all day long.

In contrast to the mother's average beauty, the daughter was stunning. She reminded him of Edith when he'd met her all those years ago at a dance. The magnetic smile, the gorgeous blonde hair, the enticing blue eyes. Unlike shy young Edith, Fräulein Stunning knew exactly what she wanted; there was an air of defiance about her, even when the foreman at the factory was barking commands in her face.

Not that the staunch Nazi cared; he was one of the few who refused to succumb to the beauty of a Jewess. In spite of official policy, Julius had observed more than one party member dallying with the forbidden fruit.

Lost in thought, he would have missed his stop if Fräulein Stunning hadn't touched his elbow, murmuring, "We need to get off."

"Thank you." He gave her a grateful nod, to which she responded with a magnetic smile.

Then and there he decided this was going to be the last

thing he saw on earth. He paused in his step, waiting for an approaching delivery truck to draw near, then launched himself into its path. A smile spread across his lips as he welcomed a rapid end to his suffering.

He hadn't reckoned with Fräulein Stunning. She must have intuited his plan and threw herself at him out of a misguided sense of helpfulness, somehow managing to roll him out of the truck's trajectory.

A crushing pain stabbed through his back as the truck came to a screeching halt next to his head. Sadness coursed through his veins at the realization his attempt to end his misery had failed. Even in taking his own life he was an abject failure.

But then, perhaps guided by God's hand, the truck lurched forward and everything around him went black.

When he opened his eyes, he saw Silvana's face. Disturbed, he quickly shut them. Recalling what had happened, he concluded that he must not have died after all, because Silvana certainly wasn't dead yet, waiting for him wherever a soul went to on the other side.

Still doubtful of his theory, he squinted half an eye open. There she was, sitting next to his bed, reading a book. But where was Edith? Shouldn't his wife be here? Some hard thing around his neck prevented him from moving his head, so he merely scanned his surroundings out of the corners of his eyes. He seemed to be in a hospital room. But where?

Something tickled his nose and he puffed hard to avoid sneezing, because his entire body hurt. That attracted Silvana's attention.

"Thank God, you're awake!" She set the book aside and bent over him, her beautiful brown eyes shining with worry. He couldn't remember ever having seen his youngest sister so anguished. "You gave us such a fright, Julius."

"I wanted to end my misery, and Edith's," he croaked, his throat dry as sand.

"Wait. I'll get you some water." She poured a glass from a thermos and held it to his lips. "Suicide is a sin. I'm so glad you didn't succeed."

He'd pondered that very issue before, and had come to the conclusion that a God who allowed the Nazis to commit atrocity after atrocity also permitted a man to take his own life, whatever religion.

"Where's Edith?" he asked.

Silvana's face fell. "They wouldn't let her inside."

"She's my wife." His thinking was still slow, so it took him a while to ask his next question. "Why are you allowed to visit, then?"

A sad expression appeared on her face. "Because you're in the Jewish hospital."

Still not quite understanding, he mused what being in a hospital had to do with his wife not being allowed to visit when his sister was. Then it hit him square in the chest: because Silvana was a Jew. Apparently the master race had to be spared from the ugly view this hospital presented.

By now he had noticed the shabby tapestry, the mold in the corners of the ceiling and the awful stench in the air. With much effort he angled his torso to look at the grime-covered linen on his bed. Well yes, the Jewish hospital certainly wasn't good enough for Edith to step inside.

He groaned. He felt like howling, since he knew he would never find the courage for a second attempt to end his life.

"A coworker of yours, Thea Dalke, saved your life. If it weren't for her, you would no longer be among us," Silvana explained.

"I shall thank her." Julius said it more because it was the socially expected answer than because he honestly felt grateful.

He was too overwhelmed by the pain in his body and anguish at the prospect of more suffering to come.

"You should. She got into quite the trouble for saving you." Silvana shook her head. "Apparently, she arrived late at work. Among other things, her salary for the day was withheld."

"Oh no." He hadn't wanted to cause anyone harm with his attempted suicide. Next time, he'd think it through properly before taking action. *There won't be a next time*, he reminded himself. Clearly fate wasn't about to permit him an easy way out.

Silvana settled into her seat again, and he looked at her thin face. The nose and cheekbones jutted out sharply and there were dark circles under her eyes. She used to be beautiful, ebullient, full of energy, now she looked old and tired. No doubt the constant harassment had taken its toll on her, too.

"Shouldn't you be at school?"

Her face turned into a pitiful grimace. "Not today."

Despite the pain clouding his mind, he was conscious enough to notice the unabridged pain in her voice. Something was off. He tried to calculate which day it was. He'd thrown himself in front of the truck on a Tuesday, so it was highly unlikely that today was the weekend. As far as he knew, there were no holidays, Jewish or otherwise, this month.

"Why not?" he finally asked.

"Oh Julius." A groan escaped her throat. "I wasn't going to tell you. You have enough problems of your own."

"Weren't going to tell me what?" He'd been right to be suspicious of the expression on her face. "Has something happened to Markus?"

"No, he's fine. It's the school." She paused, blinking a few times, before she continued. "Per decree the Nazis have ordered the closure of all remaining Jewish schools in the Reich. Furthermore compulsory education for Jewish children has been abolished."

He'd been expecting this for a while, had even warned Silvana not to engage in such a foolish endeavor as opening a Jewish school. "I'm sorry."

"You were right all along." Silvana was near to tears. That school had been her mission in life. She'd dedicated every ounce of energy to helping the students to prepare for emigration while it had still been allowed, afterward she'd devoted herself to supporting their families in every way she could. Sometimes simply by being there and letting her students cry.

Julius felt no joy in being proved right, for it was a bitter-tasting victory. "That doesn't matter anymore. What will you do now?" Even in his own precarious situation he still felt responsible for his sister.

"We don't know. Markus talked to the Ministry of Education, where he has a sympathetic contact. It seems the government is planning to turn the premises into some kind of holding center for homeless people."

People made homeless by the actions of the government, Julius thought bitterly, remembering how with a stroke of the pen, the Nazis had evicted tens of thousands of Jews from their homes two years earlier, when they'd segregated them into Jewish-only buildings and quarters. Generously he offered, "You can always move in with us."

At last, she smiled. "Where exactly would you put us up? In the bathroom or in the kitchen?"

"I guess the couch in the living room would be more comfortable."

They looked at each other, neither of them mentioning that, legally, Julius' apartment belonged to Silvana, since he'd transferred it to her name last year ahead of his attempt to escape Germany and emigrate.

"We'll see. Apparently we can stay for a few more weeks. And who knows, they might employ us to keep the homeless shelter running."

His eyes drooping, Julius found it difficult to keep the conversation going. His sister must have noticed, because she said, "You should get some sleep. There's a nurse making rounds twice a day, I'll let her know you are awake."

"Thank you. Could you please tell Edith that I'm sorry. I never wanted to cause her grief."

He watched Silvana get up, but by the time she reached the door, he'd already dozed off.

14

Joseph settled into his opulent office overlooking the Theresienstadt camp. Two days prior he had arrived at the beautiful town with his wife Liesl and his newborn son Adolf.

"Herr Sturmbannführer." An SS guard entered through the wide-open door.

"Heil Hitler!" Joseph stood, giving the perfect *Hitlergruss*, which his comrades of the first hour had invented back in 1926 when the SS was still called Saal-Schutz and worked as Hitler's personal lifeguard.

So much had improved since then, not only for Joseph himself, who'd risen from a peon to Sturmbannführer in Germany's most prestigious military unit. The only thing he regretted was that, due to the Führer's importance, Joseph didn't have direct access to him anymore like in the old days.

"Heil Hitler," the guard repeated. Both words and gesture were lacking in enthusiasm.

Joseph needed to organize a lot of training to mold this bunch of stolid men into the elite troop they were supposed to be.

"What's the matter?"

"The first transport has arrived. Would you like to be present to welcome them?"

Joseph almost choked on the sarcasm. The poor buggers arriving here had paid their entire life savings, or rather what was left of them, believing the so-called *Heimeinkaufsvertrag* purchased them a place in one of Theresienstadt's old people's homes.

Unfortunately, rumors about the true living conditions of those relocated to the East had begun to spread and Jewish subjects were increasingly unwilling to voluntarily embark on the journey.

Brilliant as always, his direct superior Reinhard Heydrich, the mastermind behind the final Jewish solution, had made plans to establish a "preferred ghetto for rich and famous Jews," long before the Wannsee Conference made concrete progress with the issue.

Theresienstadt ghetto had been chosen for several reasons, one of them being the relative proximity to the Old Reich. Compared to the camps in former Poland, it was about half the distance from Berlin. A second reason, important when trying to uphold the image of a better place to live in, was the more favorable climate.

Joseph shook his head. This had been one of the points of contention between him and Heydrich. Joseph hadn't seen the need for a preferred camp, since all Jews were destined for extermination anyway. Why squander resources on them that were urgently needed to equip the soldiers on the eastern front?

"Hitler and Goebbels want to avoid a public outcry under all circumstances," Heydrich had said.

"Sir, with all due respect, who would side with a Jew?"

"There are still people in the Reich who, for whatever misguided reason, feel sympathy for them. Not for the Jewish race per se, but for a member they know personally. A neighbor, perhaps, or a former professor, or even"—here Heydrich stared at him, wordlessly reminding Joseph that his own sister stubbornly clung to her Jewish husband—"a married relative."

Joseph pressed his lips into a thin line. Having a Jewish brother-in-law was a blemish on his otherwise spotless record. Nobody ever mentioned it, because he'd taken great care to keep his résumé clean, but Heydrich knew everything.

"To placate the weaker-minded members of the German community, it was decided to designate a preferential camp for war-decorated, rich or famous subjects. When the Jewish Council were informed, they seemed to be delighted." A cruel smile passed on Heydrich's otherwise completely expressionless face.

"Oh yes, there was quite the outcry as to how the elderly and physically handicapped people should survive the arduous journey." Indeed, the preferred outcome was that they should die en route, thus saving on paperwork.

"We assured them they'd get preferential treatment during transport as well. Second-class train cars, and then accommodation in an old people's home. The camp administration has spared neither trouble nor expense to take photographs to present to the Jewish Council."

"Really?" This was news to Joseph. Personally, he thought it was wasted effort to placate the subhumans, but he knew better than to voice his opinion. If Goebbels and Hitler agreed with spending money on Jews, who was he to oppose?

"Perhaps our most convincing point has been Theresienstadt's proximity to the famous bathing resorts of the Prague area. These fools toppled over each other, fighting over who got to sign the *Heimeinkaufsvertrag*, handing over their entire wealth without recourse."

"Brilliant." Joseph meant it. He had learned so much from

Heydrich, who'd proven to be a demanding boss. "The new arrivals are looking forward to moving into their retirement home, believing they have escaped the dreaded relocation to the East. Well, they are in for a rude awakening."

Returning to the present, Joseph looked at the guard. "Let's welcome our revered guests into our humble camp."

Theresienstadt might be better than the rest of the camps further east, yet quality in this context was relative. The entire setup was a sham. The beautiful façades of the buildings nothing more than a film set, which would put the Babelsberg Studios to shame, because behind the façade there usually wasn't even a building.

Striding toward the train station, Joseph heard the whistle of the locomotive and the screeching of tires as it came to a stop. *Räder müssen rollen für den Sieg, tires have to roll for the victory*, he thought.

Eradicating the Jews from the face of the earth was part of the master plan to resettle the entire world with members of the Master race after Germany had won the war. Then, paradisiac conditions would prevail and humanity would no longer have to constantly fight against the evil roots spreading and poisoning everything.

Joseph recoiled when the train doors opened. If this was the crème de la crème of the Jewish community, how was the rest? From the carts stumbled old, exhausted and frail people. Some barely managed to stand on their own feet and had to be supported by others.

It was a sorry crowd to look at. He inwardly groaned. He'd taken on this position in consideration of Liesl and his son, since Berlin was under air attack on a daily basis. Here, out of reach of the Allied terror bombers, she and the newborn were much safer.

Seeing the downtrodden people disembarking the train, he wondered if he'd taken the correct decision. Would he squander his talents supervising a camp for the old and frail? Oughtn't he be of more use to the Fatherland in another, strategically more important place?

His breath hitched in his chest as he believed he recognized Julius Falkenstein. A blink of an eye later, the illusion was gone and there was only an old man with white hair, shaking his head furiously at the discovery that his new surroundings bore no relation to the rosy picture of the Theresienstadt health resort with attached thermal baths. No old people's home with single rooms, care and nursing awaited him. Neither would there be shared apartments for couples, or a view of the lake.

Some seemed to realize faster than others that the whole thing was a complete fraud.

One man approached Joseph. "Excuse me, *mein Herr—*"

A guard came running along, swinging his baton in the air, but Joseph waved him away, ready to indulge the naïve bugger.

"What can I do for you?"

"This... this... this must be a mistake," the old man, dressed in a fine suit, which must have cost a fortune decades ago, huffed.

"A mistake? So did you not want to travel to Theresien-stadt?" Joseph bit back a laugh.

"I did. But this..." His gesture took in the ugly camp. "There's no lake."

"I'm afraid that's true. We never had a lake around here."

"But I was promised... here, have a look at my confirmation. I paid five hundred thousand Reichsmark for a lifetime stay in Theresienstadt in a single room with a view of the lake."

"That must be a mistake, you're right. There are no single rooms in our camp, and certainly not a lake view. What you can expect," Joseph raised his voice, conscious of the growing crowd of devastated Jews gathered around him, "are communal barracks, hard work and little food."

"No, that can't be." The old man blanched, starting to shake so pitifully, the receipt fell from his hand, wafting through the air like a feather until it settled on the ground directly in front of Joseph's shoes.

He stooped to pick it up. There was no need to read what was written on the paper, for he knew already that everyone arriving had been swindled into believing this was akin to a vacation, certainly not life in a ghetto. For a second he felt sorry for them, until he reminded himself that, however innocent and frail these people—*subhumans*, he corrected himself—they were a threat to Germany. The Führer had said so and the Führer was infallible.

To lessen the blow, he raised his voice again. "We have been forced to implement strict hygienic measures to all new arrivals. Therefore you'll be sent to quarantine barracks for a few days before entering the actual camp." He didn't mention that the barracks he'd so euphemistically referred to as *quarantine* lacked even the most basic furniture like beds or chairs. Among the guards it was known as "the sluice" and its sole purpose was to weed out those who'd succumb to sickness anyway—no need to process them into the actual camp.

Again, Joseph had to remind himself that the miserable schmucks standing in front of him weren't actual humans and empathy was completely uncalled for. Those strong enough to withstand the sluice were going to be assigned to overcrowded houses and pressed into mostly manual labor, though Jews possessing a special talent might be given work as painters, musicians or accountants.

About a quarter of the old people were expected to die of malnutrition, cold or disease caused by inadequate hygienic conditions within the first six weeks. The survivors strong enough to work would be allowed to stay in Theresienstadt, whereas the weak would undergo "a change in the present form of accommodation" to make way for yet more new arrivals. In

other words, they would be transported to the Auschwitz extermination camp.

But that wasn't something Joseph intended to dirty his
hands with.

15

Inwardly grinning, David checked on the new employees, mostly men above forty. If any of them knew that in addition to being considerably younger, their teacher also was a *Mischling*, mayhem would break out.

Once again, he silently thanked Baumann who always looked the other way when David arrived at the workshop without the yellow star on his jacket. When most of the experienced younger men had been called up, Baumann had found himself with just a handful of skilled mechanics, engineers, welders and electricians to run the ever-increasing operations.

David—or Kessel, as he was known at work—had been assigned responsibility for everything electric in both wagons and locomotives, thanks to his skills with electrical wiring and circuits.

Their entire department had moved into the mammoth repair workshop on the Reichsbahn grounds next to Tempelhof airport. It was a sight to behold: the modern locomotive hall was made of concrete and steel with a high ceiling to accommodate the locomotives. To save electricity and still provide the necessary light, the ceiling was made mostly of window panes supported by the massive steel framework.

Every morning when David stepped inside, his heart sang at the view of the majestic black steam locomotives. They came in all shapes and sizes, and he loved giving them a new life, although every time he read the ubiquitous slogan *"Räder müssen rollen für den Sieg,"* he shuddered.

He loathed helping the Nazis' war effort by *keeping the tires rolling for victory.* Even though it wasn't by choice, his work made sure the Reichsbahn locomotives transporting soldiers and equipment to the front were in the best shape possible.

An even heavier guilt weighed on his shoulders, keeping him awake at night, barely able to breathe against the bulk pressing down on his lungs: these were the same engines that pulled wagon after wagon loaded with Jewish passengers toward an unknown fate in the East. Knowing the Nazis, David didn't believe for a single second that anything good awaited those relocated.

The work itself was light, considering most of his coworkers were required to load and unload the wagons, clean them up, move them around the factory, or do other manual labor, which David was spared as overseer of the engines.

Whenever he managed to push aside the stabbing guilt over his contribution to the war effort, he was quite happy with his job. Thanks to Baumann's protection, the other foremen mostly left David alone, for which he was very thankful.

He walked over to the area where a variety of specialized tools, such as hoists, lathes, milling machines, and welding equipment were stored.

"Herr Kessel," a lanky boy of maybe seventeen with hazelnut brown hair and honey-colored eyes, called out.

He was one of the new additions to David's team, a Jewish forced worker. David automatically corrected him, "Just Kessel."

"K-Kessel," the boy stuttered, ducking his head as if he expected David to lash him for the audacity.

"Hammerschmidt, isn't it?"

"Michael Israel Hammerschmidt."

David yearned to comfort him, tell him he had nothing to fear, but couldn't afford to be overly friendly to a Jew. Due to the military importance of their work, there were always Wehrmacht and SS men strutting about the workshop, overseeing not only repairs deemed critical, but also the workers themselves.

"We don't use full names here. Just Hammerschmidt will do." Out of the corner of his eye, David noticed an SS man approaching them and added in a harsher tone, "What's the question?"

"I... I... Herr Baumann sent me to get brake replacement parts, but I don't know where."

David groaned. Baumann was irrefutably a superb mechanical engineer, but a bad organizer. He constantly sent new arrivals on errands without first giving them a tour around the expansive premises to learn where each of the spare parts were stored.

"Is there a problem?" The SS man was one of the less aggressive ones, a man who'd returned from battle with just one arm and now served his country supervising engineering tasks he didn't have an inkling about. Usually he kept to the background, content to have an easy job.

"No, Herr Rottenführer." David shook his head. "This man is new and has to be trained. If you allow, I'll show him how to do the tasks properly."

"Go ahead." The Rottenführer lingered, and David already feared he'd want to accompany them on their way to get the spare parts. Luckily, a few seconds later the man grunted and strode off in the opposite direction.

"Let's go, Hammerschmidt. The spare parts for the brakes are on the other side of the shunting yard."

The boy clearly was completely out of his depth, giving an uncertain nod. When they'd walked far enough from the factory hall to the vast outside area, where several sheds sprinkled about, housed everything from spare components needed to repair engines, boilers, brakes, and electrical systems, to raw materials ranging from steel to rubber to wood. On the way, David pointed out where everything was located and what it was used for, so Hammerschmidt would be able to run errands on his own.

"Thank you for being so kind," Hammerschmidt said, as they lugged a heavy box between them back to the building.

"No need. We're all—" David stopped himself mid-sentence. Despite the boy's open attitude, one could never be too careful. Just as they walked past the area where wagons were waiting to be refurbished, he noticed a movement. Hammerschmidt had seen it too, because he flinched.

"Did you see what that was?" David asked.

"N-no." The poor boy was shaking like a leaf in the wind.

"Better take a look." Setting down the heavy box, David went to grab a heavy iron rod. Handing a second rod to Hammerschmidt, he approached the passenger wagon. Inside, he found a young man, crouched into the corner in an attempt not to be discovered. "Hey, what are you doing here?"

The man jerked backwards, leveling wide, fear-filled eyes in David's direction. "Please. Don't hit me."

"I'm not going to hit you." David kept his eyes trained on the haggard man, who wore an old, yet well-kept suit and shoes with worn-down soles. He didn't appear to be a criminal or thief, more like a frightened fugitive. Although his entire appearance was much too clean to be a man on the run. A suspicion rose in David's mind. "Who are you?"

The man began to fumble around, before he hastily tried to

slip from the back of the wagon. David blocked his path. "I asked you a question." Whoever this man was, David wouldn't just let him disappear.

"I'm just... I was looking for a place to sleep," the man hedged.

Behind his back, Hammerschmidt hissed in a breath and David suddenly had a good idea who or rather what this man was. A Jew gone underground, a U-Boot, as these people were nicknamed for having to live submerged in the underbelly of Berlin. Unsure how to breach the topic without terrifying the man, he pulled his lip between his teeth, thinking. Finally he asked, "Are you a Jew?"

"No. Of course not." The answer came too fast and too forced, confirming David's suspicion.

Since he didn't want to give away his own heritage, he stepped sideways and pointed at Hammerschmidt, who'd gone pale with fright. "He's one too. I won't turn you in."

The man straightened his spine a bit, still shaking his head. "Thank you, but as I said, I'm not Jewish, I—"

David interrupted him. "I don't really care why you're hiding."

"It won't happen again. If you let me go, I'll never return," the man said with a longing gaze at the passenger seats he'd used as a bed. It occurred to David that these train wagons were a good choice for someone in hiding: dry and comparatively clean inside. Sheltering the refugees against wind and weather, as well as providing a comfortable padding to sleep on.

"Look. As far as I'm concerned, I never found you here. And..." Cocking his head sideways, David pensively worried his lip. "I'll make sure to leave the doors of some wagons ajar. But you, or whoever else who happens to hide inside, must be gone by six in the morning."

The man's eyes widened; relief, joy, disbelief and suspicion flashing through them in less than a second. "What do you expect in return?"

"Me? Nothing. I'm glad to help." With these words, David jumped from the wagon, beckoning for Hammerschmidt to follow him.

"Why? Thank you," the man called quietly after them.

On their way back across the huge yard, lugging the heavy box with spare parts between them, Hammerschmidt said, "That was mighty kind of you."

David stopped, looking intently at the boy. "Don't you ever mention this to anyone. Not a single soul."

"I won't." As they walked on, Hammerschmidt murmured, "You're so brave. I wish I were like you."

David's ears burned bright with the praise. Nobody had ever looked up to him before. Usually he was the maverick not quite fitting in with the rest. Perhaps the time had come when rebels were not only needed but also celebrated. Hammerschmidt's words bolstered his confidence and a plan formed in his mind.

"We could... I mean, if you'd like to help with this?" Again, David intently scrutinized the younger man's face for a reaction. What he saw was a genuine willingness to help, despite the fear etched into his expression.

"I would. I mean, I will. I do. If you think I can be useful."

Hiding a smile, David nodded. "There's not very much we can do. Since we know which wagons are going to be worked on and when, we can make sure people in hiding won't be found."

Hammerschmidt eagerly nodded.

"Every night before your shift ends, I'll send you to fetch something from the far end of the yard so you can unlock the wagons I tell you to," David explained, pleased with himself. "We might also leave a bottle of water or some soup inside... perhaps... let me find out. But no word to anyone, understood?" He paused before underlining the consequences of indiscretion. "Or we might both be shot for treason."

The threat didn't seem to frighten the young man any more than he already was. "Better shot than tortured."

"Now, that's a way to see a silver lining." David opened the workshop door, handing over the box to Hammerschmidt. "Hurry up and get this to Baumann."

A few hours later it was time for lunch break, during which all employees, including the forced workers, received a bowl of hearty soup. It was one of the perks David was especially grateful for, since the rations at home were so tiny.

His father and Amelie didn't receive free food at their respective companies, so his contribution made a real difference. During lunch he didn't speak to Hammerschmidt. Just once he caught the young man's eye, finding a fierce determination in there, giving him the assurance that he had confided in the right guy.

16

JULY 1942

Edith put on her summer hat before she left the apartment, about to step into the barely supportable heat of Berlin's city center, wishing herself back to their mansion on the Schwanenwerder island.

There, she'd relished the summer months, sitting on the terrace surrounded by shade-giving old trees and sipping a cold lemonade with her feet up and a book in her hands, or leisurely walking through the vast garden to the lake for a refreshing swim. These activities had become but a distant dream.

Forcing herself back into the present, she grabbed her handbag tighter, the scorching sunshine blazing down on her as she waited for the tram to arrive. Inside, the air was even more oppressive, filled with the heat of dozens of sweating passengers, soaking up every last bit of hot, but at least fresh, air coming in through the windows.

Fortunately her journey didn't last long. With a sigh of relief she stepped into the shadow of a building, eyeing the entrance to the Tiergarten park further down the road. Right now, she didn't have time for leisure, since she was meeting with her brother Knut.

Someone had slipped a very urgent-sounding message from him under the door last night. Anxiously she pondered what might have happened to make him want to see her immediately, rather than waiting for the weekend. Perhaps her parents or her sister Carsta were sick, or... Her hand flew to her heart at the thought and she violently shook her head to dispel the bleak images creeping up on her.

As she approached the entrance to his office in the Bendlerblock, the Abwehr headquarters, he rushed outside, an agitated expression on his face.

In an effort to lighten the mood, she joked, "Have you been standing at the window all day, waiting for me?"

His nonchalant shrug told her that, indeed, he had. It was a discomfiting discovery, to say the least.

"Let's go for a walk, shall we?" Without waiting for her answer, he took her by the elbow and led the way toward the Tiergarten. After a vigorous four-minute walk, Edith was bathed in sweat and welcomed the sight of the gigantic green trees promising shade.

The instant they stepped into the park, the air felt at least ten degrees cooler. Knut slowed his pace and led her to a bench in the shadows. This early in the day, the park was empty; no comparison to a sunny weekend afternoon when seemingly the entire Berlin population—Jews aside—sought the relief it provided from the insupportable summer heat.

Knut's eyes roamed the vicinity for passersby. When he was satisfied that no one was lingering close enough to eavesdrop, he settled down next to her. Edith's pulse ratcheted up another notch. His behavior was so peculiar; something frightfully awful must have happened.

"Is something wrong with our parents?" She was so full of fear, she could barely utter the words. Knut's shake of his head alleviated her anguish, but only for a second.

"You must make sure Julius won't be at home for the next two days." Knut's eyes betrayed his worries.

She tried to allay his concerns. "He's working all day and doesn't arrive home until late in the evening."

"No." Knut shook his head to emphasize his words. "That won't be enough. Make sure he sleeps someplace else."

"Sleep elsewhere? But where? And why?" A million questions flitted through Edith's mind. *Julius won't like that. He's old and needs his rest at night.*

"Please, Edith. It's not safe. Make sure he stays away from your apartment. He and your other tenants."

"What is going to happen?" Despite the heat, Edith was shivering.

"I can't tell you." His face was a mask of pain. "Promise me you'll make sure nobody is at your place for the next few days."

"What about me?" she asked.

At last, a smile curved his lips. "You're safe. You and Frau Goldmann. But get everyone else out of the house, the children too."

"I will. Thank you for warning me."

"You're my sister, I love you." Again, his face contorted, this time with what looked a lot like shame. "I'm so sorry that you reached the border too late. It would have been so much easier, for all of us, knowing you and Julius are safe."

Edith suppressed the urge to utter a scathing remark. Apart from Knut, nobody else in her family seemed to give a damn about Julius' well-being—and by extension her own. "Thank you so much." Curiosity, or maybe nostalgia, prompted her to ask, "How are our parents?"

"Well enough. Father is getting old and grumpy. He doesn't take well to the shortages war is causing."

This time, Edith couldn't stay quiet. "Then he shouldn't have voted for Hitler."

"True. But it's too late. We're wading knee-deep in shit."

"If you're in knee-deep, Julius and I are up to our necks." The image of herself struggling to keep her nose above stinking feces caused her to gag.

"I'm sorry." He shrugged miserably, begging for her understanding.

It wasn't Knut's fault. He was the one family member who had always stood by her and continued to support her, as evidenced by his current warning.

He glanced at his wristwatch. "I have to return to work. Promise me you'll keep Julius and your friends out of harm's way."

"Don't worry. I will." She got up, squared her shoulders and air-kissed her brother's cheek. "Take care of yourself."

"Always."

He was about to turn away when she called after him. "What about Julius' sister?"

Slowly, he met her eyes. "If she lives in the same borough."

"She doesn't."

"Then there's no need—at least not this week."

Edith looked at Knut's disappearing figure, racking her brain how to warn their household members in time not to return to the apartment for the next forty-eight hours—or however long necessary to avoid a raid. Because she was sure that was the reason Knut had warned her: an imminent SS raid to detain any and all Jews.

She returned to the bench, strategizing the best route to drop by everyone's workplace before the end of the day. Then she squared her shoulders and walked toward the bus station, ready to save her family and friends.

The first on her list was Amelie, whom she hoped to catch during her lunch break in Siemensstadt in the west of Berlin. She was lucky, because a tram going that direction approached the station just as she stepped out of the park. Edith raced toward it and jumped into the last car a split second before the doors closed.

As the conductor came around to sell a ticket to her, she asked, "Is this one going all the way to Siemensstadt?"

"No, *gnädige Frau*, you'll have to change to another line in Charlottenburg."

"Thank you." She settled on a seat, catching her breath, praying she'd manage to reach everyone before it was too late.

Forty-five minutes later she talked to the guard at the uniform factory where Amelie worked.

"I'm sorry, but I can't let you go inside," he insisted.

"Then can you please call my daughter here? It's urgent." Edith hadn't come all the way here to be sent away without relaying her message.

"You'll have to wait until the shift is over in the afternoon."

Close to tears with despair, Edith said the first thing that came to mind. "Her aunt is dying. Please, can you at least give her a message?"

Her words seemed to soften the guard. "You can give her the message yourself, albeit over the telephone. Wait here."

"Thank you so much." Edith's heart jumped with relief, then plummeted when she realized the guard would be listening in and she couldn't speak openly with Amelie.

"Your daughter is on the phone," the guard said, and handed the receiver to Edith.

"Mutti? What's wrong with Aunt Feli?" Amelie's voice shook.

"This is Edith. Please listen carefully." Luckily in this very moment, the guard stepped to the factory gate to attend to an approaching truck. Edith lowered her voice, "Amelie. You can't come home for a few nights. It's not safe. Find a place to sleep elsewhere."

"What? Why?" Amelie stammered into the phone.

"I was warned of a raid. Don't come back until you get word that it's safe."

"Alright." Amelie sounded surprisingly calm. Perhaps living on the edge for years honed the ability to accept whatever obstacles life threw at you. "Thanks for warning me."

Out of the corner of her eye, Edith saw the guard turn toward her and hastily concluded, "I'll go and let your brother know." Then she smiled at the man, "Thank you so very much."

Her heart hammering against her ribs, she escaped onto the street, taking the underground to the workplace of Herr and Frau Gerber, which lay in the south of Berlin. From there, she took a bus to the factory where Heinrich worked. It was already late afternoon when she reached Julius.

"What are you doing here?" he asked, his face full of worry. "And how did you get in?"

"I told the guard that I urgently needed to leave town because my mother is sick and had to give you the keys to the apartment."

He furrowed his brows. "I'm sorry about your mother."

"Oh no..." Edith lowered her voice to a whisper. "She's fine. But you... you mustn't return home tonight. Stay at Silvana's place until you get word that it's safe to come home."

"Wait... why?" He wasn't half as quick as the others in grasping the dangerous situation. Pain stabbed Edith's heart. Julius was getting old and frail. Even two years ago, he had been much more quick-witted.

"Knut warned me about an imminent raid in our borough." Edith sensed the foreman's disapproving stare at her back and jangled her keys, as she said loudly, "Here are the keys. I'll be with my dying mother."

"I wait to hear from you," he responded, and returned to his workstation next to a very beautiful blonde girl who couldn't be much older than twenty. Julius seemed to be friendly with her and Edith hoped that he would warn her about the raid, because she couldn't risk divulging information to a stranger.

The next person on her list was David. She'd left him till last because he always stayed late at the workshop. Still, she had to hurry up if she was going to catch him before he left the premises.

That night she returned home exhausted but happy in the knowledge that everyone was safe. The instant she opened the door, a worried-looking Helga shot out of the kitchen.

"Oh, it's you." Disappointment was etched deep into Helga's face.

The words stabbed Edith's insides, until she realized that Helga didn't know what Edith had been doing and must be out of her mind with worry because nobody had returned home. Putting her hat on the rack, she took off her shoes and settled on the sofa to massage her hurting feet.

"The others won't come home tonight—"

"What has happened?" Helga shrieked with panic.

"Nothing. Sit and I'll explain."

Giving a suspicious gaze, Helga did her bidding and settled on a chair facing Edith. "Is it very bad?"

Edith shook her head. "This morning my brother Knut warned me to make sure Julius and the others won't be home for a day or two. He didn't explain why, but was adamant that it's not safe."

"Oh dear." Helga buried her head in her hands.

"I spent the remainder of the day crisscrossing the city to catch everyone at their place of work, warning them not to come here until we send them a message that it's safe again."

"You did this? You traveled all the way to Siemensstadt to seek Amelie? And then to the other end of Berlin to Heinrich's workplace?" Helga's eyes filled with tears of gratitude.

"Yes. They're both aware, as are David, Delia and the Gerbers."

Helga's shoulders shook with emotion. "You're a hero. Thank you so much."

If Edith was a hero, then she must be a very tired hero. She imagined Julius would seek shelter with Silvana, since Knut had said her neighborhood was safe, but she had no idea where the others were going to spend the night—and would rather not know, for fear she'd tell the Gestapo if they frightened her enough.

17

The next morning, Helga was the first to get up, making Ersatzkaffee for herself and Edith, while she intently listened to the silence in the apartment. Usually this early in the morning, it buzzed with people getting ready for work, today though, there was not a sound.

Suddenly, jackboots slamming up the stairs cut through the silence. The time had come. Despite knowing that her family was not at home and she wasn't in danger of being rounded up, her hand flew to her palpitating heart.

For an instant she considered hiding in her room, letting Edith deal with whoever or whatever was to come. But her friend had already done so much, racing back and forth through Berlin in her quest to warn everyone.

The trampling steps stopped in the floors further down, giving Helga time to compose herself. Would it be possible to flee across the roof during an unannounced raid? Later, she would climb into the attic and research an exit route just in case.

Shouts, cries and ghastly begging came from downstairs, followed by more heavy steps. And then, fists slammed into her door. Despite her anguish, she welcomed the vicious sound, eager to get it over with.

The ten steps she had to cover to get to the entrance door apparently took much too long, because before she'd made it halfway, another round of smashing blows froze her in her tracks.

"Open up, or we'll break down the door," a deep voice shouted. Goosebumps broke out on Helga's skin, suddenly no longer certain that she wasn't in danger.

"I'm coming." She dried her sweaty palms on her apron, racing toward the door, fiddling with the lock until her trembling hands managed to open it.

The SS man on the other side fought for balance as the door he'd been abusing with his fists swung open. Behind him, two more soldiers stood, shoving their rifles into her face. Helga jumped backwards, raising her hands above her head, racking her brain for what to say. Seconds later, she yelled the only redeeming thing she could think of. "Don't shoot! I'm Aryan."

"You are?" a fourth man stepped inside, a malicious grin on his lips.

"I have papers. I can show you." She made to lower her hands, but he ordered: "Your hands stay up where I can see them. I'll get them myself."

"They are in my handbag, right next to the door." Her gaze wandered to the shabby black handbag, sitting next to a much nicer brown leather purse belonging to Edith. "The black one."

He smirked, motioning his men to come inside, while he took up Helga's handbag and emptied its contents onto the table in the middle of the room. Out flew all her belongings: a wallet with a few Reichsmark, her and Heinrich's ration books, a handkerchief, her employee card at the insurance company, and—finally—her identification.

The SS officer picked up the *Kennkarte* gingerly, making a show of perusing it. He seemed disappointed as he announced,

"You are, indeed an Aryan." Turning toward his colleague he said, "Helga Goldmann. Who else is on the list?"

"Heinrich Goldmann, Jew, Amelie and David Goldmann, half-Jews."

"Where are they?"

"Not here." Helga somehow managed to croak out the words.

"Tsk. You should know better than to hide enemies of the Reich. Or perhaps you don't, since you're still married to one."

"Please, I swear, they've left for work a while ago." Instantly, Helga scolded herself for giving away her family's location, except the SS knew already where every single Jew in the Reich worked and lived.

"Hm. Perhaps what you say is true. Who else is living in this apartment?"

Helga wasn't sure whether he'd addressed her, or his colleague, so she kept her mouth shut.

"Leonhard and Gisela Gerber with their three children Holger, Hans and Hertha. Julius and Edith Falkenstein," his colleague read from the list in his hand.

"The Gerbers work the nightshift and won't be home until nine," Helga said in an attempt to buy some time, her hands still raised above her head. "Their children are with relatives, but I don't know where. Edith Falkenstein is an Aryan too, and she's sleeping in that room over there." She nodded toward the main bedroom, offering, "Shall I go and wake her up?"

To tell the truth, Helga couldn't imagine her friend still being asleep after the incessant shouting, trampling and pounding on the doors, yet she hoped to spare her from being surprised by jackbooted SS men in her bedroom.

"You may," the officer graciously agreed, waving her forward. "In the meantime my men will search the place to see whether you've told us the truth."

Despite being certain that she and Edith were the only ones

in the apartment, icy clumps formed in her veins as images of a person crouched in hiding beneath the bed attacked her. But no, not even David would be reckless enough to sneak in at night after the stern warning Edith's brother had issued.

Slowly lowering her hands, she walked toward Edith's room, knocking on the door and calling out, "Edith. The SS is here. Please come out and show them your papers."

Helga didn't have to wait long. Edith was already dressed, only the half-tucked-in blouse betraying her haste as she opened the door. Fear flashed through her eyes for a split second, then she found her sangfroid and stepped into the living room as graciously as if she were to welcome a friend.

"Herr Sturmführer," she said, after a furtive glance at his epaulets. "How may I help you today?"

Her exquisite politeness impressed the man, whose expression softened. "Is your husband home?"

"I'm afraid not." She looked at him with open, innocent eyes. "He didn't come home last night and I'm beginning to worry. You wouldn't have news about him, would you?"

The SS officer shook his head, apparently unaccustomed to someone being this unperturbed by his presence. "Do you mind if we have a look?"

"Of course not, Herr Sturmführer." Edith stepped aside, inviting him with a gesture to enter her room. "Please do ascertain yourself that he's missing."

Just in that moment, a shrill hissing sound cut through the air, causing the soldiers to point their weapons at Helga's and Edith's heads.

"That's the kettle, I was just making coffee before you arrived," Helga hurriedly explained. Emboldened by Edith's example, she added, "May I take it off the stove?"

"Yes, go and get it," the officer ordered. Mere minutes later the other two soldiers returned. "We searched every room. Nobody else is in this apartment."

The Sturmführer gave a curt nod. "Ladies, I will leave you to drink your morning coffee."

"We're always willing to cooperate." Edith stepped forward, smiling pleasantly at him.

"It looks like your families got lucky," he grumbled.

"I believe so, thanks to our kind Führer who has ruled that Jews in mixed marriages and their offspring shall not be evacuated. But who am I to tell you this, you will know the rules much better than a simple housewife like me."

Helga's heart dropped into her shoes at the bold remark, fearing some kind of retaliation. The Sturmführer stared at Edith for a few seconds, before he clicked his heels, thrust out his right hand and yelled, "Heil Hitler."

Unfazed, Edith followed suit, never showing an ounce of fear. When the door finally closed behind the last of the black-clad men, Helga dropped onto the nearest chair, resting her head on the table. "I was so scared."

"Me, too." Edith stepped behind her.

Helga turned around to look at her friend. "You were absolutely amazing."

"My only goal was to convince them never to return."

"I believe you did. Your last remark was brilliant." Helga wished she possessed even half of Edith's wits.

"When I saw that man, I remembered how I used to deal with Joseph. Subtle flattery almost always works. Telling them you're on their side, while at the same time reminding them they're not above the law."

"I'll go and fetch the coffee," Helga said. When she returned from the kitchen with two steaming cups, she found Edith crouched on the sofa, trembling viciously. Putting the coffee on the table, she kneeled next to her. "What's the matter, Edith?"

"It's just... I... I..."

"Shush." Helga had never seen her friend in such a

disturbed condition. So she did the only thing she could think of and wrapped her arms around the other woman as if she were a child, rocking her back and forth, whispering soothing words. "Shush. It's over. They're gone. Everything's fine."

After endless minutes, the trembling ceased and Edith looked up at her, the desolation in her eyes hitting Helga deep in her guts.

"I don't know how long I'll be able to cope."

"For as long as you need to." Helga understood exactly what Edit was going through. She often felt on the verge of a breakdown herself and didn't know how she'd survive if it weren't for Heinrich, who cheered her up whenever she needed it most.

Despite his own precarious situation he always found the inner strength to build her up so that she could fight another day for him and for their children. Apparently now it was her turn to support Edith.

Edith dabbed a few tears from her eyes. "Sometimes I want to throw my hands up in the air and give up."

"We all have these doubts." Helga handed her the lukewarm coffee. "It's no wonder you feel drained after what you did yesterday. You single-handedly saved everyone in this household from deportation." Despite Edith reminding the SS officer that Jews with immediate Aryan family were exempt from deportation, they both knew that once the SS had them in their claws it would be too late; nobody would care about legalities then.

"I'm afraid one day I won't be present to protect Julius, and then what?"

Helga suffered from the same fears. "It doesn't help to worry about things that might happen in the future. We can only do our best in the present; for the rest we just wait and drink tea."

"I'm so exhausted," Edith whispered.

"It happens to all of us. Right now you feel as if you can't take another step, but in a few minutes, you'll get up, brush off the despair and stand your ground another day. That's how it works. That's how we protect our families."

Finally, Edith smiled. "Thank you for being such a great friend." Then she drank the coffee, got up, brushed her hands down her skirt and said, "I'd better leave for work or I won't have a job anymore."

"That's the spirit." Helga smiled.

18

In contrast to his father and sister, who'd decided to spend two nights in Oranienburg with Aunt Felicitas, David had opted to sleep at the workshop. More precisely, he planned to use the same passenger wagons he left unlocked at night for illegals.

"You not going home tonight?" Baumann asked, as he took off the heavy apron protecting him from sparks at the welding station.

"I just need a few more minutes to clean up." David didn't want to compromise his boss by making him privy to the plan.

"Want me to wait for you?"

David shook his head. "No need. I can close up shop." He'd done it before when Baumann needed to visit the Reichsbahn offices and wasn't able to return in time.

"Ain't up to anything stupid, are ya?" The older man narrowed his eyes at David.

"No. Just what's necessary."

That was enough of an answer for the man who trusted him implicitly. "Good night. See you in the morning."

"Good night." A sharp sting shot through David's guts, but

he consoled himself with the thought that he wasn't actually lying, just not telling his mentor everything—to protect him no less.

As soon as Baumann had left, David walked into the outside area toward one of the carts he'd left unlocked. It was his first night sleeping rough as a fugitive from the law, so throughout the day he'd made several trips, depositing a thermos with water, bread and a pillow inside. It was much too hot for a blanket.

Despite the heat, goosebumps broke out on his arms as he approached the train wagon, glinting in the evening sun. He didn't have a valid excuse if the police were to find him sleeping there.

Then he shrugged. The result was going to be the same, whether they rounded him up at home or found him trespassing. David harbored no illusions as to what happened to Jews who got picked up and jammed into the supposedly inconspicuous furniture vans.

The yard was big enough for him not to be seen from outside the fence, so he settled on the ground against the wagon eating his prepared dinner. Darkness would settle over the city in roughly three hours, so he decided to return to the workshop, where he scoured the trashcan for pieces of wire, breakers and other useful devices to construct a simple alarm system.

Edith's dire warning had given him chills, sending his mind spinning in wild circles. This morning, he'd hugged his family goodbye the way he always did, blissfully unaware of the looming danger. Now he realized that he might never see them again, wishing he'd told his parents how much he loved them. If Edith's brother had spoken the truth—and there was no reason to doubt him—they all teetered on the brink of mortal danger.

Throughout the day, a much graver truth had dawned on him: this could happen again anytime. Next time, they might not receive a warning ahead of the raid, leaving them with no way to evade capture. His mind wandered to the angora rabbits. In the wild, rabbits, as opposed to hares, built their burrows with one main entrance and several smaller, hidden side exits, which served as escape routes in case of an emergency.

David resolved to mimic them and devise several escape routes from their apartment, which might enable them to flee during an upcoming raid. The first step, however, would be to construct an alarm system that alerted the residents and slowed down the intruders enough to give them a fighting chance.

While he sat next to the train car, fiddling with wires, the sky erupted into flaming red, orange and purple colors at the setting of the sun. David was normally more interested in mechanical problems than in the beauty of nature, but under the looming threat of being deported, he laid his hands in his lap and sat back to enjoy the spectacle.

His own mortality hit him with an unprecedented force. Tears pooled in his eyes as he recognized the gravity of his situation. Once in the hands of the police, he was done for. They could beat him to death without consequences, they could torture him for days or weeks and then dump his mangled body into the river, or bury him alive, or... or force him to work in a quarry until he collapsed. Death by exhaustion. In that moment, David swore he'd do everything in his power not to fall into the Nazis' hands.

A slight breeze picked up, bringing much longed-for coolness with it. He gathered his things and entered the train car to get some sleep. Soon enough, complete darkness settled around him. He decided against drawing the blackout curtains in the passenger compartment, banking on the sunshine to wake him in the morning when he had to get up for work.

Still, he couldn't find sleep. The air was full of unfamiliar sounds. With his eyes unable to discern more than vague shadows, his ears worked overtime, intent on warning him of a possible danger.

The repair yard seemed to take on a life of its own, the wagons groaning and creaking as the wind hissed around their corners. A blood-chilling "Tu-whit tu-whoo" penetrated the air, causing David to press himself tighter against the wall until he realized it was the hunting call of an owl.

From far away the sound of rattling wheels wafted through the night, along with a siren somewhere in the distance, and then... steps. David's blood froze. His hands fumbled for an object to use as a weapon, wishing he'd taken a steel rod with him, just in case.

He strained his ears, but couldn't pick up a single sound. Silence again. Then, a hasty breath, a pebble bumping against metal. Someone was outside. Thinking on his feet, David came to the conclusion that whoever was there wasn't a threat to him —Gestapo or SS would have arrived with headlights, guns, dogs and lots of noise.

His jaw muscles relaxed. He willed the stranger to pass, inwardly cursing himself for not locking the door from the inside. It had seemed to be the safest option, offering a faster escape.

For a while no sound reached his ears and he relaxed, assuming the stranger had left. The soft scratching as someone opened the door disabused him of the idea. Instantly, David's pulse ratcheted up again.

"Who's there?" he asked softly.

Complete silence was the answer. Yet David sensed the presence of another human being. The smell of fear was pervasive. "I'm not going to hurt you. You can stay here, whoever you are."

Still no sound.

"Look, I'm the one who leaves the doors unlocked for

people like you and who makes sure the break in the fence line won't be repaired."

The other person puffed out a breath. "Don't try anything on me, I'm armed."

Judging by the stranger's high-pitched voice, he wasn't a grown man. David inwardly grinned, a boy was no match for him in a brawl, although he didn't intend to let it come to that, since any undue noise might alert someone who then called the police.

"Don't run away. I won't do you any harm, I promise. I'll light a candle."

"Al-right," the other person drawled, apparently intent to make his voice sound deeper. "But I will kill you if I must."

David doubted that. "There's no need. I'm on your side." Slowly he leaned toward the window, drew the blackout curtain and then fumbled for the box of matches and the candle he'd deposited within reach.

Seconds later a flickering flame threw scary shadows onto the wall in the compartment and David hissed in a surprised breath. "You're a girl."

"What's that to do with anything?" The tiny person standing in the compartment raised a long knife to keep David at bay.

"Nothing. I just assumed..." He stopped mid-sentence, feeling stupid. Why shouldn't the fugitive be a female? The Nazis pursued them as relentlessly as the male Jews. "You're a Jew, right?"

Rebellion flickered in her eyes as she responded, "No."

"So why are you hiding then?"

She sneered with derision. "You guys always think you're the only ones persecuted. And that's exactly your problem. If we'd band together and fight, we could stop this insanity."

She didn't resemble his communist and socialist coworkers, neither in speech nor in age or looks. But if she wasn't a communist, what was she then? A criminal? A political?—Both options seemed highly unlikely.

Since David didn't want to put his foot in it again, he asked, "Care to enlighten me?"

"I'm a Romani." With her chin raised, she looked like a warrior queen in the flickering candlelight. Though petite, her bare arms were sinewy and she had the most amazing electric-blue eyes.

"A gypsy?" The moment he'd spoken, he felt like a complete idiot. It was just that he'd never actually met one before. During his childhood, his mother had always warned him not to trust the traveling people, claiming they were dirty, thieving and cunning. It struck him that this particular woman looked surprisingly clean for someone in hiding.

"Tsk. That's a derogatory word. You of all people should be more sensitive."

Shame was swiftly replaced by anger at her condescending tone. "Me of all people? Who do you think you are?"

Her smug grin seemed to light up the compartment. "We already discussed what I am. You, on the other hand—" She cocked her head, her penetrating stare causing him to shiver as she seemed to dissect him, probing deep beneath his skin to find out who he really was. Just when he wanted to jump up, unable to stand her scrutiny a second longer, she said, "I'd guess you are a Jew."

"Half-Jew," he automatically corrected her, before righteous anger settled in and he hissed, "What do you care anyway?"

"I don't. How would you like it if I called you a kike?"

David wheezed. He'd never come across such an insolent woman, before, with the possible exception of his sister, who didn't count, because she was family. Grasping the last shreds of self-control, he said, "No need to insult me. Being a Jew is bad enough these days."

"Half-Jew," she corrected him, flashing her white teeth in a smile.

"Smartass."

Her smile disappeared. "My shrewdness is what's kept me alive."

David swallowed hard. He'd heard rumors about forced sterilization and atrocious medical experiments on gypsies—Romani, he corrected himself. "I'm sorry. I'm David, by the way."

She extended her hand. "Roxana."

"Nice to meet you." When he touched her small, thin hand, a jolt of electricity passed between them.

"That's a rather strange thing to say in our situation, don't you think?" Her bright smile warmed his heart.

Her remark might be true, nevertheless David felt happy in her company. To prevent her from leaving, he asked, "Have you eaten?"

A quick shake of the head was the answer.

David didn't need any more persuasion to offer her the food he'd reserved for breakfast. "Please, have a seat." As soon as she'd settled on the seat opposite him, he handed her a buttered piece of bread and some cheese.

"Butter and cheese?" Her eyes shone with the voracious hunger of a person who hadn't eaten properly in ages. As if she was afraid he'd change his mind and take the food away, she quickly stuffed every last morsel into her mouth and swallowed it down. "Who are you really? An angel?"

"Just a fugitive like you." Despite the strong impression she made on him, he didn't fully trust her yet, so opted not to tell her more than necessary. For all he knew, she might turn him in to the Gestapo, hoping to garner favors for herself.

She seemed to have read his mind. "Don't worry. I'm not going rat you out." After a pause she added, "Do you have more food?"

David shook his head. "Sorry, I don't."

"Not an angel then," she answered with a dry laugh.

"My mother would attest to that." He so wished to see her smile again. "I could bring more tomorrow, if you want."

"You would? Really?" The initial delight in her eyes was immediately replaced by distrust. "What do you expect in return?"

"Nothing." David fervently wanted her to trust him, because for some strange reason he wanted to make her happy.

"Nobody does anything for nothing." She cocked her head, studying him intently. "Are you working for the Gestapo?"

"Of course not."

"I don't believe you." Her eyes danced around the small compartment, as if seeking a way out.

Her mistrust hurt. "You can leave anytime you want."

"Are the police waiting for me outside?" She seemed not to have concluded whether she should bolt or stay.

"There's nobody waiting outside, Roxana." Then he had an idea. "Tonight's not the first time you've come here, right?"

"How do you know?" she hedged.

"From the certainty of your steps. Despite the darkness, there was no wavering, no hesitation. You knew where you were going."

"Maybe or maybe not. What does this have to do with us?"

David yearned to touch her slender hand again. Put his arms around her bony shoulders and tell her she was safe with him. But he knew she wouldn't listen. Words didn't mean anything to her, and he wondered what she'd had to endure to become so leery. Whatever her backstory, he needed to earn her trust. He'd start by offering hard evidence instead of empty words.

"Have you ever wondered why some carts are unlocked and others aren't?"

Her jaw pressed tight, she squinted her eyes at him. "Not really. I thought some of the workers here had been careless."

"That careless person is me. I usually leave a few carts open at night so people like you can find shelter."

"You work here?"

He gave a slow nod. "You weren't supposed to know. It's not safe."

"For you or for me?" Instantly, her cocky behavior returned as she cast him a smug smirk.

"For both of us."

She visibly relaxed.

"I want to help you, Roxana."

"How can you help me, if you're a fugitive yourself?"

"It's complicated." He didn't want to tell her too much, not because he feared she'd betray him—at least not willingly, but because... hell... he had no idea why he felt such a strong need to protect her. "My situation is... I'd rather not explain. It's better if you don't know too much. For your own safety."

Surprisingly, she nodded, her gaze seeking his. "I believe you, David."

His world exploded into a rainbow of colors, swirling in the air, settling deep down in his stomach, causing it to do wild and delicious flips. He had never felt like this, not even with Thea. He shoved thoughts of her betrayal aside. With hindsight, he realized the selfish girl had never truly loved him.

Roxana yawned. "I'm tired."

"Sleep. You're safe with me, I promise." He vowed to watch over her and protect her from anything or anyone wanting to cause her harm.

"I'd hope so, because if you try anything, I'll cut your throat before you have a chance to fight back."

He didn't doubt her words. After all, she'd survived years of persecution, which must account for something. "I'll wake you in the morning before the workers arrive."

"Thank you." With surprising ease, she put her knapsack below her head and closed her eyes. Mere seconds later a slight snore indicated that she'd fallen asleep.

David leaned against his side of the compartment wall, blew out the candle and opened the blackout curtain. In the almost complete darkness, only lit up by a few stars, he stared at Roxana's silhouette, her chest moving up and down with her breath.

19

After the raid in July, life had been surprisingly quiet. Yet, Julius constantly felt haunted and thus completely stopped venturing out into the street, except for work.

Work was tedious, tiring, backbreaking. The one thing making it easier was his growing friendship with the young woman who had saved his life. Fräulein Dalke's smile was a ray of sunshine he looked forward to every day. He often mused that she might be the daughter he never had.

In the beginning he'd been angry at her for thwarting his suicide plan. It had taken several days, witnessing Silvana's and later Edith's massive grief over what he'd done, until he'd come to truly appreciate Thea's quick reaction.

Yes, his life had turned into a nightmare, worse than he would have been able to imagine, yet he was alive and had hope that one day all of this was going to be over. That thought kept him going through all the struggles.

He smiled at the memory of the day he'd gifted Thea one of Edith's scarves to show his gratitude. It was a beautiful piece made of blue silk, which matched the color of Edith's eyes.

"I want to thank you for saving my life," he said, turning his fedora in his hands.

"Don't mention it, Herr Falkenstein. Anyone would have done it." She cast him her bright smile, which always seemed to light up the room and reminded him so much of Edith thirty years ago.

"Nobody else did. In fact, the Nazis would have been delighted to see me dead." Determination straightened his back. He would not give them the satisfaction of getting rid of him that easily; this was his small way to resist.

Her smile dimmed, aware that he was telling the truth.

"In any case, I want to show you how much I appreciate what you did, and perhaps make up for the trouble you received for saving me." After making sure he was taken to the hospital, Thea had showed up late for work that day and the foreman had docked her salary as punishment, in addition to forcing her to work overtime for an entire week.

Julius fumbled in his coat pocket for the scarf and proffered it to her. "A token of my gratitude."

"This is for me? It's so beautiful." Thea's eyes went wide, sparkling with delight. She took the scarf and draped it expertly around her neck, "How do I look?"

"Fantastic. It enhances the color of your eyes." Throughout their marriage, Julius had always added the finishing touches to Edith's outfits for official purposes, transforming them from simply beautiful to mind-blowing with a well-placed accessory, usually precious jewelry.

He was surprised to find almost as much pleasure in making the young girl shine with a simple silken scarf. Throughout his adult life, he'd yearned an heir to his business, now he wondered how his life with a daughter like Thea would have been. He quickly dismissed the thought, secretly glad he didn't have children to witness his inexorable decline from the top of Germany's society to the gutter.

From then on, the two of them had spent their lunch breaks together. Julius regaled anecdotes from his glamorous past, and Thea made him smile with her reenactments of famous opera scenes. It was a much-needed break in his otherwise dull day at work.

A strong urge to smoke caused him to return to the present. He walked to the cupboard to open his cigar box and settle with a cigar in the dining room. Smoking was his last indulgence in this bleak world. When he found the box empty, he remembered having smoked the last one the day before.

"Edith," he called out.

"What is it, Julius?" She looked up from her needlework—something he still hadn't gotten used to. His own wife having to patch up the holes in his suit. Back in the day, they had tailors and seamstresses doing such menial work, or better yet, he would have bought a new suit.

"Could you please get me another cigar box from the storage in the attic?" He hadn't been up there for years, mostly due to his arthritic knees.

"I brought down the last one a while ago."

"That can't be. There must be more." Already sweat was breaking out on his neck at the notion of henceforth not enjoying the comfort of his daily cigar.

Edith shook her head. "There isn't. I told you this was the last one."

He didn't remember, otherwise he would have been alarmed. "Then you need to buy new ones."

"Julius." Her voice was stern and indulgent at the same time, as if she were talking to a child. "There are no ration cards for cigars."

"Then buy me cigarettes." He knew he was being unduly harsh. Yet the prickle in his limbs seemed to increase with every passing second. He craved that smoke. He needed it. Right now.

"The Nazis cut the cigarette rations for Jews last month."

Sweat trickled down his forehead, getting caught in his thick eyebrows. He removed a kerchief from his breast pocket—at least some things hadn't changed—and wiped his face. His voice took on a pleading tone. "I need a smoke right now. Could you go to the store and buy cigarettes with your ration card. Please."

Edith gave a deep sigh and stood up to walk toward the door. There she stopped and rummaged in her handbag, fishing out a cigarette packet and handing it to him. "Here, you can have one of mine."

"Since when are you smoking?" His voice was tinged with both surprise and fascination, and perhaps disappointment at himself for not having noticed.

"A while ago." Her lips were defiantly pushed out, even as she put her hands akimbo as if daring him to disapprove.

Despite her insolent stance, he couldn't let her new habit go unmentioned. "This is such unladylike behavior. My mother would be scandalized."

"Your mother is dead." Edith shrugged.

"What has gotten into you? Not only did you take up smoking, but now you're contradicting me? Whatever happened to manners?"

Edith returned to her seat and took up her needlework, deliberately ignoring him. For the moment, he would let her get away with it. Instead he grabbed his enamel Fabergé lighter, a memento of better times, and lit a cigarette. The moment the slender stick of tobacco met his lips, he inhaled deeply, allowing the enticing aroma to envelop his senses. It wasn't the same sensation a fine cigar evoked, nonetheless the first drag satiated his craving even as a tingle traveled down his throat. Already the second inhalation soothed his anguish.

He'd always looked down on cigarette smokers, since they usually devoured their smoke in a hurry—unlike a cigar connoisseur, who savored both smell and taste to the fullest. All that was forgotten as the rush of warmth filled his lungs, the smoke meandering through his respiratory system, creating a momentary oasis of much-needed tranquility. With each subsequent inhale, Julius found himself succumbing to peaceful relaxation, the hardships of his life momentarily slipping away.

Exhaling slowly, the smoke swirled around him, forming little clouds, which he observed until Edith's voice cut through the silence. "You could at least offer to light me one, too."

"Offer you what?" He stared at her, uncomprehending.

"A cigarette." To leave no doubt, she pointed at the package lying in front of him.

"You want to smoke now?"

"Yes. I wouldn't normally, but since you started, I really need one too."

"You do know..." *that smoking is not appropriate for a lady*, he was going to say. Then he shrugged. His wife had ceased to belong to Germany's high society years ago and had been forced to join the ranks of working women. Thus, she might as well smoke if it gave her pleasure. He picked up the lighter again and then handed her the burning cigarette. "Here you go."

"Thank you."

For a while they smoked together in silence, until he asked, "Are you sure we don't have another box of cigars in the attic?"

"I'm quite certain, but you're welcome to look for yourself."

He furrowed his brows at the thought of having to climb the steep extendible ladder leading upstairs. "I might. There must be a secret stash somewhere, which belonged to my father."

"Won't they have gone bad by now?"

"Not at all. Cigars have a minimum durability of fifteen years if stored correctly." Imagining the pleasure of smoking one convinced him it was worth the climb up into the attic. "I'll have a look."

"Shall I come with you?"

"No need. But thank you."

He stubbed out the cigarette and walked out into the staircase, where it took him a while to figure out how to extend the ladder. Huffing and puffing, he arrived in the dusty attic. He hadn't been up here in years. As he slowly turned a full circle, taking in the relics of the past, nostalgia hit him square between his eyes.

An old mirror with a carved wooden frame leaned against the wall, next to it stood a wooden cabinet with beautiful intarsia, both of them long forgotten. Now he assessed that both pieces ought to receive a good price on the black market. To the right of them stood the dressing screen his mother had used in her bedroom.

If his memory was to be trusted, there should be a simple metal filing cabinet behind, which used to stand in his father's office, holding important family documents, before Julius had transferred them into a safe. When the doctor had declared smoking unhealthy for his father's cough, he'd hidden his secret stash in here, away from his wife's vigilant eyes.

Julius had never cleared the cabinet and hoped to find at least one cigar box inside. When he ventured behind the dressing screen, a gasp escaped his throat. Hidden from sight was not only the rusty bedframe he knew would be there, but also a mattress with fresh-looking bedlinen on top. For all intents and purposes it looked as if someone was, if not living, at least sleeping in the attic.

Curious, he ventured farther into the dark shadows, where he found an open hatch, leading into a small space, just big enough to hold a small person. Dismayed by the illegal activities going on under his own roof, he slumped on the bed, whose metal springs surprisingly didn't give a single squawk. Someone must have carefully oiled them to avoid any noise.

His original reason to come up here forgotten, he mentally assessed the apartment's residents one by one and quickly came to the conclusion that there was only one person reckless enough for such a bold action.

Then he got up again with some effort and walked over to the filing cabinet, where he not only found half a box of cigars, but also a collection of exquisite silverware he'd completely forgotten existed. Since it was forbidden for Jews to own precious metals, he pondered what best to do with them.

Selling it on the black market might be the best option. It would afford him more tobacco once the found stash was used up. But Julius had never done anything illegal in his life and didn't even know how to find a willing and trustful buyer.

"Julius? Everything alright up there?" Edith's voice wafted up into the attic.

He looked at his wristwatch, realizing he'd spent almost an hour lost in his memories. Edith was shouldering so many things already, he didn't want to burden her with the story of a fugitive possibly hiding in their attic, so he yelled back, "Yes. Sorry, I was caught up reminiscing."

"Dinner is almost ready."

"Coming." Her steps moved away from the ladder and back into their apartment. The aroma of the hearty soup filled the room, carrying hints of onions and simmered vegetables.

Edith ladled potato soup into each bowl, giving the Gerber boys and David a bit more than their share. Julius didn't mind, remembering how he'd always been hungry during his youth.

Reminding himself that he wanted to unmask the culprit who'd been hiding fugitives in the attic, he scrutinized every household member one by one. Right away, he discarded Edith's involvement. The Gerber parents were too occupied with their children, and too frightened of the consequences. Of their children, not even Holger at twelve was old enough to plan and execute such a crime.

The Goldmanns, however, all possessed the inner strength of truly upright people. He knew that trait from working decades in his bank, hiring employees at all levels from cleaner to vice president.

Many people were honest and fair, but few would sacrifice their own well-being for the right cause. A blush crept up his neck, reminding Julius that he had believed himself to be righteous, yet history had proven otherwise. He had not been prepared to defy an unjust law to do the right thing, and had allowed himself to become a lackey, abetting the Nazis to oppress the Jews.

Helga Goldmann would have been his first choice, but she cared too much for her family and the other residents to expose them to such a danger. Julius didn't have any illusions as to what would happen if the Gestapo found a refugee up in the attic.

Her husband Heinrich, likewise. If he were the culprit, he'd hide the illegals someplace else, where the Gestapo couldn't trace them back to his family. And Amelie... she was just a girl, not even of age.

Yes, it had to be David. He was kind-hearted and rebellious, always eager to fight for the weakest members of society. But he wasn't as clever as he thought. For example, David believed nobody knew that he and Amelie put their reversible jackets inside out to hide the yellow star and enjoy the few leisure activities available to young people these days.

Julius would put the young man to the test. Observing David closely, he casually remarked, "I was in the attic this evening."

A flickering eyelid was the only reaction. Julius wondered if he could be mistaken about his judgment, nevertheless he forged ahead. "I need someone to help me move the file cabinet." A slightly louder clink of David's metal spoon against the ceramic bowl. It was a promising start. "Could you please accompany me after dinner, David?"

"Sure." The way the young man drew out the word showed

his discomfort, leaving no doubt in Julius' mind that he must be the culprit.

"Thank you." Julius dug into the last of his potato soup, naturally without a hint of meat, while devising a plan. Once the last morsel was eaten, everyone turned to their usual chores. The women cleaned the table and the dishes, Herr Gerber reviewed the schoolwork he'd assigned his children in the morning.

"Don't wait up for me, darling." Herr Goldmann kissed his wife before he walked out the door, moonlighting as accountant for a shop owner. Julius never asked, and Herr Goldmann never explained, yet it was an open secret that several Aryans illicitly contracted him due to his stellar accounting experience.

A sense of pride warmed Julius' heart, since Herr Goldmann had honed his abilities during his time as head accountant for the Falkenstein bank, which seemed a lifetime ago. The warm sensation was quickly replaced by a chill as he remembered how he'd fired Herr Goldmann and all his other Jewish employees to please the Nazis.

Back then Julius had believed in the importance of laws and following them. All that had changed. Nothing about the Nazi regime was legitimate, thus he felt no longer a moral obligation to follow their equally illegitimate rules.

"Are you ready to climb into the attic?" he asked David.

20

David had been damp with sweat since Herr Falkenstein had mentioned the attic. The bed he'd prepared for Roxana to sleep in was hidden behind a dressing screen, albeit not very carefully.

Nobody except David had been up in the attic for months, as evidenced by the thick layers of dust on floor and furniture. He'd given the floor a good sweep to prevent visible footsteps, leaving the rest of the room untouched.

"I can't possibly accept this. It's much too dangerous," Roxana had protested when he'd proposed it.

"You can and you should. How long do you think you can sleep rough when winter comes?"

"The train cars are hardly exposed." She'd tightened her jaw in that stubborn and determined way he found so enchanting. Every part of her fascinated him, from her pitch-black curly hair, down to her small feet. She usually kept her shoes in her knapsack, claiming she was more agile and quieter barefoot.

"Please, Roxi, what if the nightguard finds you?"

"Since when does the workshop have one?"

"Every time there's a shipment of valuable raw materials."

"Then you can leave me a note of warning and I'll stay away." She crossed her arms in front of her chest, making him crazy both with worry and desire.

"Why don't you let me take care of you?" David knew she could perfectly well take care of herself. But he'd never felt such an urge to protect a woman from evil—not even Amelie or his mother.

"I don't need to be taken care of." Her eyes glared daggers at him.

David raised his hands in defense. "I know how much you despise being underestimated. I'm offering this not because I think you can't fend for yourself, but because I want to make life easier for you. Safer. Happier. Please, let me do this for you."

Finally she smiled. It took him by surprise, causing wild things to happen all the way down to his groin. "It's just, nobody has ever looked out for me."

By now she'd told him her mother had died during childbirth and her father had been run over by a car when she was four years old. Orphaned, she'd grown up with extended family inside a caravan community crisscrossing the country, where nobody seemed to notice whether she was around or not.

"I want to." David had to restrain himself from wrapping her into his arms. So far they hadn't ventured beyond an accidental touch of their hands, and he didn't want to scare her away.

"Well, I guess... alright. But on my terms." Her expression switched to stubborn again.

"Whatever you want." He'd give her anything just to see that smile again.

"I can come and go whenever I want."

"Sure."

"You won't control my presence, or tell me what to do."

"No problem."

"Nobody else will know about my existence."

"I won't tell anyone."

Returning to the present, David racked his brain how to keep his promise. He had to prevent his landlord from bumping into Roxi at all costs.

"Herr Falkenstein, if you tell me which cabinet you want moved, I'll do it for you."

"I need to look for something."

"But your knees? Do you think it's wise to go up there a second time in one day?" David was getting desperate.

"No need to worry, young man." Did David imagine this or was there a smirk on Herr Falkenstein's lips? "Go ahead please."

Climbing the ladder with the older man behind him, David peeked into the attic for evidence of Roxi's presence. True to his promise, he didn't control her coming and going, which didn't hinder him from looking up at the roof whenever he approached or left the building. She usually climbed the outside fire ladder late at night to sneak into the open roof window. When she was home—and he considered her to be home up there—it was closed.

A heavy burden fell from his shoulders, seeing the window ajar. She wasn't home, although she might arrive at any time, since it was getting dark. Taking a deep breath, he stepped onto the floor, putting his trust in Roxi's wits. She'd notice if someone was inside and would stay away.

That was both a relief and a worry at the same time, because she might believe he'd betrayed her and never return. This notion was so devastating, his stomach churned as if he'd received a punch to it.

Meanwhile Herr Falkenstein had reached the top of the latter and stepped into the attic, where he moved the dressing screen aside, revealing the bed behind. It was in immaculate condition, no trace that anyone had ever slept in there and if David didn't know better, he'd believe Roxi didn't exist.

"The last time I came up here, there was but a naked frame. Care to explain?" Herr Falkenstein asked, looking expectantly at David.

"I have no idea." David buried his hands deep inside his trouser pockets.

"Don't think me stupid, young man. I have observed you and your sister, and I know exactly what you're doing."

The breath hitched in David's lungs. Amelie wasn't involved and as far as he knew she didn't have the slightest clue about the illicit visitor. "I don't know what you are talking about. Perhaps someone found this place empty and chose to use it as a hiding place?" He emphasized his words with a shrug and a puzzled gaze.

"I was looking for a box of cigars and found this." Herr Falkenstein held up the wire David had installed as an alarm. Roxi was supposed to put it in front of the trap door into the staircase whenever she was home. It was identical to the one he'd installed next to the building's main entrance door.

Every night, David checked whether the wire was still in place, which, when someone tripped it, rang a bell to warn the residents of unwelcome visitors.

"That is mine," David said lamely, since Herr Falkenstein surely must have recognized what it was.

"It's not my intention to expose you and whoever is hiding here."

"It isn't?" Surprise, mixed with suspicion, washed over David.

"No. Rather, I'd like to propose a deal, which will benefit both of us."

"A deal?" It sounded dumb even in his own ears to repeat everything Herr Falkenstein said.

"Indeed. A deal." Herr Falkenstein settled on the bed.

"Apart from your little secret, I also found some silverware I'd long forgotten about. Since you clearly know your way around Berlin's underworld, I want you to sell it for me."

"Sell it? Me?" David mumbled like an idiot.

"Despite all evidence to the contrary, I believe you're an honest person." Herr Falkenstein looked amused. "You wouldn't cross me."

"I wouldn't." Ever so slowly, David's brain fired up again, realizing there was no immediate threat to Roxi's safety. "My family is forever indebted to you and none of us would do anything to cause you harm."

"Well, that is a questionable assertion coming from the person who exposes everyone in the building to retaliation if an illegal should be found up here."

David raised his hands. "She won't be found. She's much too wily to be caught."

"It's a woman then. I hope she's worth it."

"It's not like that. Not at all. She's a—" This time Herr Falkenstein raised his hand to interrupt David's explanation.

"I honestly don't want to know. As far as I'm concerned, I never saw anything and already forgot what we were talking about."

"Oh. Thank you." Finally, David mastered his emotions. His usual shrewdness restored, he said, "I can certainly sell the silverware for you. May I see it?"

Herr Falkenstein motioned to the filing cabinet. "It's in the lower drawer, behind the binders."

David opened the drawer. "There's nothing."

"You need to pull it out all the way."

"It already is." To make sure, David pulled the handle softly, but the drawer wouldn't move.

"You need to pull past the resistance." Amused at David's unbelieving face, Herr Falkenstein added, "This is not the occasion to be gentle. Give it a hard pull."

David did as ordered. The drawer jumped out at least six inches in such a sudden movement he lost his balance and stumbled. At the last moment, he held onto the bedframe behind him to regain his footing.

"That might have been a bit too forceful. Using your strength in moderation is a lesson which will serve you not only with hidden compartments, but with most everything in your life."

After heaving out the surprisingly heavy linen bag, David handed it over to Herr Falkenstein, who carefully opened it to expose an exceptionally beautiful set of silverware. David, who was by no means an expert, hissed in a breath, admiring the perfect craftmanship embodied by the timeless elegance, while at the same time showcasing the intricate artistry of a bygone era. Each piece had been meticulously crafted from lustrous sterling silver, sparkling in the electric light. He counted twelve place settings, complete with dinner fork, salad fork, dinner knife, soup spoon, and dessert spoon. The handles were adorned with ornate engravings, featuring delicate filigree patterns and floral motifs, meticulously hand-carved by skilled artisans.

"That must be very expensive," David murmured in awe.

"It is." Herr Falkenstein sighed. "It is also very illegal."

David nodded. "My mother was heartbroken when we had to turn in our silver and other precious things. Not that we ever had anything as beautiful as this." David remembered all too well the scene when he'd accompanied his mother to the police station, supposedly turning in her beloved silver necklace, which Father had given her.

He also remembered the dressing down—despite her obvious relief—he'd received after removing said necklace from the package they turned in.

"We all, me included, have suffered the loss of precious items." Herr Falkenstein paused, furrowing his brows. "I'm probably more guilty than others of appreciating things over people."

"Back then, Mother said to my sister: 'I love my family more than this necklace.' That sentence has stuck with me ever since."

"Your mother is a very wise woman. You are lucky to have her." Herr Falkenstein gave a deep sigh, and it seemed to David that he exhaled an entire lifetime of guilt.

"You're a very generous man." David itched to put his hand on the older man's shoulder to comfort him. He resisted, because this gesture would have been utterly inappropriate. He settled for saying, "None of us is perfect, we all need to strive to become better people."

"You're a very wise young man. It has taken me close to sixty years to realize that loving others is what makes the world go round. Many men succumb to the love of power, money, and possessions. Those things will not keep your spirits up in challenging times, but people will. So choose wisely what or whom to love and always put the ones dear to your heart first." Herr Falkenstein's expression saddened. "This might be the silver lining of Hitler's reign: that enough people realize love is worth more than anything else."

He cleared his throat. "Enough of that nostalgia. If you're going to hide an illegal here, you'll need money."

"You want me to sell the silverware and keep the money?" David swallowed in disbelief.

"Not all of it. I'm going to run out of cigars soon, and smoking is the one pleasure I can't do without." With amazing speed, Herr Falkenstein calculated a sum consisting of the price of tobacco, the amount needed for one cigarette and how many he intended to smoke each week over the course of the next twelve months. Then he concluded, "However much you can sell the silverware for, anything above that amount is yours."

"I don't even know how much it is worth," David protested.

"Easily five times the amount I need, although I don't know how much you can sell it for on the black market. So, investigate carefully and don't let yourself get caught."

"I won't. Even if I do, I will never mention your name."

"That is much appreciated." Herr Falkenstein stood and walked toward the ladder. "Good luck with your lady. Remember—choose wisely whom to trust and love."

Then he was gone, leaving David alone with his reflections.

21

Edith put a hand on her hat to prevent it from flying off, grateful for her long fur coat, which protected her from the biting cold. Her mind wandered to Julius, who had to brave the below-zero temperatures each morning with nothing but his flimsy business jacket, since the Nazis had ruled last winter that Jews didn't need to stay warm.

At least she'd managed to barter one of his fine three-piece suits for a set of long woolen underwear. She smiled at the memory of his aghast grimace when she'd presented it to him at the beginning of winter.

"I refuse to wear such an inelegant piece of clothing," had been his answer.

She chuckled. As soon as the temperature had dropped below freezing point, his resistance had endured less than a week.

As she approached the building, she pursed her lips in anger. Again, someone had left the entrance door wide open. The new tenants who'd moved into the lower floors after the original owners had been rounded up in a raid were a constant thorn in her side.

She dutifully closed the door behind her, climbing up the stairs, cursing at the dirty footprints leading up. On the first landing her breath hitched in her throat and her heart was beating like a rataplan. Both doors stood wide open.

Peeking curiously inside, the devastation caused her to jump backwards as if bitten by a snake. Dropping the heavy grocery bag in her hand, she raced up to the fourth floor, praying, hoping, begging to God... There, she was greeted by the same scenario.

The door hung off its hinges, chairs lay toppled over, drawers open, the contents spread across the floor. Panic staggered her. Inching forward, she called out, "Is somebody there?"

No answer.

She called out a second time, louder. Just as she steeled herself to venture inside her apartment, the trapdoor leading into the attic opened and a soft voice said, "The SS came and took everyone away."

Dark spots blurred Edith's vision, even as she wondered to whom the voice belonged and whether she ought to trust the owner. Moments later, bare feet dangled down from the attic. Not bothering to extend the ladder, their owner jumped down and landed with a barely audible thud next to Edith, who jumped backwards.

"Old habit. Forgive me for scaring you." The stranger was a petite young woman with pitch-black hair and bright electric-blue eyes.

The education in manners she'd received from her mother-in-law so many years ago kicked in, giving Edith something to hold on to. "Edith Falkenstein, my husband owns this apartment."

"I know," the young woman said.

"And you are?" Edith scrutinized the stranger, who looked surprisingly well-kept, except for her dirty bare feet. Very notably, no yellow star disfigured her jacket, which made Edith think that either she wasn't a Jew, or she'd gone into hiding. But what on earth was she doing here?

"You can call me Roxi."

"Well, Roxi. What are you doing in my attic?"

"I'd rather not waste time with my story, you have more important problems to solve."

Taken aback by her boldness, Edith was about to answer with a sharp remark when she heard soft steps above her head and asked, "Is somebody else there?"

Roxi nodded. "Three children. I managed to hide them before the SS arrived, but I'm afraid the people further down weren't as lucky. I heard screams, trampling and then the trucks moving on.

"Oh no." Edith leaned against the wall, feeling faint. "Who was it?"

"Couldn't see a thing."

Her curiosity about the stranger forgotten, Edith lurched into the apartment, wanting to know whether Julius was safe. After searching all rooms, she still didn't know. Most days, the Gerber children stayed at home on their own, waiting until one of the adults returned from work.

Propelled by panic, she was about to grab her handbag and head out again to check up on Julius at his place of work when Roxi shoved the Gerber children into the apartment, saying, "Here you go. I have to leave."

"Wait. You can't just..." Edith watched, speechless, as the lithe woman climbed back into the attic floor, retracted the ladder and closed the trap door behind her.

"Are they gone?" a small hand pulled at Edith's skirt.

She looked down into Hertha's anguished face. Julius would have to fend for himself; right now the children needed her more. "Yes, they are gone. You got lucky." *Thanks to the mysterious Roxi who seems to live in our attic.*

"Roxi told us to stay quiet, but we knew that anyway." Holger pushed out his chest.

"Do you know her?"

"No," all three children said in unison.

"She's mighty nice," Hans added.

"Let's make you some tea after such a fright." Edith herself sorely needed the comfort of a hot cup of chamomile tea.

As she put the kettle on the stove, she pondered what to do next. Apparently people had been taken, although she couldn't be sure who. If she was lucky, all adults in their household had still been at work and the SS had only rounded up residents from the floors further down.

Edith was appalled by her train of thought and scolded herself. *They are people, too.*

Not your people, and you can only care so much.

She didn't listen to her inner voice of reason, the guilt for having toughened up so much against human suffering weighed down heavily on her chest, making it difficult to breathe. Luckily the whistling kettle distracted her. She took it from the stove, put some dried chamomile Amelie had collected on a meadow into each and poured the water on top.

"Here you go. Now tell me what exactly happened."

The children all talked over each other, yet didn't provide useful information, except that suddenly Roxi had stood in the apartment and ordered them into the attic. The moment she'd closed the trap door behind them, they'd all heard the jackboots smashing up the stairs.

"Was anyone else at home?"

"No," Holger said.

A huge weight fell from Edith's shoulders. After drinking their infusions, the Gerber children retired to their room.

Edith, though, was too shaken to get up. About half an hour later the door opened, as Amelie and Heinrich returned home. "What the hell has happened here?"

"SS raid." Edith didn't have the energy to provide a full sentence.

"Are you alright?" Heinrich cast a very worried look at her. At the same time, Amelie began putting things back into their respective drawers.

"Yes. Just frightened."

His eyes were filled with so much kindness, Edith fought hard to hold back her tears. "I can only imagine. Did they hurt you?"

"No. I arrived not long ago to find the door open and the apartment raided."

"Was anyone else here?"

"Just the Gerber children. It seems the wire David set up to ring a bell when someone tripped it alerted them early enough to hide in the attic. They are now in their room." Edith thought it wiser not to mention the mysterious woman living upstairs.

"Shall I make you another infusion?" he asked with a nod to her empty cup.

"I can do it myself."

"No, you sit and relax. It must have been an awful shock." Heinrich hurried into the kitchen to put the kettle on the stove.

Watching Amelie cleaning up the apartment, Edith felt utterly useless—and helpless. Slowly the shock dissipated and silent tears streamed down her cheeks. It was all too much and she feared she couldn't resist a single day longer.

Morosely she sunk back into the cushions, worrying that if a Gestapo man were to appear and put divorce papers in front of her, she'd sign them this minute. Just to be done with it and get on with her life.

Herr Goldmann returned with three cups of infusion and handed her one.

"Thank you, Herr Goldmann."

"Don't you think it's about time we used first names? Please, call me Heinrich."

"Edith." She raised her cup. "Normally we ought to say cheers with wine, but I guess this will have to do."

When he broke out in laughter, her weak moment passed. Of course she wouldn't give up. She'd continue to fight for Julius, for the Goldmanns, for everyone dear to her. The Nazis would not defeat her.

One by one, the members of the household returned. Delia, David and Helga, their eyes wide with shock. News of the raid had traveled fast through the Jewish grapevine.

Helga wrapped her arms first around Amelie and then David. "Thank God, you're here. I was so worried about you."

"We're fine, Mutti," David assured her, his voice slightly trembling.

After a minute, Helga let go of her children and threw herself into Heinrich's arms. "Sweetheart, I'm so happy you're unharmed." He embraced her, caressing her back and murmuring soothing words as if she were the one in danger, not him.

Then, finally Julius arrived. Edith completely forgot her education and fell around his neck. "Thank God, you're safe."

"We knew it would only be a matter of time until they returned," Julius said, outwardly calm.

"Knut didn't warn me this time." Again, the feeling of inadequacy crept into Edith's bones. She should have visited her brother more frequently, put out her feelers with other people...

"Don't blame yourself," Julius reassured her.

Helga chimed in, "It's the Nazis' fault, not yours."

"It's all the Nazis' fault. I hate them!" Amelie stomped her foot, voicing what everyone in the room thought.

"Unfortunately, there's nothing we can do." Delia's voice was coarse, the prima ballerina but a shadow of her former self.

"We can and we should," David disagreed.

All heads turned toward him. His father said, "I hope you're not contemplating anything stupid."

"Stupid?" David scoffed. "You'd rather I walk like a lamb to the slaughter than fight back?"

"David, darling, now you're exaggerating," Helga said.

"Evacuation might not be as bad as everyone makes it seem." Julius tried to calm the waters.

"Well, if it isn't that bad, why are you all so frightened?" David concluded with impeccable logic.

Silently, Edith was on his side. If Knut and even Joseph had warned her, nothing remotely positive could be expected. But not wanting to escalate the argument, she merely observed, "Thanks to David's alarm system, the Gerber children were able to hide in the attic."

"In the attic?" David's eyes frantically traveled from person to person. "Where are they now?"

Edith scrutinized his face, puzzled by his panicked reaction, until the realization hit her between the eyes. He was sweet on the woman in hiding.

"In their room. I'll go and get them." Amelie went to fetch the children, whom everyone had been too busy to remember. "Where are their parents, by the way?"

A communal shake of the head was the answer, until Helga stated, "I believe they're working the late shift this week and won't be home until midnight."

22

The next morning Helga was preparing breakfast for everyone when a very scared-looking Holger left the Gerbers' room. "Where are my mom and dad?"

Despite the icy chill running down her spine, she gave him an encouraging smile. "They must have left early to go to work."

Near to tears, he shook his head. "They didn't come home. I slept in their bed to make sure I'd wake up."

That boy was bright and, under different circumstances, Helga would have admired him for it. Now, it only made her sad. "Perhaps they had to work the nightshift too?" Herr and Frau Gerber had been granted permission to travel after curfew because they worked in a war-critical munitions factory and were often forced to do overtime. They had never had to work a double shift before, but she was willing to grasp at any straw to avoid what, deep in her gut, she knew to be true.

"You think so?" Holger's voice filled with hope, before he cocked his head, leveling his gaze at Helga. "Or are you just saying this to calm me down?"

She patted his head. "I don't know where they are, but we must not jump to conclusions. For all we know they could have been held up by curfew or some other thing. For now, go back to sleep. I'm sure they'll be home by the time you wake up again."

But Herr and Frau Gerber never returned.

After calling their workplace from a nearby public phone, the outcome they'd feared was confirmed: the couple had left on time, but hadn't shown up for work the next morning.

"Shall I go and ask at the police station?" Heinrich offered.

"You?" A stab of fear threatened to splinter Helga's heart as she observed her husband's familiar face, which had become gaunt and tired over the last years. "Under no circumstances will you go anywhere near a police station."

"Are you going to defend me with that?" His eyes twinkled with amusement as he pointed at the raised wooden spoon in her hand.

"What if I do?" She wasn't going to let him expose himself to danger.

"Then, I'd definitely want to be there to watch the show."

Her eyes glared daggers at him. Despite her obvious scorn, her incorrigible husband took a pencil from his breast pocket and held it up like a foil. "En garde!"

Unable to curb the smile tugging at her lips, she put the cooking spoon down. His ability to make light of even the darkest moments was one of the things she loved most about him.

"What? No friendly match? Are you afraid or what?" he teased her.

"I know what you're doing, and this is not the time," she protested.

"It's absolutely the time." He gently took her hand. "We've been together so long that I can read it in your eyes."

"Really?" Naturally, she'd known this already. The same was true for her. Just by the way his shoulders were hunched or his lips pursed, she was able to read his mood.

"Yes." His gaze turned serious. "Right now, you're more

shaken than I've seen you in years. I'm afraid if I don't do something to cheer you up, you'll break down."

"Me? Never!" She shrugged, trying to brush away the truth
of his remark.

"See? You're trying to act valiantly for the benefit of
everyone else. I can see the wheels in your brain turning, trying
to come up with a solution for the Gerber children. But I can
also see that you've dug yourself into a corner."

She gave another helpless shrug. "I can't stand by and do
nothing."

His brown eyes shone with love, his warm breath brushing
her cheek. "I need you. Amelie and David need you. Everyone
in this household needs you. But that can wait. For the next few
minutes I want you to think only of yourself."

"Isn't that utterly selfish?" Helga hesitated to put herself
first, since she was so used to being the one everyone else
relied on.

"Not at all. It'll allow you to renew your energy and take up
caring for all of us again." Then he kissed her, at first gentle,
growing more passionate with every passing second. When he
let her go, his eyes devoured her with a heat that made her
remember their first years of marriage.

"Not here," she whispered.

"Hmm," Heinrich murmured against her ear. "That wasn't
my plan, but now that you mention it..." He traced little kisses
down her neck, sending tremors down her spine. Because they
shared the room with their two adult children, it had been such
a long time since she and Heinrich had enjoyed more than a
few stolen minutes together.

"But where?" Helga finally allowed herself to get carried
away by the love and passion of better times.

"Let that be my concern." He cast her a wicked grin,
making her insides giddy. After a long, passionate kiss where his

tongue explored her mouth as if it were the first time, she finally came up for breath, a rush of blood heating her cheeks.

Knowing that her husband was going to find an undisturbed place for them heightened the anticipation. Her entire body tingled. Nevertheless, she freed herself from his embrace, seizing the opportunity. "Then it's agreed upon. You find a suitable place and I visit the police station."

He broke out into laughter. "Admit it, that was your intention all along!"

"Maybe." She swatted his arm. "And now let me get back to cooking or there will be no food tonight." Seeing his hungry stare at her body, she added, "Dinner or otherwise."

"I'm going already." He agreed with a pout, yet he used her distraction to catch her mouth in another breathtaking kiss. Then he winked at her. "See you tonight."

Her entire body tingling, Helga had difficulty focusing on the cooking. When she'd finished, she left the meal to slow-cook, took off her apron and departed for the police station.

When she finally managed to speak to a police officer, Helga was told that the Gerbers had chosen to move to an undisclosed location.

Her lips twitching, she bit back a sharp retort. It wouldn't do any good to alert the police to the fact that the couple would never up and leave without their three children. A heavy weight pressing down on her chest, she stumbled outside, realizing that they had to find a safe place for the children immediately. It wouldn't take the Gestapo long to compare their lists and find them missing.

Back at the apartment, Edith was preparing to go out. "Oh, good, you're here. I need to rush out for work. Any news about the Gerbers?"

"Yes." Helga's voice sounded desolate even to her own ears.

"Oh no!" Edith needed just one glance at Helga's face to realize the severity of the situation. "They've been deported, haven't they?"

"In the policeman's words: they have chosen to move to an undisclosed location."

"Dear heavens!" A forlorn expression appeared on Edith's face, and she unsuccessfully tried to put her left hand into the right glove. "What are we going to do with the children? We can't keep them here."

"I know. It's not safe. The Gestapo will soon realize they're missing and come looking for them." Forgotten the happy moments of this morning, Helga felt like an octogenarian, all energy sucked from her frail body.

"The attic isn't an option," Edith murmured.

Helga raised a questioning eyebrow.

"Forget it." Edith finally realized she was tugging on the wrong glove and put it on her other hand. "The only person I can think of is Silvana Lemberg."

"Hasn't she had to close the school?"

"Yes, but she has connections and might know somebody who can help." Edith cast a glance at her delicate wristwatch. "I really have to rush out for work—God knows we need the money. I can visit her tomorrow."

Helga feared it might be too late by then. Any minute now the Gestapo would check their lists and realize that three children had evaded capture. She didn't want to risk anyone coming for them. "I'll take them there right now."

Surprise flickered through Edith's eyes. "She won't be able to keep them longer than a night or two."

"We need to get them out of the house, sooner rather than later." Helga's heart drummed faster as she imagined the sound of jackboots smashing up the stairs. "The SS might come looking for them any minute."

Edith's anguished face mirrored Helga's emotions. "Do you want me to accompany you?"

"No need. I can manage. You'd better be on time for work."

"Get those children to safety, whatever you do." With these words Edith rushed out.

As soon as the door closed behind her, doubts attacked Helga, crowding out the confidence she'd felt seconds earlier. So much could go wrong on their way to the former Lemberg school. Squaring her shoulders, she walked toward the Gerbers' room and knocked on the door.

"Who is it?" a thin voice asked.

"Me, Helga Goldmann."

"Ah, Frau Goldmann. Wait a moment."

From the other side of the door came scratching sounds, as if a piece of furniture was being moved, then the door cracked ajar. Helga had to bite back a laugh when she recognized the oldest, Holger, with a stick in his hand, ready to defend his siblings from intruders.

"It's really you." He seemed slightly disappointed.

"Yes." She hadn't thought how to deliver the bad news, so she simply said, "I'm going to take you to a safe place."

Instantly, tears filled his eyes, even as he valiantly tried to swallow them down. "Our parents are not coming back, are they?"

"I'm so sorry." She opened the door and stepped inside, wrapping the boy into her arms. She considered lying to the children, then decided against it. Despite their young age, all three knew about the awful things happening in Germany. "It seems they were taken during the raid last night and have been sent to the East."

"Why can't we stay with you?" Hans asked.

Helga worried her lip, then made up her mind not to spare the children the truth. Their future was fraught with danger and they might stand a better chance if they were prepared. "It's not safe here. The SS will soon come looking for you."

"Can't we hide in the attic again?" Hertha asked.

"Shush. The other woman said we can't," Holger rebuked his little sister.

Helga squinted. This was the second time in a few minutes that someone had mentioned the attic. Something fishy was going on up there. She let it go for now and instead concentrated on the task at hand. "I'll take you to Herr Falkenstein's sister. You remember her, don't you? She has visited a few times."

"She's nice. I like her," Helga said.

"But will she take us in?" Hans asked.

"That's what we're going to find out. She may only hide you for a few days, but she will know who to ask for help." Looking from one child to the next, Helga ordered, "Pack your things. Only as much as you can fit into your satchels. Meanwhile I'll go and remove the yellow stars from your jackets."

"That's forbidden!" Holger called out.

Helga swallowed down the lump forming in her throat. "From this moment on, you're going to have to do many forbidden things if you want to stay alive. Just remember one thing: you can break the Nazis' laws, but you must never do anything that doesn't feel right in here." She tapped at her heart.

"Like not obeying the law to kill our rabbits?" Hertha had tears in her eyes.

"Exactly. Now, go and pack, we don't have much time." Helga left the room and busied herself with removing the yellow stars from the children's jackets. Ten minutes later, they stepped out of their room in single file, faces earnest, satchels slung across their shoulders. Helga's heart shattered into a thousand pieces at the sight and she sent a quick prayer to heaven. *Please keep them safe.*

As she handed them their starless jackets, she explained, "From now on, until I tell you otherwise, you're to call me Mutti."

Hertha's eyes opened in panic and Helga patted her head. "We're going to pretend you're Aryans. Don't speak to anyone, unless asked a question, and then keep your answer as short as possible." She looked at the oldest. "Best if you do the talking for your siblings, if needed."

Holger grew a few inches with pride. "Don't worry, Frau Goldmann, I will take good care of them."

"You have to call me Mutti, remember?"

"I won't forget again, Mutti," Holger said with an earnest expression.

Fighting back the tears, she observed the three youngsters. They knew all too well what was at stake and she inwardly gave thanks that her own children were already grown up. Not that this guaranteed their safety, but at least they were old enough to cope—after a hopefully happy childhood, despite the circumstances.

The alarming sensation in her gut intensified, so she wasted no time propelling the children down the stairs, out of the house, onto the sidewalk and around the corner. After marching two blocks, they arrived at the tram station.

Hertha looked up to her with terror-filled eyes. "But we aren't allowed—"

"Shush." Holger cut her short. "She's our Mutti and we are allowed to do anything she does, right?"

"Right, Holger." Helga tousled his hair, scolding herself for not explaining things properly in her rush to leave the house. After glancing over her shoulder, she crouched down and said, "To keep you safe, we need to pretend you're my children. Call me Mutti and do as I say. That's why I took the yellow stars from your jackets, so everyone will assume you're Aryans and

allowed to do anything they are allowed to, including taking the
bus. Understood?"

All three children nodded with serious faces.

23

The tram arrived and Helga gently shoved the children inside, waiting for the conductor to check her monthly pass, when a hot flash of fear reminded her that she had no idea from what age children needed their own ticket.

David and Amelie had always owned monthly student tickets, but since Jews weren't allowed to use public transport anymore, the Gerber children didn't.

Doubts filled her mind. Shouldn't the children be at school? Would the conductor question where she was taking them and why? Just as she was about to scream with anguish, she felt Hertha's small hand sneaking into hers. Taking a deep breath, she willed the panic away. She had to be strong for the three youngsters.

When the conductor, an older man with only one arm, approached them, Helga plastered a pleasant expression on her face while she squeezed Hertha's hand.

"Tickets please," the conductor said.

She showed him her monthly pass, racking her brain how to ask about tickets for the children, who behaved miraculously sangfroid.

"Beautiful children you have. My daughter recently gave birth to my first grandchild." A happy smile spread across his face.

"Congratulations to your daughter. I can only imagine how much joy that little bundle brings to your family."

His eyes narrowed. "We all need joy these days. Her husband was on home leave for the birth, but had to return to the front yesterday. It was hard for my daughter." Fear struck his eyes when he realized that his words might be considered defeatist.

Helga seized the opportunity with both hands. "I'm sure you and your daughter are great patriots and she will raise her wonderful child with pride until her husband returns home a war hero."

The conductor gratefully accepted the bridge she'd built him. "We are indeed very proud of our son-in-law. I would do my duty at the front, too, if I hadn't lost my arm in the last war."

"We all do our duty to the best of our abilities. Being a conductor helps keep the wheels rolling for victory." Even as the hated slogan left her mouth she wondered whether she'd laid it on too thick. Apparently not, because he smiled and turned to the next passenger without asking for the children's tickets.

The weight plummeting from her heart was so massive, she could have sworn she heard the impact.

When they disembarked from the tram, Holger sidled up to her. "I was so worried he would ask why we're not at school."

Helga tousled his hair. "I would have come up with a believable excuse, but I'm glad I didn't have to." She gathered the three children around her and explained, "Take each other by the hand, we need to walk from here and it's going to take us about half an hour."

She had mulled over this decision for quite a while and finally opted not to transfer to the bus which stopped directly in front of the entrance to the former Lemberg school. She couldn't face having to deal with another conductor.

When they reached their destination, the breath hitched in Helga's chest at the sight of several SS men standing guard in front of the main entrance to the premises. Apparently it hadn't been such a good idea to come here.

Unfortunately the guards had seen her. One of them strode toward her. "*Halt!* You aren't allowed to walk here."

Despite cold sweat trickling down her back, she put on her most innocent expression. "I'm so very sorry, officer. I wasn't aware this street is closed."

"What do you want here?" He wasn't impressed by her show.

The Lembergs had recently been forced to move into the gardener's house—more a shed than an actual house—at the back of the complex. Feverishly racking her brain, she remembered a gate partly concealed by ivy, with a path leading up to their new living quarters.

"We accidentally got off the tram one station too early, and now we have to walk around to the other side of this building." She hoped the guard wasn't versed in the public transport lines.

The guard continued to eye her suspiciously, but broke off when blond, blue-eyed Hans smiled up at him and said, "When I'm grown up, I want to be in the SS like you."

Helga's heart stopped beating for several torturous seconds. Nothing happened. The SS man's face softened.

"You'll have to be very disciplined and train hard."

"I know."

"Please excuse him, officer. My son is fascinated by soldiers." Helga jumped into the conversation, sending Hans a warning gaze to keep his mouth shut.

"Our nation needs heroes."

"We certainly do." She smiled, knowing her understanding

of hero would certainly not match his. "We shouldn't take up any more of your time."

"To get to the other side, you have to return from where you came and turn left at the next crossing."

"Thank you so much, officer." Helga grabbed Hans' hand and turned on her heels, the soldier's stare boring deep into her back. Only when they'd turned the corner did she finally relax and pause.

"I told you not to speak unless spoken to," she scolded him.

"It worked, didn't it?" Hans pushed out his lower lip.

"It did, but it could have gone wrong." Helga reflected on the situation. "Thank you for helping out. Next time, wait until I give you a sign."

The SS man had sent them on quite the detour and it took another ten minutes before they finally stood in front of the gate in the wall surrounding the gardens.

No bell was in sight, so she opened the unlocked gate. A queasy feeling settling in her guts, Helga ushered the children through and knocked on the door, which Frau Lemberg personally answered.

"Frau Goldmann! Has something happened to my brother?" The usually effervescent woman had dark shadows beneath her eyes and a look of alarm on her face. Before Helga managed to answer, Frau Lemberg's gaze fell on the children. "I'm very sorry, we were forced to close the school."

"That's not the reason I'm here. Can we come in, please?"

Frau Lemberg's eyes frantically darted around. "Make it quick. It's better no one sees you."

Helga wondered whether this had anything to do with the SS men she'd spotted at the main entrance and if she should rather try her luck elsewhere. For lack of other options, though, she followed Frau Lemberg inside.

"Would you like some water?" Frau Lemberg asked.

"Yes, please," Holger answered politely.

"And an *Ersatzkaffee* for you?"

Nodding, Helga explained, "Please excuse the unannounced visit. The SS raided our house yesterday." Noticing the fear creeping into Frau Lemberg's gaze, Helga added, "Your brother and Edith are fine. These children managed to hide, but their parents weren't as lucky. Apparently they arrived home just as the SS were leaving. They were taken."

Frau Lemberg let the awful news go without comment. "Let's get you that water I promised—you must be thirsty." She disappeared into the kitchen and returned moments later with three full glasses. "Here you go. Can you quietly play for a few minutes?"

Holger nodded. "We won't make a peep."

When Frau Lemberg beckoned, Helga followed her into the kitchen, watching as she filled the kettle with water and put it on the stove, apparently reluctant to broach the topic. When she finally turned around, her eyes were filled with sorrow. "The children can't stay here."

It was as if someone had pulled the rug out under Helga's feet. Gasping for air, she struggled against the wave of desperation threatening to drown her. "Just for a few days, until we find another place for them, please."

"They are not safe here. The Gestapo have turned the school into a holding camp for the Jews about to go on transport to the East."

An image of the Gerbers sitting on the ground just a few meters away, awaiting their fate, hit Helga deep in her stomach. Maybe being sent to the East wasn't as horrible as everyone believed it to be, and the children would be better off with their parents than in the care of strangers. She shrugged the vision away. If both Edith's brothers had warned her about evacuation, it must be godawful.

"I had hoped you'd know someone who might take them in.

We would keep them, if it weren't for the fear that the Gestapo might return at any minute to pick them up."

Frau Lemberg took a deep breath. "Most families have been evacuated already and the rest seem to be gathered in the former school building, awaiting their destiny. I'm surprised my husband and I haven't been targeted yet."

"Is there a Christian family who might take them?" Helga was getting desperate. Under no circumstance was she going to return home with the children. She'd never forgive herself if she failed to protect them.

"I wish there were." Frau Lemberg took the kettle from the stove, pouring it over the Ersatzkaffee.

Helga was mesmerized by her efficient movements. "I wonder why we are doing this?"

"Doing what?"

"Drinking Ersatzkaffee. I don't know a single person who actually likes it, and yet we all drink that stuff." When Frau Lemberg stared at her as if she'd gone crazy right in front of her eyes, Helga added, "Isn't this the same as the persecution of the Jews: nobody I know condones it, and yet nobody tries to stop it."

Frau Lemberg shook her head. "That is a rather philosophical interpretation. We drink Ersatzkaffee because we need the feeling of a hot drink in our stomach, whereas not helping our neighbors... people have a thousand reasons for that, ranging from fear, greed, or indifference to condoning the actions of the Gestapo. Although I do think the people who approve are in the minority. But when the majority fail to speak out, the minority's actions are left to run unfettered."

Helga took the offered drink, savoring the slightly bitter aroma of chicory root. It lacked the fine nuances and complexities found in genuine coffee. Still, she found Frau Lemberg's words to be true: the hot, bitter liquid gave her the fuzzy sensation she craved so much in this crazy world.

"How can I make sure the children are safe?"

"You can't. We can only pray."

"There must be someone willing to take them. Anyone." Helga was ready to throw herself to her knees and beg.

"I can't promise anything. There's a pastor from the Swedish Victoria Parish in Wilmersdorf. A few of my students have mentioned that he helped them. Apparently, he's been obtaining food coupons and issuing forged baptism certificates."

"That would be wonderful. Thank you so much."

"Don't thank me too soon. I don't know him personally. Let me see if I can get in contact with him." Silvana raised a hand to her recently grayed hair. The tiredness in the gesture betrayed how worn out the former school director must be.

"In any case, I thank you for at least trying. I'd keep the children if I believed them to be safe with us."

Silvana let out a heartfelt sigh. "I know. I'll keep them overnight. If he can't help, you must take them back. It's too dangerous with the SS crawling all over the premises."

Relief washed over Helga, so strong she almost kissed Frau Lemberg on her cheeks. Since that was utterly inappropriate, she simply offered, "If you need anything—for them or other children—please let me know."

Frau Lemberg gave a sad smile. "What we need is for Hitler to stop persecuting our people."

"I wish I could help with that." Helga meant it. Given the opportunity to meet with this evil man, she'd go there with a knife in her handbag, prepared to take him out. That's what his politics had made of her.

24

Joseph sat in his office, overlooking the main street of the Theresienstadt camp. He took great pride in the immaculate facades, the cleanliness of the pavement and the orderly behavior of the residents.

Theresienstadt was the flagship of the camp system, meant to show the world, and especially the German population, how well the Nazi government cared for even their archenemies. It existed to silence all rumors and concerns about the evil treatment of Jews, because Hitler, and Goebbels by extension, cared above all about public opinion.

Regrettably, up to this day, the general public was not steadfast enough to accept the wisdom that these vermin had to be eradicated. Instead, many people were falsely guided by empathy and kindheartedness—valuable character traits under normal circumstances, except the German Reich was entangled in a war for its very existence.

Only the extermination of every last Jew on earth would ensure prosperity and freedom to the German nation for millennia to come. Yes, Joseph was proud of his contribution to the Fatherland and did his best to suppress any compassion he might feel toward the Jewish pest.

Shame at his own weakness slashed his guts, as he repented his atrocious betrayal to the honorable cause. It had happened fifteen months ago and still weighed heavily on his conscience. Back then, he'd sneaked into Edith's apartment to urge her to flee the country to save herself and her husband.

It had been wrong to let his emotions rule over logic. Just because Julius Falkenstein was married to Joseph's sister didn't make him any less dangerous. If anything, the reverse was true. If he could, he'd travel back in time and redeem himself by delivering Julius to the authorities instead of warning him.

To stamp out that black mark on his otherwise clean record, he dutifully grabbed a thick folder to pore over the statistics his accountant had provided for him. This prompted another pang of guilt. A decade ago, after the Night of Broken Glass, he'd let another Jew escape for sentimental reasons. A former schoolmate, Heinrich Goldmann, who was married to the girl Joseph had been sweet on before he met his first wife.

Joseph shrugged the guilt away. Those reckless actions belonged to the past. He had become a better man, one who didn't allow himself to be carried away by undue sympathy. These days he prided himself on maintaining absolute control over his emotions, to the point that he had no qualms about doing away with one of the subhumans, whoever it might be. If required, he'd send his own sister to her grave for the crime of staying married to a Jew.

So far, this hadn't been necessary, because Hitler was generous toward those misguided souls who'd been lured into loving the hideous enemy.

His eyes ran down the columns of numbers representing the new arrivals versus the departures. There was a constant influx of mostly old, rich subjects, who weren't used to hard work.

They inevitably succumbed to the squalid living conditions within a few weeks and joined the departure column.

Through trial and error, Joseph had found a way to maintain equilibrium in the camp's population, whereby the departures were offsetting the new arrivals. Theresienstadt had become a well-oiled machine, doing away with the Reich's enemies in an effortless, natural way.

At least he didn't have to deal with what Heydrich had called "the ultimate threat" when he'd presented Joseph and Reiner Huber with his genial plan for the final solution to the Jewish problem at the conclusion of the Wannsee Conference.

"The idea is to put them to use first," Heydrich had explained. "The weaker ones will be sent to factories or camps, the able-bodied will be transported eastward to work on road construction projects. Undoubtedly the vast majority will drop out through natural selection. Thus we only have to eliminate the remainder."

"Why exterminate them if we can further exploit their labor?" Joseph had asked, enthusiastic at the notion of hundreds of thousands of workers for the struggling armaments industry.

Heydrich, in his inimitable detached voice had elaborated, "Even the most resilient object will be depleted at some point, so it won't be of further use to the Reich. But, given the chance to recuperate, it will procreate and become the nucleus of a new, more virulent strain of the Jewish race. It's necessary to destroy that seed."

"I understand..." Reiner Huber had said.

Joseph had liked the hard-working, ambitious man, who'd sadly been assassinated by the French resistance during a visit to Paris last year.

A glance at the clock told him it was time for his daily briefing with his two aides. Punctual as always, the knock on the door came at the exact second when the hand turned the full minute.

"*Herein*," he bellowed, giving permission to enter.

The two men in their late twenties were poster child SS men: tall, blond, with bright blue eyes, always eager to serve Führer and Fatherland. Almost looking like twins, they approached Joseph's desk, giving a Hitler salute perfect in form and execution. It was a joy to watch.

A warm feeling in his heart, Joseph stood up, reciprocated the salute and shouted a heartfelt, "Heil Hitler." Then he motioned the two aids, Mayer and Helm, to sit down.

"Sturmbannführer." Helm held out a sheet of paper. "We've received new orders from headquarters."

"Let me see." Joseph grabbed the paper, running his eyes over the text, furrowing his brows. "They advise us to keep extra capacity for a huge delivery by the end of February."

"Does it say how many arrivals we are to expect?" Mayer asked, practical as ever.

"About three to four times our monthly intake in just one transport."

"That will be difficult to achieve with natural attrition, even if we step up the work quota and punishments," Helm said.

Joseph leaned back, assessing the situation. Helm was right, they'd never be able to generate enough departures through the usual measures, not even by further reducing food allowances. "We also have to keep in mind the ability to process the corpses, since the crematorium is constantly working at capacity."

"Yes, Sturmbannführer," Helm and Mayer said in unison, sitting up straighter. Joseph couldn't have been prouder of them if they were his own flesh and blood. Unfortunately, he'd been forced to disavow his two sons by his first wife due to a trace of Jewish blood in their genealogy. In weak moments, he wished they were here with him instead of Mayer and Helm. It would be such a joy to train his sons to become consummate SS men.

"We'll have to relocate some of the weaker subjects to another camp. Arrange for their transport to Auschwitz—they have the capacity to deal with large amounts of arrivals," Joseph ordered.

"Yes, sir." Helm and Meyer stood, gave the perfect *Hitlergruss* and clicked their heels before they left Joseph's office. They would execute the task with swift precision. Meanwhile, he picked up the telephone to arrange a train for the transport.

When he was done, he looked out onto the camp's picturesque main street, musing what kind of plan warranted such an order from headquarters. As far as he knew, there weren't many Jews left in the Reich.

In any case, it didn't matter. An SS man's task was to execute orders, not to question them. If Heydrich, or anyone else, deemed it important, they'd let Joseph know. If not, he had better things to do than waste his time speculating over the fate of subhumans.

He decided to call it a day and surprise his sweet wife Liesl by arranging a performance of the camp theater troupe tonight, just for the two of them, while the nanny took care of their newborn son.

Yes, life had become infinitely better since Hitler had come to power.

25

FEBRUARY 27, 1943

Julius waited until the foreman looked the other way before he stretched his hurting leg. It had been raining a lot and his rheumatism was acting up in the humid cold. This morning he'd even needed Thea's help to disembark from the tram in front of the factory.

Sitting long hours on the high chair, punching holes into metal, certainly didn't help. Furtively glimpsing at the clock on the opposite wall, he returned to work, occupying his mind with a complicated percentage calculation while his hands continued to perform the required task.

One day he'd counted them: 25,386 times the same movement during his shift. To say the work was boring would be an understatement, and he would have gone crazy by now if he hadn't resorted to keeping his mind busy with mathematics. Spending his working hours in the company of numbers helped him to escape reality.

Today, he was solving a particularly tricky calculation, estimating the difference in weight of a pallet with metal pieces before and after perforation. He was close to adding the final numbers in his head when the siren roared.

Irritated faces looked up all around him, since it was much too early for lunch break.

"What's going on?" he muttered.

"Who knows. Perhaps an important visitor," Thea, who was filling in for her sick mother at the neighboring workstation, answered.

Regardless of the cause, Julius welcomed the respite, using it to stretch his arms and legs. He broke off when the foreman bellowed, "Every Jew is to assemble in the yard. Put your work tools aside, take off the aprons and walk single file downstairs."

A shudder ran down Julius' spine. Whatever this was about, it couldn't be anything good. As he followed the command, Thea, agile as always, ventured toward the window. When she turned around, her face was white as chalk. Her gaze met his, forming a silent "Hide" with her lips.

"They've come for us," his other neighbor whispered, the fear thick in his voice.

"Why should they? We're essential workers." Julius had been clinging to this belief for such a long time, he wasn't going to be disabused of it.

Thea returned to Julius' side, having grabbed their coats from the rack. She handed Julius his. "Here you go."

He admired the young woman's sangfroid and told himself to keep his aplomb, even as he observed that most of the Jewish workers were in different states of panic, far from the orderly single file the foreman had demanded. People ran around like headless chickens, and soon the bottleneck formed by the exit door to the staircase became impassable.

Thea tugged at his hand. "Herr Falkenstein, I have found a hiding place in the storage room in the basement. It's big enough for the two of us."

Julius was sorely tempted to take her up on the offer, but he acknowledged that his rheumatic knees would never allow him to descend the stairs fast enough. If he attempted to hide in the storage room, he'd not only be discovered, but he'd also endanger her.

"I can't. My knees," he whispered.

"I'll help you."

"Unless you carry me down the stairs, it won't work." They were approaching the exit door. Within seconds they would reach the staircase and once the crowd had shoved them through, there would be no way for either of them to get to safety. "Look, I won't make it. But you will."

"Please. You can do it," she begged.

From outside, he heard voices bellowing orders. This gave him an idea. "They'll check us against a list. They always have lists, you know that. If both of us go missing, they'll send a search party."

Her face fell.

"Don't worry. I'll cover for you."

"But how..."

By this time they'd reached the staircase. He pushed Thea toward the basement. "Go. If you escape, please tell my wife what happened." A second later she disappeared into the looming darkness, and he followed the mass out into the huge yard where the SS were waiting. The chilled air hit him like a slap in the face and he silently thanked Thea for her foresight in grabbing their coats.

Everybody else was coatless, their work clothes offering no protection against the winter temperatures. Stumbling along with the crowd, cold sweat dropped down his forehead. Instinctively, he reached for the kerchief he used to wear in the breast pocket of his three-piece-suit, only for his fingers to find the edges of the yellow star sewn onto his jacket.

The days of wearing elegant suits were long over. At least for him.

"Faster! Lazy scumbags!" one SS man shouted, while another one wielded his rifle to drive the panicked workers into an orderly line. Alas, without success. He must have recognized the futility of his efforts, because he began herding them into groups instead.

Then, a third SS man strutted forward. He was at least forty years old, boots polished to a shine, his uniform impeccable and his face a mask of exceptional arrogance. Julius inwardly flinched; he knew that type, had dealt with them for decades in business—never a pleasant experience. This man was convinced of his own importance and harbored contempt for everyone else.

The shoulder lapels classified him as Oberscharführer, which confirmed Julius' character assessment. A mid-level non-commissioned officer, useful to lead a small unit, but not intelligent enough to rise up in the ranks.

The Oberscharführer didn't allow Julius time to muse, because at the snap of his fingers, a younger SS man raced to his side with the ubiquitous list, proffering it to his boss as if it were a treasure. And perhaps it was.

Not wasting a second, the Oberscharführer bellowed at the assembled crowd: "When I call your name, you shout 'Present'. Loud and clear. Understood?"

The collective murmur of agreement caused the Oberscharführer's lips to twitch in disgust, apparently having expected a more enthusiastic reply. Then he read the first name from the list.

The blood chilled in Julius' veins. He fully intended to keep his promise to cover up for Thea, but he hadn't expected the SS to call out the names right there in the yard. He'd hoped to be given the opportunity to explain that Thea had left early this day due to sickness, an accident or whatever, which wouldn't be possible now.

"Abrams."

"Present."

"Allgeier."

"Present."

The Oberscharführer went on rattling off names, receiving a more or less firm response to each. But always a response. Julius didn't have time to weigh the pros and cons or calculate the odds and come up with a plan.

"Becker."

"Present."

"Dalke."

His heart racing at full speed, Julius swallowed hard and called out in the highest-pitched voice he was capable of: "Present."

A bead of sweat threatened to drop into his eye, yet he made no movement, listening intently. Time appeared to slow down, stretching the instants between his answer and the next name on the list into a seemingly infinite expanse.

Julius was as good as dead. He didn't delude himself into believing that his work colleagues would stand up for him. Images flashed through his mind at breakneck speed. The constraints of time loosened their grip on reality, and he perceived every detail of his surroundings with heightened clarity.

Despite having worked here six days a week for several months, having walked across the yard a thousand times, it wasn't until this very moment of anguished expectation that he actually saw the huge lime tree standing in one corner. A slight breeze gently rustled the leaves, sunlight filtered through the foliage and painted dancing spots on the gravelly ground.

The peaceful vastness of the present was sliced through by a shout: "Dostert."

Julius' knees gave out as his lease on life itself was renewed.

"Present."

When the Oberscharführer called out the name "Falkenstein," Julius answered almost with jubilation, despite the fact he'd condemned himself to whatever the Nazis had in store with this group.

At least Thea was safe. She was young, agile and clever, she'd find a way out of this hell –and perhaps Edith could pull some strings when she learned that Julius had been taken. It was a long shot, yet the only hope he held.

His relief didn't last long, because as soon as all names on the list had been called out, the SS men made generous use of their rifle butts, herding the workers into the waiting trucks. "Make it quick! Slovenly bastards!"

Swept along by the people around him, Julius was sucked toward the truck's black maw. Every cell in his body screamed in panic, his brain ordering his legs to move in the opposite direction. But deep down he knew there was no escape. The courtyard was surrounded by high walls, trucks blocked the only exit road, and... a thick rifle butt hit him on the shoulder. "Go! Or do you need a special invitation?"

Not bothering to answer, Julius swallowed down the yelp, ignoring the pain in his arm, accepting that from this moment onwards he would be at the beck and call of the SS. They could do to him—with him—whatever their sadistic little hearts desired. If he wanted to stay alive, he'd better follow their orders.

Strangely enough, after unsuccessfully trying to take his own life, he wasn't about to let the Nazis take it from him without a fight. So he hurried forward until he reached the big, black abyss. Without hesitation he jumped up—but failed to heave himself inside.

His bad knee refused to bend and he fell back like a sack of potatoes. Just as another rifle was about to smash down on him, Carsten, a young worker from his department, grabbed Julius by the shoulders and boosted him upwards, all but shoving him into the crammed truck.

Crawling on all fours, he managed to get inside, just to

witness how the dreaded punches hammered down on Carsten's back, resulting in an ugly cracking sound.

"Aaaargh." Carsten winced through clenched teeth as he escaped into the relative safety of the truck.

"Thank you," Julius said, though he wasn't sure the other man heard him, because more people crammed in, shoving him further to the other end. Behind Carsten was a heavily pregnant woman who had failed in her first attempt to climb into the truck.

There was nobody behind her to lend a helping hand and those inside the truck were scrambling to find their footing. Just as someone turned around to help, two SS men walked up to the woman, took her by her arms and feet and swung her back and forth, then threw her onto the platform like a pig in a slaughterhouse.

Julius shuddered at the adequacy of the comparison, for they would all be worked to death in one of the relocation camps in the East. Finally, the pandemonium stopped, the door slammed shut and darkness settled over the scared people. Together with the loss of eyesight, the occupants seemed to have lost the faculty of speech.

The only sound audible was the cranking up of the motor, followed by bucking as the truck rolled out of the factory grounds. Julius was too consumed with panic to think, until a raspy voice asked, "Where are they taking us?"

"Who knows." Judging by the sonorous organ, the speaker must have been the chief welder, a man like an ox with biceps bigger than Julius' thighs. For some reason, Julius drew comfort from his presence. Not because he believed the welder might force a way into freedom for all of them, but simply because he was there. Perhaps a guardian angel watching out for his folks. Julius snorted at the ridiculousness of the thought. Guardian angels didn't exist in real life, certainly not in the Nazi state.

The vehicle careened around corners, hurling its human

cargo left and right, fighting for purchase. After what seemed like an eternity, it finally came to a halt, the back doors were opened and everyone was ordered outside. Carsten showed up beside him, jumping down from the truck bed and turning to extend his hand to help Julius down.

Once outside, Julius blinked into the strong sunlight, which was hurting his eyes. Ostensibly they had been taken into the yard of a military garrison.

"Must be the Hermann Göring Barracks," Carsten said, as he jumped forward to catch an unconscious elderly woman, covered in grime. Behind her, a young girl about Thea's age staggered from the truck, blood running down her face. Despite the pain in his knee, Julius held out a hand to the girl and steadied her as they were prodded toward a building, which turned out to be an empty vehicle depot with few windows, the smell of oil and gasoline permeating the air.

More trucks arrived with more people. The SS soldiers who'd come for them must have been much more brutal than those who had arrived at Julius' workplace. Many of the newcomers had broken bones, bleeding lacerations, or swelling bruises. One woman stepped into the vehicle depot with as much dignity as possible in spite of her torn dress, which indecently exposed her underwear.

"Here, take this," Julius offered her his coat.

"I can't possibly..." she protested feebly, even as she gratefully took the garment.

Yet more people were shoved inside the building. Heartbreaking scenes of panic unfolded, with mothers screaming for the babies they had left at home when they set off for work. Unaccompanied children wailed incessantly, begging for their parents. Spouses frantically searched for their other half.

At least Julius had the reassurance that Edith was safe. Out of her mind with worry once she realized he'd been taken, but safe at home in Helga's company. Hot and cold shudders raced down his spine as he discerned that this action had been different from the usual roundups. It must have been a thorough sweep for every last Jewish resident in Berlin. The final push to reach the Nazis' dearest goal: to render the capital *judenrein*, cleansed of Jews.

Another, more violent shudder caused goosebumps to break out all over his body when he realized that his beloved sister Silvana and her husband Markus must have been taken, too. Frantically, he searched for them, weaving through the throng of desperate people, insane with fear for their loved ones.

In the crowded hall, people begged to be relocated to a different holding camp closer to their home, for a sip of water, for a bit of straw to sit on, for a piece of cloth to hang around their shoulders to keep warm.

After searching the entire place up and down, left and right, Julius finally accepted that neither Silvana nor Markus were present. He'd met a few business acquaintances from the past, neighbors, casual relations, work colleagues, but none of the people he held dear. And to his great relief, there was no sign of Thea Dalke. This gave him an intense bout of Schadenfreude. At least one Jew would continue to defile the Nazis' sacred Reich.

At last he found a place to sit down on the cold ground. The concrete walls protected against the wind, but did nothing to ward off the bitter chill of a February night. Deprived of his coat, he hunkered down with chattering teeth, in too much distress for a coherent thought. To add insult to injury, his rheumatism didn't take well to the dank air, causing his joints to stiffen painfully. Even when he dozed off, the ache in his knees woke him multiple times throughout the night. Jammed between bodies, he carefully shifted around, trying not to kick anyone.

It seemed, fate—or rather the Nazis—had finally caught up with him, no matter how rich or famous he used to be.

26

Edith shuffled upstairs, exhausted from a long day at work. At least today she didn't have household chores to do before dinner, because it was Amelie's turn to cook the evening meal. In contrast to Edith, the young woman was always full of energy, no matter how long or arduous her shift sewing uniforms for the Wehrmacht had been.

Secretly, she envied her for her youth, which equipped her to deal with the hardships Nazi rule threw at them. At the same time she pitied the girl for a youth lost to harassment, ostracism and war. Indeed, there was no winner in all this. Not the pure-bred Germans, not even the members of the SS riding their high horses and looking down on everyone.

The recent defeat of the 6th Army at Stalingrad had resulted in approximately half a million Wehrmacht soldiers killed and another hundred thousand captured. Every single family in the nation had lost a relative, friend or neighbor. Furthermore, the defeat had driven home the fact that the Wehrmacht wasn't invincible, as everyone had seemed to believe; Germany might not even come out the victor in the war Hitler had instigated.

Edith sensed a change in the population's prevalent sentiment from jubilation to cautious concern and anger. The propaganda ministry had stoked this anger, blaming the Stalingrad debacle, along with every other known evil, on the Jewish World Conspiracy. For weeks now, Edith had been exposed to an ever-thickening tension, and it seemed inevitable that the common fury would culminate in some kind of violent explosion.

Nonetheless, the mood in Berlin had been strangely calm. Perhaps her constant anxiety over Julius' safety had caused her to exaggerate the dangers. Perhaps the Stalingrad defeat served to engender a more realistic view of the war. She didn't dare get her hopes up, yet she silently prayed for the German public to realize that Hitler was the bad guy, not the Jews.

When she opened the apartment door, her gaze fell on the empty dinner table. Disappointment settled in her gut as she shrugged out of her coat, hanging it on the rack. It wasn't like Amelie to neglect her chores.

"Anyone home?" she called into the eerily silent apartment, which normally at this time of day bustled with activity. Silence was the only response. She walked into the kitchen, to find it empty, the only sign of life a used coffee mug in the sink.

A dreadful chill crept up her spine. She assured herself of the time with a second, third and fourth glance at her wristwatch, followed by a look at the clock hanging on the wall in the living room. It was dinnertime, no question. The other household members should be home by now, perhaps with the exception of David, who often worked late into the night at the locomotive workshop.

The door opened and a cheerful Helga walked in, swinging a brown paper bag in her hand, "Guess what I got!" One glance at Edith and the empty table behind her was enough to turn her face into a stone grimace. "Why is nobody home yet?"

"I don't know."

"Amelie! David!" Helga screamed and raced off into the room David had shared with his sister since the Gerbers had been taken. "Thank God. You're here!"

Edith witnessed through the open door how Helga hugged and kissed her son as if he were a baby.

"What's wrong, Mutti?" His voice was hoarse, his cheeks burning red.

"Were you here all day?"

"I went to work in the morning, but Baumann sent me home immediately." Several sneezes attested to David's sickness.

"Where's Amelie?"

"Should be home soon. What time is it?" Even from afar Edith registered that he was not yet fully aware of his surroundings.

"It's past dinnertime already."

"Really? I must have slept all day." His voice broke, causing a violent cough.

"Did Amelie come home? Or your father?" Helga insisted with desperation.

"I don't think so. If they did, they didn't wake me." David rubbed his eyes, turning his head left and right, dispelling the sleepiness which was holding him in its grip. "I'm sorry. I don't know."

Helga turned to send Edith a plea for help. But all Edith could offer was a shrug. She was as clueless as the Goldmanns, although... she quickly shoved away the images of SS men beating Julius and hauling him off to some unknown place. That mustn't happen. Ever. She offered what she hoped was reassurance: "I'm sure they were just held up and will arrive any minute, laughing at how worried we are."

"You're glowing with fever. I'll make you a broth," Helga said after feeling David's forehead. She'd barely left the room when he dozed off again.

"Do you think I should take him to the doctor?" Helga asked, worry in her eyes.

They both knew this was but a dream. No Aryan doctor was allowed to treat a Jewish patient and the few Jewish doctors left were so overwhelmed, they only took on the severest cases— even then they couldn't do much without medicine.

"I think a hot broth will do." Edith followed her friend into the kitchen. "He'll be fine."

"I know." Helga turned around, her eyes swimming with tears. "I fear for the others."

Edith heaved a groan. "Right now there's nothing we can do but wait."

"What if they are already on a transport?" Helga's eyes frantically danced between the soup she was preparing and her coat, carelessly thrown over a chair. "I should go and look for them."

"Where would you go?" Out of her mind with worry herself, Edith somehow found the inner strength to think logically.

Helga shrugged. "Around and about."

"It's past curfew, they must have sought shelter somewhere." At least Edith hoped so. Despite the recent Allied bombings and the nightly blackout, there was no general curfew in place, just Jewish people had to stay off the streets after 8 p.m.

The soup on the stove bubbled up and Helga automatically took the cooking spoon to stir it. "What shall we do with David?"

"He's safe here. At least for the moment." Edith pondered whether she should tell Helga about the hiding place in the attic, but given the bad shape David was in and the awful cold up there, she decided against it. Nevertheless, it gave her an idea. It was a long shot to count on the mysterious guest to have more information than everyone else, yet she waited until Helga was fussing over her son, before she stepped outside, let down the attic stairs and climbed up.

"Roxi, it's me, Edith. We met a few months ago when you rescued the three children."

No answer.

"I won't come up, but if you are there I want you to know that none of the Jewish members of our household returned from work this evening." Edith bit her lip, thinking. "David is in bed sick, so he was spared. Still, I'm worried about him, too. If this was some kind of concerted raid, he'll have to go into hiding."

Finally she heard soft steps and Roxi's voice. "Are you alone?"

"Yes. David's mother is with him. Everyone else is missing."

"I know where they have taken them." The slim woman peeked out from behind the folding screen, her eyes searching the room, before she walked out into the open. "You sure there's no Gestapo in the house?"

"Very sure." Edith held her hands up to show she came as friend. "You would have heard their jackboots clomping up the stairs.

"Right."

Since Roxi didn't seem inclined to share further information, Edith asked, "Do you know what happened?"

"Yes. It was given the code name *Judenschlussaktion* and it was supposedly the final sweep to catch every last remaining Jew in Berlin. I've seen their trucks driving through the city all day. Most of the captured were taken to the Herrmann Göring Barracks, whereas the half-Jews and those in mixed marriages are held in the Rosenstrasse."

"The Office of Welfare and Youth Welfare of the Jewish Community?" Edith asked, incredulous.

"Exactly. The Nazis have turned it into a holding camp."

"How do you know all this?"

Roxi took a step backwards. "Never ask this kind of question. It makes you suspicious."

"Me?" Edith was indignant. "If I wanted to harm you, I would have called the Gestapo months ago."

"I thank you very much for your hospitality, but now I must leave. This place isn't safe anymore." Roxi had already turned on her heel, but she paused for a second. "Tell David to go underground. He's in danger, too. If he wants to contact me, he knows where."

Before Edith had time to respond, Roxi slung a knapsack on her shoulders and disappeared through the open rooftop window.

Edith needed to take a few deep breaths to regain her composure, before she stepped down the ladder, stowed it away and closed the trap door leading to the attic. She pushed exceedingly hard to move it back into place.

"Where have you been?" Helga greeted her upon her return.

Edith chose to answer with a question of her own. "How is David?"

"Weak with chills and fever. I had to spoon-feed him the broth."

"He needs to leave the house." Edith closed the door behind them.

"Whyever? You can't kick him out in his condition."

"Helga, please calm down. It's not safe here. Apparently the Gestapo raided the entire city, rounding up every single Jew in an attempt to 'cleanse' the city."

"How can you say this?" Helga flopped on a chair and buried her head in her hands. Her slim shoulders were shaking.

Edith walked up behind her, putting a palm on her back. "It seems the Jews from mixed marriages were taken to Rosen-strasse."

Helga's head jerked up. "How do you know this?"

Edith remembered Roxi's words. *Never ask this kind of question. It makes you suspicious.* It did ring true. Of course, Helga was above suspicion. But she wasn't about to divulge her source even to her. The less people knew about Roxi, the better. "The grapevine."

"You learned all this in just a few minutes? Who told you? And more important, is this person trustworthy?"

"It doesn't matter. We'll go first thing in the morning and find out whether our families are there."

"What if they've been deported by then?"

Edith felt her friend was on the verge of falling apart, so she said in her sternest voice, "Pull yourself together. I need you to have a clear mind if we're going to get through this."

Helga looked up, anger flaring up in her eyes, followed by sadness and then by understanding. Finally, she nodded. "You're right. Do you have a plan?"

"Not exactly. First we need to ensure David is safe. Molly-coddle him all night if you want, but make sure he's gone by dawn in case the Gestapo return to search for him. In the morning, we'll pack a few necessities for our family members and leave for the Rosenstrasse."

"I need to go to work." Helga feebly protested.

"Who cares about work when our loved ones are missing?"

Finally, Helga's face lit up. "You're right. Years ago I promised that Hitler wouldn't take my family away. And as sure as I'm standing here, I'm going to fight to my last breath!"

"Now that's the spirit," Edith said, relieved. Together they would get through this.

27

Amelie ignored the pulsating pain in her arm where the SS man had smashed her against the truck because she'd helped an elderly man climb up. As far as she could tell, nothing was broken, just an agonizing pain where soon an ugly bruise would form.

They had been taken to a building which she recognized as the former Office of Welfare and Youth Welfare of the Jewish Community in the Rosenstrasse. She'd been here on errands; it lay smack dab in the center of Berlin, not far from the Spree River and St. Mary's Church. The street itself was a dead end, only about three blocks long.

When they'd disembarked from the truck, she had sought an opportunity to escape, but the Gestapo had planned their raid well. All entrances to the street were blocked and only trucks with Jewish prisoners were let through. If she'd tried to escape, she would have been shot on the spot.

The first thing she noticed inside the building was a musty smell, attesting that it had not been used or aired for some time. It took a while for her eyes to adjust to the semi-darkness. The entrance hall was filled with waiting people. Seeking a familiar face, she weaved through the crowd until an orderly with a yellow star on his jacket walked straight up to her.

"Come with me," he said, his eyes drooping with exhaustion. He led her and several other women up a flight of stairs, pointing to a room on the second floor. "In here."

The moment she entered, Amelie gagged violently. It was empty except for a few straw mattresses on the floor and a bare bulb hanging from the ceiling. Reluctantly, she walked further into the dimly lit room, itching to turn on her heels but knowing that was not an option. Even if the orderly didn't stop her, what would she have gained? The arrival hall downstairs was no better than this stinky hole.

Dread was closing in on Amelie like a gigantic vice. To keep it at bay, she took a deep breath, only to gag again at the awful stink. Closing her eyes, she willed herself to imagine a beautiful rose garden, an explosion of vibrant hues of green and red, the air filled with a sweet and intoxicating fragrance. As she strolled along the meandering paths, she stretched out her fingers to brush against the soft petals, inhaling their delicate scent.

After some minutes, calmness settled in her mind. Armed with the delightful images she'd conjured up, she opened her eyes again to confront the dire reality. Several women were crouched on mattresses along the wall by a boarded-up window through which faint shimmers of sunlight streamed inside.

No one moved or acknowledged the arrival of the newcomers. She went on her tiptoes and peeked through the cracks in the boarded-up windows, spotting a small patch of the street. Sometimes a pair of SS men with rifles slung across their shoulders marched into her field of vision, but mostly she only saw the advertising column plastered with Nazi slogans.

Amelie settled on one of the vacant straw mattresses, which turned out to be dank, explaining the awful smell. The screeching of brakes when yet another truck arrived, presumably to unload his cargo of unlucky Jews, interrupted the silence at regular intervals. A constant trickle of women was led into the room, until many hours later, it finally stopped.

In the evening, an orderly showed up, pointed at Amelie and said, "You. Come with me."

She was too afraid to ask where he was taking her, so she followed him wordlessly down the stairs to the ground floor, grasping her hands together in an attempt to suppress the trembling. When he stopped in front of a room that had been converted into a kitchen, she almost wept with relief.

"Take this and distribute it evenly." He held out two loaves of bread. Amelie wondered how she was supposed to break it into equal parts. He seemed to be able to read her thoughts, because he produced a butter knife. "Bring it back to me and don't do anything silly. And for the love of God, don't let the SS see it, or we'll both be in trouble."

She cocked her head, asking herself how the orderly had gotten his position. Was he simply a man ordered to do this job, the same way he'd requested her to help him, or was he a collaborator, buying his own life by betraying others? She inwardly shook her head, intending to give him the benefit of the doubt. "Thank you."

Just as she turned to take the food upstairs, a man from the crowd sitting in the entrance hall jumped up. "Amelie!"

The bread all but tumbled from her hands as she rushed toward the gaunt figure. "Vati!"

She threw herself into his arms, letting him embrace her, soothe her, comfort her. His presence alone was enough to raise her spirits. It was as if someone had lifted a veil, letting her assess the situation with a clear mind.

All the inmates in the Rosenstrasse had one characteristic in common: they were related to Aryans, as a partner in a mixed marriage or the child of such a marriage. Her hopes soared that the Nazis would be lenient with them.

"Are you alright?" Father asked, pointing at her face.

She hadn't realized it until now, but as her fingertips stroked her cheek, they found a long blood-crusted scratch. "It's nothing, I didn't even notice." She thought it better not to tell him about the bruise forming on her upper arm. "Does Mutti know where we are?"

"I don't think so. Apparently everyone was rounded up at work. My poor Helga will be worried out of her mind."

The newfound hope percolated. Her mother had been the pillar of the family for such a long time, protecting them against the worst of the Nazi harassment. She was capable of throwing herself in front of the fiercest SS man to keep her family safe, but if she didn't know where they were... They might be long-deported by the time Mutti found out. Amelie's brain went into overdrive, feverishly trying to conjure a way to get a message out.

"Is David here, too?" Father asked, the worry etched into his face.

"No." Amelie's heart filled with warmth. "Baumann sent him home because he was sick. I saw him briefly as I was leaving for work."

Father's face lit up. "Your brother is resourceful, he'll find a way to evade arrest."

Amelie stepped backward, gazing at the loaves of bread in her hands. "At least they're feeding us. If you need anything, I'm upstairs in the third room to the left. Holler out and I'll come to see you.

"I love you, my darling." Her father kissed her on the forehead. "Now go or you'll get into trouble."

"I love you, too. We'll get through this together. Just don't let them take you anywhere." It felt strange to tell her father to be cautious, since usually he was the one watching over her. "Promise you'll fight tooth and nail to stay inside the building. As long as we're here, Mutti can find and free us."

He ruffled her hair. "You've grown into a very fine young lady. I'm so proud of you."

Amelie choked back her tears and pressed his hand one last time, then she returned to her room to distribute the food. A shy-looking girl about her own age lingered in the corner of the room and she invited her to share the smelly mattress. The other girl happily accepted.

"I'm Miriam, and you?"

"Amelie."

They didn't ask each other about their lives or their families, because everyone in this building had similar experiences to share. Amelie merely longed to be in the company of a friendly soul who made her feel she was not alone in this world.

She would have preferred to sneak downstairs to seek out her father, but since men and women were strictly separated, she didn't dare. Instead she sufficed with sending him her good wishes, hoping he'd pick up the optimistic vibes.

As night fell, she lay on the mattress, snuggled up against Miriam's warm and soft body, listening to the noises. Nobody talked or whispered, yet the air was filled with breathing, rustling, snoring, weeping and croaking. Some women whimpered in their sleep at the physical or psychological wounds the Nazis had inflicted on them, others groaned as they moved around to find a more comfortable sleeping position.

Hours later, Amelie dozed off, her last thought being that she was still alive and in Berlin. Perhaps tomorrow the sky would look clearer.

28

David woke up shivering with cold. He was lying in a puddle, his bedsheets moist with his own sweat. Fighting the dull ache in his bones, he stretched his limbs and put his feet on the ground, feeling for his slippers.

Shaking from the chilly air, he somehow managed to walk into the kitchen, intent on boiling himself water to drink.

"You're awake." His mother surprised him, sitting up from the sofa, where she must have fallen asleep last night. "How are you?"

"Freezing."

"My poor boy, go to bed, I'll make you a hot flask." She was already on her feet, ushering him back into his room.

"My bed's all wet with sweat."

"Then take your sister's. I'll change the linens in the morning."

"Where is she anyway?" David faintly remembered his mother and Frau Falkenstein being extremely upset about something.

"Go back to bed, I'll explain in a minute."

Too exhausted to protest, he trotted off, covering himself

with Amelie's thick down blanket. He started when the door opened and his mother came in, holding a steaming mug and a hot-water bottle in her hands. "Here you go."

The hot liquid ran down his throat, warming him from the inside, while the bottle returned heat into his shivering bones from the outside. Helga settled on the bed and looked at him with a serious expression on her face.

Feeling much better, he asked, "What is it? Tell me."

"Amelie and Heinrich, as well as Herr Falkenstein and Delia, were taken yesterday. It seems the Gestapo made one final sweep through Berlin's factories, arresting every single Jew they could find."

Swallowing hard, it took David a few seconds to find his voice. "Looks like I got lucky then."

"At least for now." Helga looked exhausted.

Though feeling wretched himself, he put a hand on her knee. "Tomorrow I'll help you to find them."

She shook her head, tears pooling in her eyes. "We're pretty sure the Gestapo will come looking for you once they find you missing, which means you have to go into hiding, at least for a few days."

He'd never seen his mother this rattled, not even when his father had been arrested during the Night of Broken Glass. Normally, she was the pillar of the family, using her status as an Aryan to protect them from the worst harassment. She'd confronted his former school director when classmates had beaten him, she'd fought tooth and nail to find a landlord who would rent to a *jüdisch-versippt* German, a woman who was married to a Jew. In short, she'd always been there doing whatever was needed to keep her family safe.

Right now he sensed that she needed a strong shoulder to lean on. Someone to tell her everything was going to work out. Ignoring the pain in his limbs, he laboriously sat up, wrapped his arms around her and propped his burning cheek against the top of her head, rocking her upper body back and forth the same way she'd done so often when he was a child.

"Don't worry, Mutti. We'll get through this."

That's when she started weeping. Her tears soaked his fresh shirt, her inconsolable sobs tore his heart into pieces. His wonderful, loving, strong, courageous, optimistic, energetic mother was bawling like a baby.

After a long time, she whispered, "I love them so much. I don't know how to live without them."

"Shush. Father and Amelie are not dead."

"How do you know?"

"I just do. And you better believe me." He tried to sound sure and optimistic despite his own doubts.

She sniffed. At least her sobbing stopped. For a few minutes she stayed motionless in his arms, leaning against his chest. Somehow she seemed to draw strength from the embrace, because her spine gradually straightened until she finally extricated herself from his embrace. "Thank you so much. I needed that more than you can imagine."

"It was the least I could do for you."

His mother surprised him with a smile. "You might be a head taller than I am and strong like an ox, but you'll always stay my little boy and I'm not going to allow Hitler to take you away, too. Here's what we do: you go to sleep and get better, meanwhile I'll pack your things and wake you at six in the morning, so you can go into hiding."

He bit his lip. The notion of having to leave the bed sounded like torture. "You sure you don't want my help in finding Father and Amelie?"

"I'd rather have at least one family member in freedom than all of you arrested."

Nodding his agreement, David slunk back beneath the covers, completely exhausted from the conversation.

"Now sleep," Helga ordered.

"I will." He dozed off before she even closed the door.

David was jarred awake by the sound of fists pounding on the door. He shook his head to dispel the nightmare, but the pounding wouldn't stop. Finally, soft footsteps came from the neighboring room, his mother's voice calling out, "I'm coming. Don't shoot."

In a split second he was wide awake, his eyes roving over the room, searching for a way to escape, despite knowing there was none. The window opened to the street, where surely the Gestapo had parked their cars. Even if they didn't spot him and shoot him, he wouldn't be able to get anywhere, four floors up on a blank wall.

He silently cursed himself for not checking on the alarm system last night. The ringing bell would have given him the time needed to use the emergency escape route through the roof. Now it was too late, because the soldiers pounding on the apartment door stood between him and the trap door into the attic.

Knowing the SS men were coming for him, he jumped into his clothes, plus an extra jacket, stuffing his pockets with whatever useful utensils he found in his haste.

"What can I do for you?" Helga asked in a voice that didn't betray the fear she must be feeling.

"We're looking for David Goldmann."

"My son is sick in bed."

"He has to come with us."

"On what grounds do you take my son away? What has he done?" Helga stood her ground.

"He's a dirty Jewish pig."

"I'm Aryan."

"That'll make him a dirty half-Jewish pig," another voice said derisively.

"You can't just take him away. I have rights," Helga protested.

"Go file a complaint if you wish," the man snorted. "And now either you tell us where your son is hiding or we'll smash this place to pieces."

David had heard enough. One last glance around his room to check for anything he might find useful in captivity and he stepped through the door. He stiffened his spine and calmly said, "I'm here."

His mother sent him a pleading look, worry etched deep into her features. As he passed her on his way to the door, she grabbed his hand, squeezed it and whispered, "I'll find you and get you out."

He squeezed her hand for an instant, then two SS men grabbed him under his arms and dragged him out of the apartment. Downstairs they manhandled him into the waiting truck, already full of other stragglers waiting to be shipped off.

They stopped two or three times to gather more prisoners. Then the truck drove and drove and drove. Since his mother had told him the mixed breeds were being taken to the Rosenstrasse, his anguish grew with every passing minute. It shouldn't take that long.

Finally, the truck stopped. They were ushered outside, just as the sun was rising above the horizon. David jumped from the platform and took a moment to stretch his aching limbs. An error, as he found out instantly, because an SS man rammed the hilt of his gun into David's ribs. "No dawdling, you filthy scum."

David sucked in a pained breath, not wanting to give him the pleasure of knowing how much both the blow and the insult had hurt. Somehow, he managed to square his shoulders and walk toward what looked like a vehicle hall in a military barracks. This certainly wasn't the Rosenstrasse building.

Cold sweat dripped down his back. They must have mistakenly, or by sheer malice, sent him to a holding place for full

Jews. It didn't need a genius to figure out this was bad. Very bad indeed.

A chill settled into his bones, sucking the fight from him, urging him to give up. He stumbled forward, thinking of his parents, Amelie, and Roxi. He hoped she was safe, somewhere. Hiding up in the attic she should have had time to sneak away through the rooftop window when the soldiers came.

The men in front of him slowed down, and David stepped aside to avoid bumping into them. Another mistake. A split second later, an SS man slammed his elbow into the side of David's jaw. Swallowing down a howl of pain, he hastily sought shelter in the crowd.

After passing the bottleneck of the doors—driven on by blows from rifle butts to whoever wasn't fast enough—he recoiled at the unbearable stench inside. The huge vehicle hall was filled to overflowing with thousands of people.

As David was pushed further into the throng of bodies, he noticed a few buckets along the wall, overflowing with what he recognized as human waste. Gagging, he looked the other way. Weaving his way through the crowd to find a space to sit down, he passed an elderly man with dried, caked blood covering the side of his face. Twice he blinked until he accepted the truth that this man was his landlord.

Julius Falkenstein recognized him, too. He pointed to his right and moved aside. "David, sit with me."

"Thank you, Herr Falkenstein."

"Julius, please. I reckon the time for formalities has long passed."

"Julius." David swallowed hard, finding it difficult to forgo traditional respect and call the distinguished man by first name. Nevertheless, it seemed fitting: captured in a stinking hall, reduced to supplicants, who had the time for phrases of civility? "It's an honor."

Herr Falkenstein—pardon, Julius—said with a wry twist to

his lips, "I'd love to say the honor is all mine, but"—he made a grand gesture that encompassed the entire garage—"this place is not all that hospitable, it seems."

Now it was David's turn to grin. He'd never seen Julius' humorous side. "How long have you been here?"

"Since yesterday, when they rounded us up at work."

David nodded, feeling the need to explain. "I was sick at home. They came for me in the small hours."

"Is Edith unharmed?" Julius' face was a grimace of sorrow.

"Yes, your wife and my mother are both at home. My mother said they're holding those with Aryan relatives in the Rosenstrasse, so I was astonished to be brought here. And I certainly hadn't expected to come upon you."

Julius' attention perked up. "Please, tell me more."

David related everything he remembered his mother explaining to him and answered quite a few follow-up questions, until Julius declared, "We'll need to make our status known."

"Our status?" The fever was coming back, weakening David's mind. His thoughts seemed to crawl through thick layers of cotton, not allowing him to grasp the meaning of Julius' words.

Patiently the older man explained, "It seems the Nazis are separating the captives into groups. Those who have someone to speak for them, and those who don't. I believe people like us with Aryan spouses or parents will be treated more leniently than the rest."

Through a leaden tiredness weighing down on him, David nodded. Currently he didn't care either way, as long as he was allowed to lie down and sleep.

But Julius would have none of that. "We'll approach the SS officer in charge immediately and inform him that they've brought us to the wrong place."

"Later..." David mumbled, yearning to lie down in the space Julius was about to vacate.

"No. Now. Get up." The order was given in a low voice, nonetheless it brooked no argument, much like David's mother when she ordered him to wash his hands before dinner. Despite his awful exhaustion, David obeyed. Struggling to push himself up from the concrete floor, he followed the older man like a windup doll.

"Where are we going?" David still didn't comprehend the plan.

"To find someone who will listen and get this mess straightened out."

"What if they'll beat us for being so bold?"

Julius stopped to look at him with a deadpan expression. "And here I thought you were a rebellious young man, involved in all kinds of illegal activities."

At this reference to their black market deal and Roxi's presence in the attic, David began to protest but stopped when he noticed the slight quiver of Julius' lip. "I am."

"Then, what are you afraid of, young man?"

He really needed to get a grip on himself. If Julius was trying to get them both transferred to Rosenstrasse, he needed to support the old man in any way he could.

Soon enough they stood in front of what seemed to be the main office.

"What do you want?" the guard demanded.

"I'd like to talk to the officer in charge," Julius countered.

"Oh, would you? Well, let me see if that's possible," the guard smirked, leaning over to peek into the office before barking back a laugh. "Guess his schedule's full today. Try again tomorrow, Jew."

"We are, in fact, not Jews at all," Julius stated in a surprisingly authoritative manner. "This is the reason why I need to talk to your superior."

The SS man locked eyes with Julius, his face a grimace of contempt, but when Julius calmly returned his gaze for a full half minute, he relented and waved them on into the office. David found the spectacle quite amusing, since he'd never heard of the SS giving in to anyone, least of all a Jew.

"What's your problem?" the officer behind the desk asked, barely looking up from his list.

In the blink of an eye, Julius transformed from inferior supplicant to cultured businessman. "Herr Unterscharführer, there seems to be an unfortunate misunderstanding. My friend is a privileged half-Jew and I am married to a Christian woman. Neither of us should be here."

The Unterscharführer finally raised his head and stared at them. "Nonsense. Everyone with Aryan relations was taken to the Rosenstrasse, if you ended up here, you're a Jew." Then he dismissed them with a wave of his hand. David's shoulders slumped in defeat. He was about to turn on his heels, when a hand touched his shoulder.

"With all due respect, Herr Unterscharführer, there must have been a very unfortunate oversight. Both of us, indeed, are who we say and we can prove it to you, if you so wish." David watched in awe how easily the man who had once operated one of the largest banks in Germany slipped back into a role of power, as if begging for their very lives was no different from a boardroom negotiation.

"Ahh. That's what everyone claims."

"My name is Julius Falkenstein. It may sound familiar to you, since I used to own the Falkenstein bank."

"One more proof you're a Jew." A smirk appeared on the Unterscharführer's lips.

Finally, David found his voice. "Herr Falkenstein is married to a Christian woman."

"Is he now? And you? To whom are you married?"

"To no one. My name is David Goldmann and my mother is Aryan. Her maiden name is Helga Raabe."

"Quite the clever plan the two of you have cooked up. So where's the proof?"

"You may always send someone to ask my mother," David offered.

"Hm. Why should I go to all this trouble for a Jew?"

"Because we're privileged Jews and Hitler himself has ruled that we should be exempt from certain regulations." Julius seemed very sure of himself.

"Nobody will ever find out."

"My wife will."

"And my mother," David added.

The Unterscharführer narrowed his eyes at them, gauging the situation. After several seconds he gave a curt nod. "To the Rosenstrasse camp it is, then. If I find out you've been lying, you'll wish you had never been born."

"Thank you very much." Julius was all poise, whereas David's knees threatened to give out under him.

They were ushered into the yard, where two other people waited. Soon after, the small group was shoved into a police car with windows and driven to the Rosenstrasse building in the city center.

"That was a very brave thing you did," David said to Julius.

"Was it?" Julius held out his gnarled hand to show him how much he was shaking.

"Being courageous doesn't mean not to be afraid, it means to confront your fear and act regardless."

Julius' eyebrow shot up. "You're a very wise young man. Much like your father."

David felt his ears burn at the compliment. "He's a wizard with numbers, unlike me. I was never good at school."

"There are different types of intelligence and I hear you're as much a wizard as your father, but with mechanics. Your mother speaks highly of you, telling everyone that you can repair anything and everything."

If possible, David's blush burned even brighter. He'd always assumed his mother was disappointed over his lack of good grades at school. "I... thank you."

"Don't thank me. It was your mother praising you to the skies." Julius leaned back in the seat as they drove through the streets of Berlin. "You know what I regret most?"

"That they didn't allow you to cross the border?" David remembered well the despair when the Falkensteins had returned after supposedly making it to safety in Switzerland.

"Actually no." Julius gave a sad smile. "That was something beyond my control. No, my biggest failure was not to see how all of this would end. I sincerely regret having dismissed Hitler as a clown who wouldn't last longer than a few months. If only I had listened to Edith instead of being complacent, I would have put up a fight back in 1933 when there was still a chance to prevent all this madness."

"You think Hitler cannot be stopped?" David recoiled in horror, because that meant they were all going to die.

"Not by us, at any rate." Julius stared at him intensely. "That doesn't mean you should stop fighting, because every life saved is a victory, even if it's only for another day. In my opinion, Hitler's defeat may be achieved exclusively by the Allies. If they don't overpower the Wehrmacht on the battlefield, then Germany is truly lost."

29

After the shock of David being arrested before he had a chance to go underground, there was no chance for Helga to find sleep. Consumed with rage and anxiety, she went into the kitchen to brew *Ersatzkaffee*.

"Make one for me too, please."

Helga jerked around, looking at Edith as if she were a ghost. "Why aren't you asleep?"

"It's kind of difficult to sleep through a bunch of SS almost smashing our front door to pieces," Edith said with a wry expression.

"They took David." Helga's entire body began trembling so hard she had to set down the kettle.

Wordlessly, Edith embraced her, leading her to the sofa in the living room. As soon as she sat down, the dam broke and tears began streaming down her cheeks. "They took him and I didn't do anything. What kind of mother am I? Letting the Nazis take my child away."

"Shush." Edith settled next to her, holding her tight. "It's not your fault. There was nothing you could have done."

"I should have told them—"

"Shush. Antagonizing them would only have resulted in you being arrested as well. That wouldn't have helped David one bit."

"I should have gone with him," Helga sobbed. "Wherever the Nazis have taken my family, I should be too. We belong together." Her flood of tears impeded her speech. "Heinrich... Amelie... David..."

Edith got up and disappeared first into the kitchen and next into her room. When she returned, she held two cups in her hands, offering one to Helga. Sniffing the strong aroma, she said suspiciously, "That's not Ersatzkaffee."

"It is. With a big shot of brandy." Edith shrugged and grinned. "Don't tell Julius I raided his secret stash."

Another wave of pain hit Helga's heart and she cried out, "He'll never know. They've taken your husband too."

"Shush. Helga, please. Drink." Edith all but shoved the cup into her face.

The hot, strong beverage flowed down her throat, warming her from within. It soothed her senses and at the same time the alcohol infused her with new energy. After the first few sips the world didn't look as bleak anymore.

"See, it's only half bad," said Edith, who'd been closely watching her expression.

This time, Helga didn't break out into tears. She breathed deeply, savored the bitter, pungent aroma in her mouth and took another sip. When she'd emptied the cup, she put it on the coffee table, locking eyes with Edith. "That was good. And now let's go and fight to get our families back."

"That's the spirit." Edith's face twinkled with mischief. "Although we probably should get dressed first."

Helga looked down at her stockinged feet poking out beneath her pajamas. "I guess we should."

Half an hour later, the two women were on their way to the Rosenstrasse. Helga didn't know what she had expected, it certainly wasn't the spectacle that awaited them on their arrival. They weren't the only ones to disembark the S-Bahn at the station Börse. A handful of other women did the same. The big surprise came when they climbed down from the platform to the street; loud chanting wafted toward them.

"What are they yelling?" Edith asked.

Helga perked up her ears, yet understood only snippets. "Something about men." Anticipation coursed through her body, propelling her forward with the need to get to the bottom of this. "Hurry up. There are others here already."

"It seems so, which is good."

They hastened along until they arrived at a small alley where a few dozen women had gathered, apparently for the same reason Helga and Edith had shown up—to inquire the whereabouts of their husbands and children.

"Look at this," Helga said in awe. "This is amazing."

"Amazing in a good or bad way?" Edith asked.

"I guess it's both. It means the Nazis arrested plenty more families, or these women wouldn't be here, but it also means they came to get their loved ones back. Which is good for us, since there's strength in numbers." At least Helga hoped so. The Gestapo easily intimidated even the most valiant person.

"Are you here to inquire about your family, too?" Helga asked one of the women standing in the crowd.

"Yes. I came here as soon as I heard the rumors."

"So, it's true then, they are being held here?" Edith asked.

The other woman shook her head. "There has been no confirmation. A while ago, someone peeked out of a window and shouted something, but he was immediately pushed away. Afterward the SS barricaded all the windows."

Looking upward, Helga observed the boarded-up windows, some evidently old, while others sported new-looking planks. Her mind was in turmoil. It must be true then, prisoners were held inside. Unfortunately there was no way of knowing if her family was among them. She turned around to look at Edith. "Do you think we should split up? One of us stays here, the other one goes to Gestapo headquarters to try and find out something?"

Edith bit on her lip, before she hesitantly offered, "I'll pay the Gestapo a visit. Perhaps I can also get some information about Silvana and Markus. I'm pretty sure they were taken during the raid, too."

The pain emanating from her friend hit Helga so hard, she swayed, struggling for balance. She had no comfort to offer, not even an uncommitted *I'm sure they'll be fine*, because, being fully Jewish, Edith's in-laws would be anything but fine. "You do that. We'll meet up for a quick meal at the apartment, let's say around six tonight?"

Edith nodded and turned away. Just as Helga was about to put a question to one of the women who'd been there when they arrived, Edith turned back and asked, "What about work? Aren't we supposed to go to work?"

"Didn't you tell me this very morning that rescuing our families is more important than work?" Helga jutted her chin, ready to take on Hitler, the Gestapo and the rest of the world.

"Right. To hell with work. See you tonight. Stay safe." The next moment Edith was gone, leaving Helga forlorn.

A few seconds later, the woman she'd spoken to earlier said, "Look, there are more people coming."

The crowd had grown to about thirty people, mostly women and children, among them a few men—even one in Wehrmacht uniform, whom Helga considered to be very brave.

Several times women approached the gate to inquire about family members. Invariably they returned without the desired information. Around noon an SS man with a megaphone in his hand stepped into the street and announced, "You can all go home now. If any of your family members are inside, you'll be informed in due course."

A few women turned toward the S-Bahn station, their shoulders slumped in defeat. Even as Helga contemplated whether she should stay or leave, a housewife in front of her shouted, "Give me my husband back!"

Her yell rippled through the crowd like a jolt. Helga instinctively stood taller as she joined the rallying cry. "Give me my husband back!" Seconds later, the entire crowd screamed, "Give us our husbands back! Give us our children back!"

An exhilarating energy streamed through Helga's body as she walked up to the SS man with the megaphone to his mouth. Whatever he was saying was drowned out in the collective shouts of angry relatives, demanding to get their loved ones back.

Realizing that nobody was heeding his authority, a fearful expression crossed the SS man's face and he quickly vanished into the building.

"Ha, we frightened him," one woman said.

For a long time nothing happened. Another woman ventured toward the guard, just to be shooed away. Beside Helga, a mother told her daughter, "Go to Aunt Elsie's house, she has an extra key for our home."

The girl dashed away, leaving Helga with an idea forming in her head. Emboldened by the presence of the other women— the crowd was still growing—she walked up to friendliest-looking of the five SS men guarding the sole entrance.

"Step back. I don't know whether your husband is inside or not," he said, even before she had a chance to open her mouth.

"Please, *mein Herr*." Helga wrapped her shawl tighter around her shoulders to ward off the chilling breeze. "My husband has the only key to our place. Without it, I'll have to sleep on the street."

He shot her an awkward gaze. "Ma'am, I really am not allowed to give information."

To emphasize her words, she shook her shoulders as if shivering. "You surely don't want a good Aryan woman to die from exposure in this cold?"

"I'm sorry, I can't let you inside."

"Might you just ask for Heinrich Goldmann and tell him his wife needs the keys for the apartment?"

At last he sighed. "Stay put. I'll see what I can do. I'm married myself, wouldn't want my missus out here in the cold."

"This is so kind of you," she said with her sweetest smile, despite her blood boiling, because he didn't seem to care about the humans held captive inside. Helga waited for endless minutes, her confidence shrinking under the hostile stares of the other SS men, until he finally reappeared in the doorway, holding a key in his hand. "Here you go, Frau Goldmann. Your husband is well, and your daughter, too."

"Thank you so much." Helga pocketed the key next to her own.

"If you want my advice..." She didn't, but since he'd been nice enough to inform her that both Heinrich and Amelie were alright, she nodded. "Get a divorce. Then I can help you to get your daughter out."

She'd heard this abhorrent suggestion too many times to get worked up over it the way she used to, so she simply cast him a sour smile. "I will certainly consider it."

"Don't wait too long—once she's sent on transport, nobody can get her back."

These words had the intended effect on her and she quickly hurried away, fighting against the ice threatening to congeal her blood. Would Hitler finally break her by forcing her to choose between her husband and her daughter? Should she give up one to save the other? Could she?

"Did they tell you anything?" one woman asked her.

"Yes, both my husband and my daughter are inside," Helga replied. "He told me only because I pretended that my husband had the only key to our apartment."

"Clever idea. I'm Veronica, by the way." Veronica linked arms with Helga and the woman on her other side, forming a living wall. "They're not going to get past us." Then she began chanting, "Give us our husbands back! Give us our children back!"

Helga swayed with the crowd like a wave in the ocean, moving left and right, shouting until she was hoarse. For several hours nothing happened, apart from half-hearted attempts by the SS guards to disperse the crowd.

When darkness fell, the small street was filled with people. Hunger sent sharp pangs into Helga's stomach, reminding her she hadn't eaten since morning. Her toes had long since numbed from the cold and she hardly felt her fingers as she set off for the S-Bahn station to return to the apartment and meet up with Edith for dinner. When the train pulled in, a number of women disembarked, probably having come straight from work.

"Down there," Helga told them, as she stepped into the wagon. "There's a huge crowd keeping guard."

At home, Edith was preparing a potato casserole. As soon as she saw Helga, she threw her hands up in horror. "Goodness, your lips are blue. Let me make you some hot coffee."

"Heinrich and Amelie are in the Rosenstrasse, but I've heard no news of David or your husband," Helga whispered while she followed her friend into the kitchen, where she settled on the small stool they normally used to reach the upper shelves. "What about you?"

Grief contorted Edith's face. "I arrived too late. It seems Silvana, Markus and everyone else from the holding camp in the Lemberg school were put on a train last night."

"I'm so sorry," Helga heaved.

"Silvana was always so full of energy, so ebullient, so kind. She refused to leave when she had the chance, claiming her mission was to prepare her students for emigration as best as she could. And now she's gone." Edith did not shed a tear, yet

Helga detected from the tremble in her thin shoulders that she was barely holding on.

"She's not dead yet," Helga said, hoping it was true.

"You don't know that!" Edith turned around, her beautiful blue eyes swimming with unshed tears. Just as Helga feared her friend was going to crumble under the sorrow, she squared her shoulders. "We must not give up. Ever. Now tell me what exactly what you found out."

Helga shared with her the events of the day, concluding with the heartening arrival of more women to join the protest.

"We'll return later tonight and stay there until they release our families, but first we eat." Edith ladled casserole onto two plates and carried them to the dining room. Over dinner she explained her plan. "I believe it's important to show presence. The SS will be counting on us to tire of protesting and leave. That's the moment they'll strike and haul the prisoners away. A cloak-and-dagger operation, if you will. So we need to make sure there's always someone on location."

Her eyes wide open with amazement, Helga listened to Edith laying out an elaborate plan.

"You and I, we'll take turns. One of us keeping up the protest, while the other one can go grocery shopping or prepare meals. We'll also pack a thermos with food and hot drinks against the cold. And"—she looked up from her plate—"since your trick with the key worked so well, the guards might be amenable to delivering food packages to the captives. We'll make some and hide messages of support inside."

"How did you come up with all this?" Helga asked in awe.

"I might have led the life of a spoiled society lady, but my strength has always been in organizing events, juggling schedules and catering to our guests' preferences."

30

Julius had been pleasantly surprised by the conditions at the Rosenstrasse—not that they were comfortable, but compared to those in the Herrmann Göring Barracks, they were almost luxurious. Being married to a German woman clearly came with benefits. David had taken good care of him, miraculously organizing a straw mattress and even a blanket, along with bread and a bowl of soup.

In the morning he woke to the sound of female voices chanting. He pricked his ears to discern the words. Since all ground-floor windows were boarded up with barely enough gaps to allow sunlight to filter through the slats, he couldn't make out more than "... children."

"What's going on?" Julius asked David, who was just coming awake by his side.

"Don't know." David yawned, stretching his limbs. "Let me go and find out." Within seconds he was on his feet and sauntered over to the entrance, where a young man wearing the yellow sash with the word "*Ordner*", orderly, stood smoking a cigarette.

Just the sight of it set Julius' nerves tingling with the urgent need for a smoke. He fumbled in his breast pocket, only to realize he'd used up his last cigarette the night before. While he was racking his brain for a way to satisfy his craving, the entrance door opened. A sudden burst of light blinded him. Along with the light came loud chanting. "Give us our husbands back! Give us our children back!"

Goosebumps broke out on his back at the realization that he and everyone else in here had not been forgotten. Out there people were fighting for them. He wondered whether Edith might be among them, clamoring for the Nazis to liberate her husband. He'd probably never find out, since it was doubtful that the Nazis would ever release them, however much the women chanted.

After another group of arrested people were ushered in, the door closed again, effectively blocking out sunlight and reducing the chanting to the background. It was still there, like the distant humming of a train.

David joined him, an excited grin on his face.

"Did the orderly give you valuable information?" Julius asked, moving aside to make room for him.

"A lot, but guess what I saw peeking through the open door?"

"A large group of mostly women chanting?"

"Yes. And..." David paused as if he was about to spill a secret "... my mother was there! Next to your wife! How's that?"

"Marvelous." Warmth settled deep inside Julius with the blossoming hope that perhaps their fate was not yet sealed.

"It gets better, though."

"You have more good news?"

"She saw me! My mother saw me and gave me a thumbs up, while she mouthed "Father" and "Amelie," so I assume they're both here as well. I tried to convey to your wife that you're here with me by putting up both my thumbs, and I think she understood, since her face lit up."

"That was very kind of you. Thank you so much." Julius was so moved by that simple detail, he had difficulties holding onto his composure. "Now go and find the rest of your family."

"I will, but first I have to tell you what the orderly said. He's a former classmate of mine and insisted I should not volunteer for anything, under any circumstances. Not if they look for mechanics, not if they promise work or a better place. He implored me to keep my head down and remain unseen."

"That sounds counterintuitive. Surely, if they are looking for mechanics it is because they need them for some sort of work, which must be much better than the alternative."

"Or it could be a trick." David pursed his lips pensively.

"We might never know for sure." Julius mused. "How well do you know the orderly?"

"He was my classmate at the Lemberg School."

A fierce stab to his intestines made Julius wince at the mention of his sister's school. From what he'd picked up on the grapevine, the arrests organized under the harmless-sounding sobriquet Fabrikaktion, factory action, had been anything but: they had been the concerted final action to rid Berlin of every last living Jew.

Surely Silvana and her husband had been arrested along with most everyone else, and he feared for their well-being. Why had she been too stubborn to leave Germany when it was still possible? He caught himself, realizing that he'd been the same way, albeit for different reasons.

"Are you alright?" David asked.

Julius shrugged off the morose thoughts. Now was not the time to repent unwise decisions. He needed to keep his wits about him if he was to have any chance of getting out of this place. "I'm as fine as can be expected, despite being exhausted."

"Everyone's bleary-eyed, it's not exactly a comfy hotel they're keeping us in."

Julius gave a dry laugh. "That is very true, young man.

Now, about your friend the orderly. If you feel he's trustworthy, we should definitely heed his advice." He rubbed his chin, flinching at the three-day stubble beneath his fingertips. After stealing his citizenship, his bank, his mansion and his personal wealth, would the Nazis also take his decency by turning him into an unkempt, unshaved, stinking derelict, sleeping in his day clothes?

It was another thought he brushed away. "I'm inclined to believe your friend is right. The Nazis don't want to cause a fuss, so they might ask for volunteers to test their process for whatever they have in store for us."

David ran a hand through his hair, apparently coming to the same conclusion. "Promise you won't speak to anyone until I'm back."

Julius swallowed down a laugh. "I could be your grandfather, young man, there's no need for you to take care of me."

"I want to. My family owes you so much. You and your wife have been extremely generous and saved our necks more than once during the past years, the least I can do is make our imprisonment a bit more comfortable for you." David put a hand over his heart and lowered his voice to a whisper. "Deep in here, I just know we're going to survive this. So, keep strong."

"I will. Now go and find your family." It was all Julius could do to keep the amusement out of his voice. David's kind efforts were a refreshing change to the prevailing indifference all around him.

David trotted off toward the orderly. After exchanging some words, he pinned an identical yellow "*Ordner*" sash on David, presumably to allow him to roam freely around the premises. Since there was nothing else to do but wait, Julius leaned against the wall, scrutinizing his fellow prisoners.

Every single one looked the way he felt: tired, dirty and crumpled. Most of them sat motionless, staring straight ahead with empty eyes, some lay sleeping on the floor, snoring, others crying or whimpering. A few men had children by their side and tried to engage them in some kind of play. For once Julius felt grateful that he didn't have a son. At least his offspring would not have to witness the horrors which had befallen his country.

His arthritic leg began hurting fiercely, taking his attention off the crowd while he wriggled to find a comfortable position on the hard straw mattress.

Outside, people continued to chant. He drew comfort from the knowledge that Edith was among the protesters. She, and the world, had not forgotten about him. Her actions also instilled him with pride for his soft-spoken, pliable wife. When had she turned into the strong lady standing up for justice? He regretted having underestimated her and promised to tell her what a marvelous woman she was if he ever got out of this ghastly place.

Then he closed his eyes, trying to get some sleep. He soon gave up the attempt, since the thick fear permeating the room made it impossible to relax. After some time, David sauntered down the stairs, the happy expression on his face a stark contrast to the dreary environment.

"I found them." David settled next to Julius on the mattress. "They're both fine."

"Why didn't you ask them to join us?"

"It's not allowed. Amelie is upstairs in a women-only room and my father has been assigned to one of the rooms in the back. Apparently there's an order to this chaos and nobody is allowed to leave their assigned space."

"At least you had the chance to talk to them."

"I warned them about volunteering." David produced a package of cigarettes from his pocket, offering it to Julius, "Want one?"

"Thank you very much." Julius was about to refuse the gift, but his obsession was too strong. "I wouldn't normally, but I'm at the point where I would kill just to get my hands on something to smoke."

"Then take them all. I really only smoke when I'm bored." David pushed the package toward him.

"No, I can't possibly accept this."

"Please, do. I'll go and see whether I can find out more information. Apparently, I'm an orderly now." David got to his feet and walked into the direction of the exit, where he talked to his orderly friend. Julius watched both of them disappear in the direction of the SS office.

31

"You saw him, too, didn't you? I haven't been imagining this, have I?" Helga asked for at least the tenth time.

"No, you aren't hallucinating. David was standing in the doorway, winking at you."

"That means something, doesn't it? At least he's alive." Having the three people she loved most in the world taken from her within twenty-four hours had taken a heavy toll on her emotions.

"It does." Edith linked arms with her. "Do you believe David wanted to tell me something with the two thumbs up?"

"Since he looked directly at you, I'm one hundred percent sure he meant to say that your husband is in there, too."

"I don't want to get my hopes up too much..." Edith's expression was utterly forlorn.

The slumbering guilt stabbed Helga's heart painfully and she squeezed her friend's elbow. "I'm so sorry about Silvana. Don't give up hope yet."

"Disperse! We're going to shoot everyone who's not leaving!" a Gestapo officer shouted from the entrance to the tiny street.

An icy shiver ran down Helga's spine. The order had been clear and concise. The protest was over. Out of habit, her brain processed the command and ordered her feet to move, along with Edith, who still linked arms with her. The crowd scurried to take refuge in nearby house entrances.

No shots rang out.

They waited.

Nothing.

One by one, the protesters left their cover, walked out into the open street and took up their positions again. It wasn't an active decision, at least on Helga's part. It was more like she was magnetically drawn back to her previous spot in front of the Rosenstrasse building, driven by the desire to get her family back.

"We're not leaving," Edith said, softly first, then louder.

"We're not leaving?" Helga repeated.

"We're not leaving!" the crowd chanted.

"We'll stay here until you release our husbands!" Edith screamed.

"We'll stay here until you release our children!" Helga responded.

"We want our husbands back! We want our children back!" the crowd yelled.

Helga was too exhausted to comprehend what was happening, yet she was captured by the spirit of the masses, shouting in unison with her co-protesters, demanding that the Gestapo release their loved ones.

It didn't take more than a minute at most until the Gestapo disappeared around the corner, perhaps to deliberate a better way to get rid of the unwanted protesters. Because one thing was certain: there was exactly one door to the Rosenstrasse building, and none of the captives could be sent on transport to some horrible place without passing the gathered crowd of relatives.

"I never thought it would work," Helga said.

"Me neither." Edith retrieved a thermos from her handbag, pouring hot coffee into a mug.

"Then why did you shout? Weren't you afraid you'd be arrested?"

Edith took a sip and offered the mug to Helga. "You know what? I stopped being afraid long ago. If we don't step up and stop this madness, nobody else will. And who knows how much worse it will get."

Helga needed a while to process the truth behind the words. "You're right. The Nazis have taken my family, what more can they do to me?"

"Torture and kill you," a rail-thin young woman with black hair and sparkling blue eyes said.

"Roxi, what are you doing here?" Edith asked.

Helga looked at the two women. This girl didn't look like the kind of person Edith usually associated with. "You two know each other?"

"Briefly," Roxi said.

"You shouldn't be here, it's not safe." Edith insisted.

"Because they will arrest me? As your friend so nicely put it, the Nazis have taken my entire community and now the man I love. It's become personal."

Edith shrugged, giving Helga the impression there was more to Roxi than met the eye. Since neither of them cared to elaborate, she decided not to press for answers. Some things were better left unspoken.

"Would you like a hot coffee?"

"How'd you get that?" Roxi's eyes lit up with delight.

"We came prepared with thermos bottles and lunch packages."

Meanwhile the SS had recovered from the shock of being openly defied by a bunch of housewives and drove into the narrow street in a Kübelwagen—an open-roof military vehicle with machine guns mounted on the back.

An SS man pointed his gun directly at Helga, shouting, "Leave now or we'll shoot."

Despite the icicles forming in her veins, she stood perfectly still, locking eyes with him. He was a young man, a bit younger than David. His hair was perfectly slicked back beneath his cap, exposing a clean-shaven, boyish face.

Helga was done being afraid.

Feeling the support of so many women standing behind her, she linked arms with Edith and Roxi and raised her chin. "You are murderers!"

The youngster behind the machine gun opened his mouth wide. Perhaps he was issuing a command. Perhaps he was surprised. It didn't matter. Not to Helga.

Whatever he might have wanted to say was drowned out by the crowd surrounding her and yelling, "That's what you are! Murderers! A disgrace to our nation! Give us our husbands back! Give us our children back!"

The crowd fell silent. Pure adrenaline flooded Helga's system. She seemed to hover a few inches over the ground, propelled onward by the combined power of these women, determined not to give up. Not this time. Not when it had become personal.

Tension flooded the air, billowing from wall to wall, echoing off into the sky, a long, howling expression of pain. She gazed at Edith, perceiving the same fearless resolution in her face, then at Roxi's steely expression, which hardly hid the traces of heart-wrenching grief. With these two by her side, she would not surrender.

The women seemed to be as surprised by their own violent reaction as the SS, because for a minute, nobody moved.

No one spoke a word.

Then, something unexpected happened. The soldiers

lowered their machine guns and the Kübelwagen drove away. Once the roaring vehicle disappeared around the corner, silence reigned, interrupted here and there by a few scattered sobs.

"Was that it?" Helga whispered in awe.

"I doubt it." Roxi worried her lower lip.

"For now they're gone. It's a promising development," Edith said.

"No doubt, they'll return." Helga didn't trust the Nazis as far as she could throw them.

"A war is not won with one battle alone." The wiseness of these words was amazing for a woman as young as Roxi.

"Are you going to tell me who you are?" Helga probed.

A beautiful smile lit up the younger woman's face. "I'm just another tenant in your building." Then she was gone, as suddenly and silently as she had appeared.

A tenant? Helga asked herself. She'd met all the tenants in the building at one occasion or another, and she'd certainly never come across this mysterious person. Turning to face Edith, she said, "Do you know her?"

"Actually, I do. She was the one who saved the Gerber children during the raid last year."

This statement made no sense. "She did?"

"Yes. She's been hiding in our attic."

"In our attic? And you knew about her? What if the Gestapo had found her? They'd have punished all of us! Do you have any idea how dangerous this is?"

Edith seemed to enjoy this conversation much too much, because her eyes twinkled with mischief. "Now you're talking like a good German housewife, not like the fierce woman who'd throw herself into an SS man's path to prevent him from deporting her loved ones."

Helga glared at her friend. "That's completely different."

"Is it really? Are we supposed to be loyal only to our immediate family and not care about anyone else?"

The accusation stung deep in her soul. "Of course not, but..."

"But what?"

"Hiding her in our attic is dangerous. She's a complete stranger, who's to say she's not secretly working for the Gestapo?" Helga didn't believe Roxi was capable of such a betrayal, nevertheless she hung onto every straw to justify her—admittedly shameful—opinion that hiding a stranger in need was a dangerous mistake.

"I believe your son knows her very well." Edith dragged out the word *very* in a way that made Helga flush.

David was a young man in his own right, but thinking that he and that girl engaged in... She quickly shook off the idea. In her mind he continued to be her little boy, despite his twenty-three years.

Edith seemed to read her thoughts and added, "They're both old enough. I believe at his age you already had two children."

"I actually was pregnant with my second one." Helga corrected her automatically, as if that detail made a difference. She shrugged, mulling over the new information for a while, before she said, "I guess you're right. But why does he have to endanger all of us by hiding her in our building?"

"Because he's a good man."

32

Another long day passed, followed by a restless night. David was grateful for his task as orderly, or he would have gone stir-crazy with boredom sitting around doing nothing.

His job gave him the opportunity to focus his mind on something other than the imminent danger and the horrible situation they found themselves in. And, more importantly, it allowed him to freely roam the premises, walking from room to room, checking up on his family and friends.

He'd never expected to find so many friends and acquaintances here. It seemed as if half of the remaining Jewish population was gathered in the Rosenstrasse building—the privileged half, he reminded himself. He'd witnessed the deplorable conditions in the Hermann Göring Barracks, where the full Jews had been jailed. No doubt they had been deported to some unspeakable place by now.

Despite no exact knowledge what happened in that circle of hell called Auschwitz, merely the whispered name sufficed to send shivers through the toughest of men. David surely didn't want to find out first-hand, since not a single person who'd been sent there had ever returned.

Roxi's lovely face flitted through his mind, the delicious hours they'd shared in the attic learning one another's bodies. He shrugged off the memories, praying she was safe. He trusted her cleverness to avoid all officials, a skill learned straight from the cradle. Being an outcast all her life had honed her sixth and seventh senses, enabling her to smell danger from a mile away. If she didn't want to be seen or heard, she had the eerie talent to move like a ghost among the living without leaving a trace.

He'd grappled with that trait of hers for a long time, had often cursed her for vanishing into thin air for days on end, just to rejoice when she showed up again, letting him know with a knock, a hidden leave or some other sign that she was eager to see him.

Finally, a smile broke out on his face and warmth flooded his heart. The Gestapo was no match for her stealth. They'd never find her if she didn't want to be found.

"Hey you," one of the SS men called out to David, beckoning him to approach.

"Yes, sir, what can I do for you?" Years ago, David had learned not to antagonize government officials.

"These women on the street are protesting for you."

"Yes." Since David didn't know where this conversation was going, he considered it best to appear open-minded and not to suggest anything himself, which might later be held against him.

The SS man grinned like a fool. "That's German loyalty. Really have to give them that. You have someone out there too?"

David pondered how best to respond. The SS man knew David was either a mixed bred or married to a German woman. "I should hope my mother is out there too."

"She might be. Your name's Goldmann right?"

David nodded.

"Look I shouldn't be doing this. Some of the women want to give food packages to their relatives. The one asking said her name's Goldmann."

His heart jumped with delight, yet he somehow managed to stay calm. "There are many Goldmanns."

"Never mind. I told them that they can prepare small lunch boxes and hand them over to me. No messages. No tools, knifes or anything. Just food." The SS man locked eyes with David. "You're going to search and distribute the packages for me."

"Yes, sir." David intuitively stood a bit straighter. If the Nazis allowed contact, even if only in the form of lunch packages, they probably didn't plan to kill the captives.

"If I find out you've been neglecting to remove forbidden items, I'm going to personally hand you over to the Gestapo, understood?"

"Absolutely." David's knees threatened to buckle, because that had been his plan.

"Well then. Here's the first package. It's for Heinrich Goldmann. Examine it and search for the rightful owner."

Under the SS man's scrutinizing stare, David opened the package, his heart hammering against his ribs as he unwrapped the brown paper, like he'd done a thousand times with the breaktime snacks his mother had packed for him. Inside were two simple sandwiches.

"Open it."

He did as ordered, peeling the upper side away. The luscious smell of ripe plums wafted into his nostrils. Water pooled in his mouth at the memory of his mother's trademark jam, made of plums from Aunt Feli's orchard. Fortunately, there was no hidden message inside, just the lovingly made bread with his mother's homemade jam. It was a message all by itself. *I love you. I haven't forgotten about you.*

Tears sprung to his eyes, the emotions threatening to overwhelm him. He showed the package to the man, before putting it back together with nimble fingers. "There's nothing inside."

"Alright. Find the recipient and come back for the next one."

With a spring in his step, David made his way to one of the back rooms in search of his father. He found him crouched on a straw mattress, mumbling endless numbers under his breath. It was a habit he'd adopted when bookkeeping, always prompting himself with the numbers he was about to add with his slide rule.

"Heinrich Goldmann," David said loudly. His father looked up, meeting his gaze with a question. "I have a package for you from your wife."

The brilliant smile on Heinrich's face lit up the entire room. "Thank you so much. Did you get one, too?"

"Not yet. This is the first one. Mutti put her plum jam on the sandwich." Again, David fought back the tears.

"I knew your mother would fight for us." Heinrich's expression grew wistful. "I love her so much. Not a single day went by in all these years that she wasn't my first thought in the morning and my last one at night."

David yearned to sit next to his father, sharing memories. Unfortunately he didn't have the time. "I have to get going, the officer said there are more packages and I have to distribute them all."

"Good for you. Bringing hope and love to the people in this dark place." Heinrich was visibly shaken, as he reverently broke a piece from the sandwich and offered it to David. "Here, take this."

"Thank you, Vati." David took the bread, holding it to his nose and inhaling the familiar scent until it conjured the image of his mother standing in the kitchen. She wore an apron over her dress, her dark hair tied up into a ponytail. All around her was a mess of fresh plums, cut into halves to remove the stone, sugar, and slices of apple. A sweet concoction was bubbling on the stove, soon to be poured into jam glasses.

For once eager to help, David and Amelie stood close by, secretly hoping to snatch a plum or two and taste a spoonful of the jam in the making. These were happy memories of a time long before Hitler and his cronies ruined everything. "I'll return later. Save me some."

"I will. I love you."

The rest of the afternoon David hustled up and down distributing packages to the inmates. Wherever he went people looked at him in awe, as if he were Saint Nicholas distributing gifts to the poor.

Tired and immensely happy, he decided to pass by his father for the promised piece of bread and jam before retiring to his assigned place next to Julius.

"Do you have a few minutes to sit with me?" When David nodded, Heinrich moved to make space for him. "How was your day?"

"Exhausting but good. It's so heartwarming to deliver the packages and see the joy in the recipients' faces. Honestly, I feel like Saint Nicholas."

"Although it seems these days he only brings gifts to the Christian children, letting his companion, Servant Rupert, administer whiplashes to the Jews."

The inner joy David had felt all day dissipated. "What have we ever done to deserve this?"

"Nothing. Not you or I, anyway. Probably none of the people in this detention center either. This is not about rewarding the good and punishing the bad. It's exclusively about the worldview of one man and his power to enforce it."

"We have to band together and rise up."

Heinrich cast him a sad gaze. "I believe it's too late for that. Look at how few of us are left. One of my biggest regrets in life is not to have nipped things in the bud when it was still possible. I should have protested early on, lobbied against Hitler, or at least openly voiced my criticism. Our generation has failed yours."

A wave of emotions choked David to the point that he

wasn't capable of responding. Instead, he simply leaned against his father's shoulder in silence for a few minutes, until a screeching siren pierced the air.

Bombing alarms had become a common occurrence in Berlin during the past weeks. Instead of getting used to it, David became more acutely aware of the dangers with every raid.

"What, now? Seriously?" David's eyes raced toward the exit to the basement. There was no way all the people crammed into the building would fit into the bomb-proof shelter—if there even was one.

Havoc ensued when people scrambled up, attempting to race downstairs just like David had intended to. He feared he'd be trampled to death in the stampede when a shot rang through the air and a voice bellowed, "Everyone stay in your places."

After ordering the inmates to stay put, the SS fled the building to get themselves into the safety of a nearby shelter. With the windows nailed down, they locked the men and women inside, helplessly exposed to the British bombers.

"Oh my God, they're leaving us in here to die," someone howled.

"Wasn't that their plan from the beginning?"

"Hoping the Tommies will do their dirty work for them."

David himself was torn between horrible fear of a direct hit and the hope that the English bombs would finish off the German government as well as anyone who supported it.

"But what can we do?"

Heinrich's voice cut through the noise. "There's nothing we can do but calm down and pray."

One man shouted, "I'm not going to be a sitting duck!" He got up and walked over to the window, smashing the glass and fiercely jiggling the thick planks nailed across the frame from the outside. After several unsuccessful tries, he screamed in frustration and returned to his place, his hands bloodied from shards and splinters.

David inwardly shook his head at such a waste of energy. Even with a crowbar it would be almost impossible to break through. A loud explosion interrupted his thoughts. Instinctively he covered his tingling ears with his hands; from experience he knew that more bombs would follow.

His father snuggled tighter against him, putting an arm around his shoulders, like he'd done so many times when David was a child.

"I'm afraid," David admitted.

"Me too."

Another bone-chilling screech passed above them, followed by a dull thud. The old building shook and shuddered, as if it wanted to get rid of annoying bugs. Plaster fluttered from the ceiling, settling on the heads and shoulders of the people crouched on the floor. A terrifying thought struck David. "Amelie. She's up on the second floor."

He was already scrambling to his feet, but his father held him back. "Don't. You can't do anything for her."

"I must at least try." He was desperate to rush upstairs to protect his little sister.

"Believe me, I'd rush up in an instant myself if I believed it would have any effect beyond exposing ourselves to snitches."

"How can you think of being ratted out by someone when Amelie is up there, in danger of being hit by a bomb?" David gritted his teeth to keep the boiling rage at bay.

Heinrich sighed. "If a bomb hits this building, we're all dead, regardless of which floor we're on. The only chance for survival is in the basement, but the SS have sealed it so nobody can escape."

A hot, raging fury snaked up David's spine, threatening to overwhelm him, lashing out at anyone who happened to be within distance.

"Breathe and pray," Heinrich said, knowing his son all too well.

"I'm not religious, remember?" David spat, fighting hard to regain self-control. Being Jewish was the reason for the harassment he suffered and he surely wasn't going to pray to a God who allowed his people to be persecuted in such a cruel way. Neither did he want to worship a God who encouraged his followers to torture members of a different religion or race.

His stint in the Zionist training farm had taught him that faith never offered a solution, since most Zionists burned with hatred and the need for revenge. No, he was done with religion once and for all.

"Then think of someone you love. It will help you to keep things in perspective." Again, Heinrich's face took on a dreamy expression, which was quite incongruous amid this bedlam. Without a shadow of doubt, he must be thinking about Helga.

"You know, sometimes I'm jealous of you and Mutti," David admitted.

"As a young boy you once told me that you were going to marry your mother as soon as I died, so you could protect her."

Shame washed down David's spine. "Goodness, I didn't mean to..."

"I know." Heinrich patted his hand, just to squeeze it painfully hard when another blast shook the very foundations of the building. "You were maybe four years old."

David puffed out a breath to clear his nose from the dust and debris thickening the air. "The two of you love each other so much."

"We love Amelie and you as much, or maybe more, just in a different way. When you were children, Helga loved both of you to bits. Now that you're grown up, she does her best to give you the freedom you need. As parents we will always love you, but we also know that one day in the not-so-distant future you will leave our house to start your own family with a girl you love. That's just the way life works." Heinrich scrutinized David's face. "What happened with Thea, by the way?"

"Thea?" An acute pain stabbed his insides. He'd been deeply, madly in love with her, whereas she'd considered him merely a convenient diversion. Soon after he'd moved to the training farm in Luckenwalde, she'd made out with another man behind his back. He had never confessed to anyone, not even Amelie, his utter heartbreak.

"She and I broke up when I went to the Zionist camp, because she didn't want to move to Palestine."

"What a shame. She's such a polite and well-mannered girl, and good-looking too." Heinrich winked at him.

"It simply didn't work out with us." He wasn't going to badmouth Thea by telling his father that her lovely façade didn't measure up with her selfish interior. She could be kind and generous, but only if it suited her own goals. In Thea's life she always came first; others were merely a means to reach whatever her heart desired.

Deep inside, his stomach fluttered thinking of Roxi, who was the complete opposite to Thea, both in looks and in character. Roxi had never expected anything from him; in fact she'd been rather reluctant to accept his help, since she was so fiercely independent. She'd never promised anything either, nonetheless she'd been incredibly generous even to the point of endangering herself by hiding the Gerber children.

The glow of the fiercely blazing buildings in the neighborhood penetrated the slats and illuminated the room as bright as day. Another ear-splitting blast crowded everything out of his mind as he prayed—to a God he didn't genuinely believe in—to save his and his father's life.

"Do you think Mutti is in a shelter?" he asked when the ground finally stopped shaking.

Coughing plaster, dust and debris from his mouth, Heinrich seemed to crumble with sorrow. "I wouldn't put it past her to stand outside right now, defying not only the Nazis but the Allies as well." A trace of happiness dislodged the sadness and he continued. "That's why I love her so much, although, believe me, she drives me out of my mind with her stubborn determination to stick with me against all odds."

"What else is she supposed to do? You're her husband, after all."

"I told her in no uncertain terms to divorce me to save herself and you children."

David gasped. He'd never considered the difficulties of living in a mixed marriage. "What did she tell you?"

Heinrich laughed. "She was close to stoning me for even suggesting she should choose between her children and her husband."

"That does sound like Mutti." David bore his eyes deep into his father's. "Whatever it's worth: Despite the circumstances, I could never have wished for better parents than you."

His father's eyes became misty. Another, more distant explosion saved him from having to answer. "It looks like the Tommies are done for tonight."

"I hope so. It's a strange feeling. Obviously I want them to win and kill all the Nazis they can, but I sure don't want to become collateral damage."

"I can relate."

In the wee hours of the morning, the air raid stopped as suddenly as it had started, leaving only the stink of sulfur and burned flesh hanging heavily in the air. David returned to Julius' side, hoping to get a wink of sleep before he got up in the morning to distribute packages of love and hope to the inmates awaiting their fates.

33

The Rosenstrasse women organized taking turns, so the building was never unguarded, but each one of them would have time to shop for groceries, go to work, or sleep. On the third day, Edith prepared breakfast, inwardly recoiling as she looked at the forlorn table, set for two instead of six.

Even half a year ago the apartment had been filled with life, hosting three families plus one former ballerina turned maid. The three Gerber children ran around, noisy and dirty, the way children were. A tear slipped from her eyes as she remembered how often she'd scolded them to be quiet because one or another member of the household needed to get a wink of sleep after a nightshift.

What would she give now to hear their fresh voices in the tomblike silence that had settled over the apartment. Neither she nor Helga were in the mood or condition to talk much after completing their turn in the Rosenstrasse, chilled to the bone by the icy temperatures and hoarse from chanting.

A big sigh erupted from her chest, as she pondered how long they might uphold the protest. Would the Gestapo be right in their assessment that the crowd would soon grow tired of shouting and disperse? She hoped not.

After a silent breakfast, she and Helga wrapped themselves in their warmest coats, an extra pair of socks, gloves and woolen scarves. At least their families were somewhat sheltered inside the building, since they had to make do with flimsy jackets after the Nazis had stolen the winter clothing from the Jews.

Her heart painfully squeezed thinking of Julius' rheumatic knees, because she was sure that the Nazis wouldn't provide their prisoners with a bed and eiderdown, and most certainly they wouldn't waste precious coal on heating either.

"Ready to take on another day?" Helga asked.

"I am." Just when they stepped out of the apartment in the now deserted building, she heard heavy footfalls stomping up the stairs.

"I pray it's neither the SS nor the Gestapo," Helga whispered, her face pale beneath her pugnacious expression.

"You think they've followed us home and are now going to arrest us?"

"I wouldn't put it past them to get rid of the protesters in such a clandestine way."

"Well, here he comes," Edith stated dryly as she spotted the field-gray Wehrmacht uniform.

"Good morning, Edith," the man said. The unexpected greeting caused her to stumble, and she would have tumbled down the stairs if he hadn't jumped to catch her.

"Knut!"

He smiled ruefully. "Did I scare you? I should have announced my visit, but since you don't own a telephone..." Jews had been forced to turn in their telephones some time ago.

"It's just... yes, you almost gave me a heart attack," Edith said, hugging her brother. "What brings you here?"

"I heard about the Rosenstrasse protests."

"You did?"

"Despite Goebbels' best efforts at censorship, everyone in Berlin must have heard about it by now. You know how fast gossip travels through the grapevine. This is something people can identify with. Respectable German wives fighting for their families."

"Actually, we were just on our way there," Helga joined the conversation.

"I hope you didn't come to talk me out of it. Julius is being held there, as is Helga's family." Edith steeled herself for an argument with her brother, preparing to rebut any point he'd throw at her.

Much to her surprise, he broke out in a boyish grin. "Would it help?"

"No."

"I know, so I came to protect you." He exaggeratedly put up his hands in defense.

"Protect me from what?"

"From getting harmed. I have it on good authority that Hitler has instructed Goebbels to stop that protest, albeit without risking a public scandal. I believe the tactic is to scare you women shitless." Perceiving her raised eyebrow, he quickly added a mumbled "sorry," before he continued. "They think they can just wave a few machines guns in your faces and you'll rush away to never return."

"They tried that already. It didn't work." Edith bit on her lip, remembering how afraid she had been.

"Well, in any case, I'll come with you. They won't dare to shoot at me in uniform."

"Are you sure this is a good idea? Won't you get into trouble?" Helga asked.

"I don't care if this does get me into trouble," he told her with a wry twist of his mouth. "Edith is my sister and I'm going to make sure she doesn't get harmed. So, let's go, ladies."

On the suburban train, another surprise awaited them. As

they got ready to disembark, the conductor announced, "Attention, please. This train will not stop at Börse. All passengers headed for the stock exchange will need to continue to the next station..."

"I can't believe they closed down the station," Edith said.

"It's standard procedure to prevent too many people gathering in one place, especially when the government expects some kind of trouble."

"We're definitely going to raise hell."

At the sight of Helga's rebellious expression, Edith had to bite back a giggle.

"We'll walk from the next station, it's less than ten minutes." Edith was already figuring out the shortest route in her mind. After losing their car and then moving to the city apartment, she'd grown adept at finding her way around the city center.

Helga, however, was seething. "Those damn rats. I've half a mind to scratch out the eyes of any SS man who gets in my way."

Her outburst caught the attention of a small group of women standing next to them in the crowded wagon. "Excuse me, are you by any chance headed to the Rosenstrasse?"

Edith shot a warning gaze at Helga, then answered with a question of her own. "Why would you want to know?"

"My sister and I..." The woman paused, clearly intimidated. "See, we believe our brother-in-law is being kept there."

"Is he a Jew?"

"Yes." The stranger's whisper was barely audible.

"The privileged Jews are held there, all others have been sent to different holding centers."

"He's married to our other sister," the stranger responded. "We want to help." It was as if someone had switched on the sunlight in the wagon. Other Aryans were coming to stand up for their Jewish relatives. A rush of euphoria coursed through her veins and she suddenly felt certain that Julius would cheat death once more. The Nazis would have to give in and let the Rosenstrasse inmates go free. They were too afraid of public opinion.

"You can come with us, we're headed there," Edith offered as the train pulled into the next station.

"Thank you so much. I'm Emma Dirkens, by the way." They didn't get the opportunity to shake hands, because the crowd was pushing through the doors and out into the street.

Edith craned her neck, trying to orientate herself, though she oughtn't have worried because, apart from a few stragglers, every disembarking passenger was heading in the same direction, which incidentally was where she presumed the Rosenstrasse building lay.

As they followed the procession, Edith introduced herself. "I'm Edith Falkenstein, and this is my friend Helga Goldmann. We're both married to Jews."

"You are two very brave women. I know what my sister is going through."

Biting her lip, Edith kept walking at a brisk pace. She turned her head to look at the stranger. "Why are you doing this? You must be aware it's dangerous."

"It's... we've kept silent much too long. They took our neighbors and friends and acquaintances. We don't want them to take our family as well."

Edith nodded, tears welling up in her eyes. Apart from Knut, nobody in her family seemed to spare a thought for her well-being, much less Julius'.

As they reached the Rosenstrasse, Edith gasped. "There are hundreds of people! At least twice as many than when we left last night."

"And none of them looks as if they're about to be scared away," Helga added.

"It's high time someone stood up to Hitler." Knut marched next to her.

"I thought you were fully behind his ideas, given the career you've made for yourself in the Abwehr." Edith tried to keep the trace of accusation out of her voice.

Knut bent forward and put his lips next to her ear, so nobody could eavesdrop. "Would you be surprised if I told you not all is what it seems?"

It was such a jaw-dropping revelation, Edith was stunned into silence. Her little brother, who'd always been pliable, rarely putting up a fight, was standing in the first row, protesting the arrest of Jewish people and hinting at rebellion.

After hours of chanting, linking arms, and sharing a thermos with hot coffee and cheese sandwiches, Edith observed an elegant woman stepping into the road. She was wearing her pitch-black hair in a modern pixie style and was wrapped in an absolutely stunning white mink coat of the finest quality—Edith had seen many of these coats during her marriage to Julius Falkenstein—combined with a matching hat, a brown leather handbag and gloves.

It wasn't her exquisite clothes, though, which took Edith's breath away, but the precious party badge awarded only to the longest-standing members of the NSDAP. If Knut had been brave coming here in uniform, this woman was the epitome of... what? Courage? Insanity? Humanity? Edith elbowed Knut. "What could she possibly want here? A party member of the first hour?"

Knut shrugged. "Beats me. Whatever her motive, it's a brave act of defiance."

Beside her, Helga gasped and frantically waved at the fur-clad lady, shouting, "Felicitas! Over here!"

"You know that woman?" Edith asked in awe.

"She's my sister. Felicitas Ritter, widow to Oranienburg's mayor, Ernst Ritter."

While Felicitas Ritter weaved her way through the crowd, Edith muttered, "But... she's... she wears... the party *Bonbon*."

"Despite being a Nazi she loves Heinrich and the children, and she has always come through for me and my family."

"Helga! When the radio announced some minor issues surrounding the arrest of privileged Jews, I rushed to your house, but nobody was there." Felicitas glared at her sister. "I have to come all the way here, by public transport no less, to find out this is a veritable protest and you're in the thick of it."

"I'm sorry." Helga's face was a grimace of misery.

"Why didn't you tell me? Didn't you know I would support you?"

"We didn't plan this protest, it just kind of happened."

"Well, now I'm here." The next moment Felicitas raised her fist into the air and joined the crowd chanting, "Give us our husbands back! Give us our children back!"

In a lull a few minutes later, she turned and fixed her gaze on Edith. "You must be Edith Falkenstein. Helga has talked so much about you, it's a pleasure to finally meet you."

"The pleasure is all mine." Edith didn't mention that they'd met on several occasions about a decade earlier, because she didn't want to embarrass the other woman. "We're grateful for all the support we can get."

Then she proceeded to introduce Knut. Even out on the street, protesting against the government, there was no need to forget manners. "This is my brother, Knut Hesse. He works for the Abwehr."

Felicitas held out her leather-gloved hand for him to shake. "We're so thankful for your service."

Helga rolled her eyes. "Do stop it, will you?"

"What? Our heroic soldiers protect us from the Slavic barbarians as well as the British child murderers."

Helga shook her head and whispered softly enough so only Edith heard, "I love her to bits, but I have no idea how an intelligent person like her can buy into Hitler's narrative of foreign countries attacking us and not vice versa."

It was a question Edith had often pondered herself since her family had bluntly declared that Julius, a man they'd liked and admired for many years, was to be eradicated because his Jewishness alone made him the root of all evil. "I guess we will never comprehend."

"In any case, I'm grateful for her support. But how can she believe Jews are bad while at the same time adoring Heinrich and her niece and nephew?"

"People are very good at compartmentalizing." Edith had been reading up on psychological behavior even before Hitler came to power. It had helped her to foment fruitful relationships with people in the society, where everything seemed to be driven by business interests rather than genuine affection. "They can absolutely believe one thing and still do the opposite, because subconsciously they believe they're exempt from certain rules. Just think of the Catholic Church torturing women believed to be witches while at the same time preaching to love thy neighbor as you love yourself."

Knut overheard her last remark and joined the conversation with a surprisingly bitter undertone. "Bigotry is rampant."

Edith had the impression there was more to his outburst than met the eye. "I need something to eat, will you accompany me to a café around the corner?"

"Sure. Shall we get you something?" he asked Helga and Felicitas.

"That's very kind of you, but we'll go for a snack after you return," Felicitas said with a pleasant smile.

"Alright. See you later." Edith's feet were numb with cold and her fingers stiff, ever since she'd drunk the last drop of hot Ersatzkaffee an hour ago. Though that wasn't the main reason she wanted to go the café; she needed to talk to Knut in private.

"My treat," he said as he ordered hot coffee and buns, handing over his ration booklet to the sales woman.

"Thank you." She wrapped her hand around the cup, feeling the warmth seeping back into her body, and wiggling her toes in the shoes. "How are things with you?"

"Me?" Knut hedged. "Nothing special."

"Why are you working with the Abwehr if you don't condone Hitler's actions?" Her gaze lingered on his face, trying to read his hidden thoughts.

He shrugged. "Because it's the best place for me to be."

She wouldn't get any answers from him by asking directly, so she decided on a more subtle approach. "Why did you come here?"

"I already told you: to prevent you from getting harmed."

"Do you really think you can do anything if the SS decides to shoot me?"

"No." He took a bite from his bun. "I'm banking on the fact they won't shoot at me in my uniform, and thus won't dare to shoot you either while I'm at your side."

"That's kind of you. I wish more people would stand up against the Nazis."

"I wish so too. They've gone too far." He lowered his voice to a barely audible whisper. "Hitler is running the country into the ground. After the defeat at Stalingrad there's no way for Germany to win this war."

Edith tore her eyes wide open. "How can you say this?"

"Because it's true." He leaned across the small table so his mouth hovered next to her ear. "We lost close to half a million men, killed or taken prisoner. At the same time the Wehrmacht is spread too thin, fighting in Africa, keeping occupied Europe under their thumb, helping out Mussolini in Italy, etcetera. There's no way we can win this war, not when America has teamed up with Russia and England."

A shimmer of hope entered her heart, giving as much

warmth as the hot beverage had. "Do you think it'll be over soon?"

"No. Hitler will fight to the last man and people will follow him. Just look at Joseph and his blind loyalty. It's been impossible to have a reasonable discussion with him for years."

Edith sighed. "I miss him. I miss the wonderful brother he used to be. The one who stood up for justice."

"He thinks what he's doing is the right thing, which is so sad." Knut looked down at his clasped hands. "He dropped you like a hot stone because you didn't divorce Julius. He'd drop me in a split second if he knew—"

Edith raised an eyebrow, wondering what dark secret Knut might harbor that would cause their older brother to turn against him. "You're not in love with a Jewess, are you?"

"Certainly not. Don't worry, nobody will ever find out."

"That does make me worry about you." She put her hand on his arm, shocked when she felt him trembling. "If I can do anything to help."

"Thanks for the offer." He chuckled. "But first, let's get your husband back."

34

To keep her hands occupied, Amelie unraveled thread from her dress and weaved it into long braids, just to unravel it again once she was done. Suddenly an SS man stomped into the room and assumed a military posture, feet hip-width apart, back straight, chin raised.

She suppressed a groan. It was the same man who'd trembled with fear during the air-raid alarm the day before.

"Who threw the subversive note out of the window?" he bellowed.

The women looked at each other, half bemused, half appalled. It was impossible to open the thoroughly nailed-shut windows.

"I'm asking for the culprits!" Spittle flew from his mouth, as his eyes roamed across the mass of destitute women. When no one moved, he stepped forward, glaring at them. "If five volunteers do not come forward by the time I count to three, I will pick the guilty ones."

Instinctively Amelie hunched her head between her shoulders, clinging to her braided threads like a lifeline.

One brave woman stood up and said, "You must know that

the accusation is completely absurd. None of us threw a note, simply because the windows are boarded up."

"You... you... insolent Jewish bitch. You'll pay for this! I won't allow you to talk to me like that." His face glowed purple, the vein in his temple pulsating ferociously. For a moment Amelie feared he was going to attack the woman, who stood there utterly calm.

Nobody came forward to plead guilty for a crime they hadn't committed, so the SS man randomly chose four more victims and forced them to follow him downstairs.

Fear froze Amelie's blood as she looked after them, walking to an unknown fate. A minute later David entered the room, a little box in his hand. "This is from Mutti."

"Thank you." Her hand was trembling so much, she dropped the package when she reached for it.

"What's wrong?" David asked. His expression grew somber as she relayed the incident. "The poor sods. I'm glad you weren't among them."

A wave of guilt washed over Amelie. "I should have done something."

"There was nothing you could do."

"You always tell me that we should band together and fight the Nazis." Amelie felt the rage inside her displacing the fear.

"True, but not while you're a prisoner in this damn building with no way to break out."

"How's Father?" She didn't want to dwell on her miserable feelings.

"Holding on. I came to tell you splendid news. You'll never guess who's out there protesting." He grinned like a maniac.

"Mutti?"

"That was an easy guess. After all, you're holding her package in your hands." He poked her in the ribs.

"Then who?"

"You have three guesses."

Amelie rolled her eyes at him. "You're such a child."

"If you don't want to know, I can always leave," he teased her.

She was too curious to let that happen, so she furrowed her brows pensively. "Hmm. Let's see." She rattled down the names that came to her mind. He shook his head, until she finally begged, "Come on, tell me."

"Aunt Feli."

"Really?"

"With fur coat, *Bonbon*, and all."

"She's wearing her party badge?" Amelie shook her head at the brazenness of her aunt. Or maybe the badge was intended as a shield if the Gestapo wanted to arrest her.

"She is. And there's someone else."

"We don't have any other relatives in Berlin." All members of Father's family had been deported the last year.

"You remember Frau Falkenstein's brother? The Abwehr officer?"

"He was at the farewell party, right?"

"Yes. He's out there wearing his uniform."

A lightness came over Amelie, pushing the fear away. "That's amazing. I'm starting to believe we might get out of here."

"We will, either way."

"I meant alive."

"I know, sis." Someone shouted from the staircase and David quickly bent forward to hug her. "I need to run. Keep the faith."

"You too. Tell Father I love him, if you happen to see him."

Then he was gone, leaving Amelie with a huge smile. Everything would work out just fine.

35

Joseph sat in a meeting room in Prinz-Albrecht-Strasse. The housewives' protest, as he and his colleagues dubbed the unpleasant demonstration, was proving to be a veritable pain in the behind.

On the first day, the SS elite had laughed about the little wives coming out of their holes to cry for their husbands. Everyone, Joseph included, had bet that the women would soon lose their courage. After standing in the icy temperatures for a few hours, everyone expected them to be too exhausted, cold and hungry to return the following day.

But the opposite had happened. The women continued to shout their demands, undeterred by the police presence. More and more relatives of the captives poured into Rosenstrasse for support. The pesky housewives organized themselves into shifts so the building was never left unguarded. In a constant ebb and flow, new demonstrators showed up, while others went away to work or run whatever other errands.

Each evening the tiny street was bursting at the seams with casual protesters dropping by after leaving work for the day. It wasn't a matter of destitute women in mixed marriages anymore. Aryan relatives and even Wehrmacht soldiers in uniform joined the protests on occasion.

On the day after the horrendous bombing attack by the British air terrorists, a few women seized the opportunity and climbed the charred remains of the walls of a bombed house on the opposite side of the street. From there they attempted to catch a glimpse of their relatives by peering into the windows of the upper floors.

"What have you done to disperse the housewives?" asked Klemps, the man from the propaganda ministry.

"We shouted orders at them, had police wave guns in their faces and fire warning shots into the air," Joseph's superior answered.

"And?"

"I'm afraid the measures taken didn't have the desired effect. The protesters rush into nearby house entrances for shelter, but as soon as our policemen stop threatening them, they're back chanting."

"Arrest them," Klemps demanded.

"We arrested approximately ten women yesterday. The others were visibly shaken, yet they still didn't budge."

"How is this possible?"

"It's definitely unprecedented." Joseph felt sorry for his superior who had to explain the irrational behavior of a bunch of females.

"This cannot be allowed to go on. We're four days into this attack on the government's authority and no end is in sight. Any suggestions?"

"Shoot them all!" Joseph's superior bellowed.

Some SS members murmured agreement, while others paled at the notion of murdering hundreds of German women, some of whom might be related to them. Even the most upright SS man might—against his will—be related to Jewish scum, as Joseph knew from first-hand experience.

Klemps shook his head. "Unfortunately, I have orders from Goebbels not to do that. He's afraid it might lead to an even greater uproar. These women are part of the German community, after all."

"They shouldn't have married a Jew then," someone mumbled.

"I agree. My biggest regret is that I couldn't convince Hitler to annul existing interracial marriages."

Joseph wheezed. Such a critical statement might be considered treason. Klemps must have realized his blunder, because he quickly added, "Our Führer had good reasons for his decision and it certainly was the best way forward."

"If intimidation doesn't work and we're not allowed to kill them, what is left?" The question hung in the room, thickening the air, all but suffocating the attendees. There was only one answer to that question, which nobody dared to voice. It was inconceivable. Akin to admitting defeat.

The heavy silence that followed pressed heavily on Joseph's lungs. He fought the urge to harrumph. He clasped his hands together, staring intently at the toecaps of his shining boots. Just when he thought he couldn't take the pressure anymore, someone said, "We could release the privileged Jews."

A fist smashed down on the table, causing everyone in the room to raise their eyes in fear.

"Impossible! Hitler wants Berlin free of Jews and we will deliver his wish," Klemps trumpeted.

The uncomfortable silence wafted through the air, touching each man with brutal intensity, until finally Joseph dared to raise his voice. "Perhaps if Goebbels was informed, he might ask our Führer for his opinion in this tricky issue, since none of us can match his providence."

Several men nodded. "Yes, our Führer will know what to do."

Klemps looked at Joseph, his brows furrowed pensively. "Sturmbannführer Hesse, is it?"

"Yes." A bad feeling gripped Joseph's gut at being singled out.

"Aren't you related to the Jew Julius Falkenstein?"

Dread crept up his spine. "Unfortunately, yes. Our entire family has disavowed him and our sister Edith many years ago."

"Well, it might be time to freshen up on your relationship with her." Klemps held a finger to his cheek.

"To what purpose?"

"Her husband is among the detainees in the Rosenstrasse and she might well be one of the protesters. She used to be very influential. If you can convince her to stop that ridiculous protest, the grapevine will do the rest."

Joseph groaned inwardly. He'd tried time and again to make his sister see reason and renounce her ill-fated marriage. He frantically racked his brain for an excuse to get out of this doomed mission. "With all due respect, I have tried countless times again and again to talk sense to her. Her only response was to stubbornly defend her husband."

"Then you'll have to do better this time." Klemps knocked on the table. "The meeting is over, we'll reconvene tomorrow morning. By then I want results."

Sweat trickled down Joseph's back. Edith wouldn't be intimidated by threats. But if he didn't deliver results... he swallowed hard, inwardly cursing his obtuse sister. Why wasn't she as sweet and pliable as their other sister, Carsta, who hadn't shed a single tear when her husband Rudolf was killed on the battlefield?

Instead, she'd praised Rudolf for his heroic death and thanked the Führer for protecting Germany from her many enemies.

"Do you want me to come with you?" Joseph's superior knew about the difficult relationship with Edith.

"No, thank you. I believe she'll be more open-minded if I appeal to her sisterly love for me."

"Clever idea. Good luck."

Edith approached the apartment building with the distinct feeling of being watched. Panic ratcheted up her pulse when she heard heavy steps behind her. Accelerating her steps she unlocked the door with trembling hands.

Just as she turned to shut the door, she saw a man in SS uniform. Fear knocked the breath out of her lungs, followed by relief when she recognized Joseph. However much he'd bought into the Nazi ideology, he wouldn't cause her physical harm. At least she hoped not.

"What are you doing here, Joseph?"

"Can I talk to you for a minute?"

"There's nothing to talk about." She made to slam the door in his face, but his reaction was too quick. His foot was in the door, keeping it ajar, before she had a chance to lock him out.

"That was not nice, Edith." The set jaw gave him a hard, even cruel, appearance and she began to doubt her assessment that he wouldn't hurt her.

"We're long past niceties."

"Really? That's your thanks for me warning you to leave the country?"

She shrugged, giving him a glance over. Their estrangement was mostly his fault—because he valued Hitler and his stupid ideas over his own sister. In any case, he looked as if he was going to force his way inside, so she let the door go. "Come in. What do you want?"

"I need to talk to you in private. It's about your husband."

"His name is Julius," she bristled.

"I need to talk to you about him," he insisted, his eyes completely devoid of emotion.

"Oh, what now? Your Gestapo friends arrested him and every other Jew in the city. He's being held in the Rosenstrasse," she quipped.

"That's the reason I'm here. Can we talk in your apartment?"

"Be my guest!" She swept her arms with a sarcastic flourish, letting him know that he was absolutely not a welcome guest. Then she climbed the stairs, not looking back to see whether he followed her or not. For all she was concerned, nothing good was going to come out of this conversation. Most likely it was another attempt to coax her into agreeing to a divorce.

As she unlocked the door to the chilly apartment, because there was neither enough money nor rations for coal to heat, she purposely made no move to offer him a drink or a seat like any polite person would do. Instead, she glared at him and demanded, "What's so important you came all the way here? In your uniform no less."

If he was insulted by her hostility, he didn't show it. "I had hoped you'd be open to reason." When she didn't even blink, he continued, "You might have heard about the unfortunate house-wives' protest in the Rosenstrasse."

"That's what you call it? May I enlighten you that those courageous women are fighting for their families? The very institution Hitler always touts as being the nucleus of the German nation?"

Joseph gave a sour smile. "So you've heard about it."

It was rather unusual for him not to rise to the bait. Whether she wanted to or not, she had to give him credit for his self-control. If only learning to keep his hot temper at bay hadn't been achieved through such horrendous circumstances.

"In fact, I have." Edith slightly bowed her head.

"I assume you're too intelligent to be involved."

"Indeed I am—involved, I mean." She gave him a sardonic smile, proud of her participation in the protests.

Joseph let out a sigh and shoved a hand through his carefully combed hair. "Apart from endangering yourself, you're shedding a bad light on the family. Has it ever occurred to you how badly this makes me look?"

"You've come all this way to tell me my actions might harm your career?" she asked sweetly, while inwardly seething. How could he bemoan the possible harm on his career when Julius was fighting for his very life? Joseph's selfishness felt like a punch to the stomach.

"Partly, yes, because everything you do reflects on me, whether you want to acknowledge that or not."

"I'm sorry for putting my husband's life ahead of your career." Her face a mask of pure innocence, she added a good measure of sarcasm to her voice.

"That's forgivable, if you find your way back to the right path. You're still an influential woman. Would you consider publicly renouncing these protests and calling for logic and reason?"

"Why should I?" She looked at him, half aghast and half bemused.

"For the good of our nation. This protest has been going on too long already, it's liable to sway public opinion in favor of the Jews, making the evacuations much more difficult." From the hard line of his mouth, Joseph was getting desperate at her being deliberately obtuse.

Edith, sensing a chink in his armor, dared to hope that perhaps not all was lost and she could still make him see reason, appeal to the humanity she knew he possessed.

"Wouldn't you reckon that's a good thing? For my part, I'd rather Julius returned home instead of being deported to some godawful place." She pointed her finger at her brother. "Deep in your heart, do you genuinely believe what the Nazis have been doing to Jews is right?"

"Of course I do. Jews are not real humans. They belong to

an inferior race, intent on destroying the Master Race, if we let them." Joseph repeated the phrases she'd read so often in official Nazi propaganda.

His assertion hit her deep in her soul, sending shivers from head to toe. She was shocked into silence by the bone-chilling realization that Joseph had turned into a veritable monster. The brother she had loved and admired for most of her life had ceased to exist. The man standing before her, claiming that Jews weren't real humans, had himself ceased to be a human being. He had traded places with a callous, heartless fiend, void of the slightest trace of empathy.

When she finally recovered her faculty of speech, she said, "You're a lunatic. How can you speak like that about Julius, whom you've known and liked for many years? Who bailed you out of prison? Who generously helped all members of our family when in need? How can you?" Exhausted, she broke off, her anger giving way to tears of despair bubbling up from deep down in her soul, because she knew with certainty that Joseph had lost any remaining sense of humanity.

"He might be one of the few rare exceptions, but since we can never know for sure, it's better to eradicate them all."

"Eradicate?" she screamed "What do you mean by this?"

Joseph visibly bit his tongue. Whatever he had been about to divulge, he wasn't supposed to share. He mumbled, "It was just an expression."

Edith looked at him, terrified and somber at once. "I don't recognize you anymore. What happened to you?"

"Nothing happened to me!" Unable to control to his temper any longer, he lashed out. "You're the one who's a disgrace to our family!"

Edith observed him for several seconds, before a surprising calm settled over her and she responded, "In fact, you're the one who's a disgrace, not only to our family but to humanity as a whole."

"Don't you dare disrespect me!" he screamed at her, his fist twitching as if he was about to smash it into her face.

"The Nazis stopped showing me respect years ago, so why should I respect them?" In contrast to her brother, Edith had found her inner peace. She was done being afraid. It was a surprisingly liberating insight. She would do whatever was needed to fight against this government, even if it cost her own life. She'd been complacent far too long.

"Because... you... I... this is all your fault! Why did you have to get married to a Jew? And why did you have to stay with him? You could have divorced him, and everyone would have been happier for it—"

"Everyone except Julius and me, who are arguably the two most important people in our marriage."

Joseph's face contorted into a grimace, showing he was holding onto a thin thread of patience. Despite the explosiveness of the situation, Edith relished the power she had over him, cracking his armor of emotionlessness.

Gnashing his teeth, he snarled, "I came here in peace. You are nothing but belligerent. Why can't you for once think about anyone besides yourself?"

"About the poor little SS soldiers perhaps, who haven't succeeded in harassing innocent housewives into submission? Am I supposed to think about them?"

Her smug grin blew a fuse in his brain. Before she was able to anticipate his reaction, he reached out and slapped her face hard enough to leave a dark red imprint of his hand.

Edith ignored the fierce burning on her cheek. She wouldn't be cowed by his physical attack, so she stood taller, her voice dripping with ice. "I'm not afraid of you, Joseph. If you've come here as an SS officer, go ahead and arrest me. But if you've come here as my brother, I expect your apology. Now."

Completely rattled by her resistance, he hesitated, apparently gauging the situation. "I'm sorry, Edith. I shouldn't have slapped you, but you were making me so angry."

She silently shook her head, not satisfied with his apology.

"Look, I'm in a very difficult situation here," he explained. "This protest has to end. The propaganda department has tasked me with enlisting your help to persuade the housewives to stop. If you talk to them, woman to woman, they might well end this little uprising." He paused for a moment, giving her the impression he wasn't being honest. "I have full authority to grant immunity to everyone who leaves the Rosenstrasse without making a fuss."

"Ach, Joseph, you severely overestimate my leverage and underestimate the determination of these women. Every one of us is ready to fight until our last breath for what is most important to us: our families. If Hitler insists on taking from us those we love most, I won't be the only one who'd rather die than comply."

"You can't be serious." His jaw dropped at her bold statement.

"I am. Just like the Wehrmacht soldiers go into battle, ready to die for their Fatherland, we are ready to die for our families." She put a gloved hand on his arm. "If there's still kindness in your soul, go back to your superiors and tell them to release our loved ones, because we will never stop protesting."

But there was no kindness left in Joseph. His face transformed into a steely mask, devoid of any kind of emotion. "I'm sorry you feel this way, Edith. If you don't help me to end this protest, I'll make sure your husband will be the first one to be deported." Then he clicked his heels and shouted, "Heil Hitler!"

A second later he had vanished, leaving Edith shattered to the core.

THE NEXT DAY

Early in the morning an SS man strode into the room and hollered, "Julius Falkenstein."

Julius flinched, looking toward David sitting next to him. Since the young man had taken on duties as orderly, Julius relied on his judgment.

"I guess you'll have to go and see. They called you by name." David shrugged. "Pretending you didn't hear will only make it worse."

"You're probably right." Julius steeled himself for the worst as he acknowledged his presence and made to scramble upright. After sleeping all night on the hard, damp mattress in the unheated room, his limbs were stiff and his rheumatism acting up.

The SS man made no attempt to help and neither did any of the other inmates for fear of feeling the butt end of a rifle if they moved. Somehow Julius managed to get up and walk toward the entrance, though every cell in his body was filled with a leaden dread.

"Follow me." The SS man led the way to the office. At the threshold, he clicked his heels, and announced, "Julius Falkenstein is here." Then he turned around and left, leaving Julius to his own devices.

"Don't dawdle, I don't have all day," the commanding officer huffed.

Julius' mind swarmed with ghastly images of him working in a quarry, lashed by the Gestapo or dying from starvation. Regret stabbed him like a red-hot rod. Why on earth hadn't he listened to Edith and emigrated in the 1930s? He'd now be sitting in a beautiful country mansion in England, reading about the horrors in Germany in the newspaper.

He swallowed his fear and stepped into the office, hesitantly approaching the desk, behind which the officer throned. Through the window behind him, rays of winter sunlight streamed inside, painting a halo around his head. It conjured up a perverse image in Julius' brain. The officer was as far away from being the Savior as the snake in paradise.

"You need to sign here and here." He pushed a few papers over to Julius.

True to his upbringing, Julius diligently read the papers he was supposed to sign, until the officer lost patience and snapped, "Sign this, alright. Or do you want to stay here?"

Emboldened by the possibility of signing his own death warrant, Julius gathered the nerve to ask, "What is this, if I may ask?"

"Your discharge papers, stupid Jew! If you want to be released, don't ask questions, or I'll change my mind and have you deported."

Relief vying with suspicion, Julius concluded that, with or without his signature, the SS was going to do with him as they wished. So he took the pencil lying on the desk and signed with what he hoped was a confident stroke, despite his trembling hands.

"There you go." The officer stamped the discharge paper,

handed it back to Julius and added, "Present yourself at the labor office tomorrow morning to be assigned a new job."

For a lack of anything better to say, Julius responded with, "Thank you."

"Now, get out of my sight."

As he exited the office, a long queue of waiting men was forming, all of them observing him with fearful eyes.

"They released me," Julius said, relying on the Jewish *Mundfunk*, the rumor mill, to spread the news throughout the building in no time at all. Prodded onward by another guard, Julius didn't get the chance to return to his spot and say goodbye to David. He sent a prayer to heaven that the entire Goldmann family would soon be released as well and they'd all reunite at home.

That same evening, Julius opened the last bottle of a vintage Bordeaux wine from his hidden stash in the attic to celebrate their freedom. Around the table sat Helga, Heinrich, David, Amelie and Edith.

"We, along with everyone else held captive in the Rosenstrasse, have been very lucky. We owe our freedom, our lives, to the courageous protests of our wives!" he toasted, kissing Edith on the lips.

At first she shrank back, because he'd never kissed her in the presence of others. Then she returned his kiss, leaning into his embrace. "I'm so glad you're back."

"Me too, my darling." He smiled at her.

"I already saw myself on a train to the East," Heinrich admitted as he wrapped his arm around Helga. "We are so blessed to have you."

"Thanks, Mutti, and thanks Frau Falkenstein," Amelie said. "The rumors in there were running wild, but the moment we heard women out there demanding to get their families back, I knew we'd survive."

"Really? I always feared the Nazis would simply shoot the protesters." David hungrily eyed the food on the table.

"They certainly threatened to do so. They fired shots on several occasions, although I got the impression the SS didn't actually want to kill good German housewives. Nobody got hurt." Helga's face showed the exhaustion of too little sleep and too much excitement over the course of the past week.

"I feel so guilty I couldn't get to Silvana and Markus before they were deported. They must believe I abandoned them," Edith admitted, full of guilt.

"Don't ever think this way. You did everything you could," Julius tried to reassure her. But he understood the sentiment, because he, too, was stricken with guilt about being safe while his beloved sister had been sent away to face an unknown fate.

He'd been clinging to the notion that the rumors were just that, though deep in his soul he knew that everyone going on transport was going to face unspeakable horrors. If only she'd followed their other sister Adriana to London when it was still possible.

He raised his glass again. "I want to remember those who can't be here with us. My sister Silvana and Markus, the Gerbers and their children, Delia, along with so many others of our friends and relatives. May each one of them find the strength to endure the fate which is awaiting them. My biggest hope is to see them again after all this is over."

Personally, he had lost his illusions about the Nazis' intentions regarding Jews, yet he wasn't willing to give up hope. If not in this life, then at least in the next one, he yearned to see his sister again.

"To everyone we love and have loved during our lives," Heinrich added.

Everyone drank from their wine glass. The liberation of the

Rosenstrasse inmates had been an unexpected victory, but they knew it would not change the Nazis' policies going forward. They had lived through too many horrors since Hitler had come to power. As long as he existed, Jews would be hunted, harassed, deported, and killed.

Edith nudged him. "What are you thinking?"

"I wish I had listened to you and emigrated years ago."

"Me too." Her voice was laced with sadness, indicating she derived no enjoyment from having been right under the circumstances. "If it makes you feel any better. I never imagined it getting as bad as it is."

"No more moping around," Heinrich said with a strong voice. "We're here to celebrate that we're still alive and together."

Helga smiled. "As long as we stand up for each other, we'll survive this. News from the front is encouraging. Germany will lose this war, sooner or later, then we can recover what is left of our lives."

"What is next?" Amelie asked with a small voice.

"In the morning the labor office will assign each of us a new workplace," Julius said.

David stomped his feet. "Nazi scum! Of course they won't let us return to our previous workplace for fear our colleagues will learn what happened and side with us."

Julius suspected that David had not only loved his job at the workshop but had also somehow used his position there to hide illegals. "It is what it is. That doesn't mean you have to stop doing good."

Helga's eyes opened wide and she fixed her son with a stern expression. "Am I the only person in this household who didn't know about your clandestine activities?"

Flushing under her gaze, David mumbled, "I didn't want you to worry."

"You risk everyone's lives hiding people in our attic and tell me not to worry!" Helga was practically screeching.

While poor David seemed to shrink under her scolding, Amelie squared her shoulders, defending her brother. "We should follow his example and help where we can. Just look where turning a blind eye has got us."

That was an argument nobody could refute. After a long silence, Julius spoke: "Perhaps there's truth in her words and we old people can learn something from the recklessness of the youth."

Helga glared at him for a moment, then hunched her shoulders as guilt entered her eyes. "I guess we should. I'm just not brave enough."

"You're incredibly brave." Heinrich squeezed her hand. "Without you, Edith, and the other women out there protesting, none of us would be here."

"But... you're my family... you're everything I have. It's easy to be brave when your family's lives are at stake."

Much to everyone's surprise, the usually quiet Edith spoke up. "Helping others is the right thing to do. If everyone only fights for their relatives, the Nazis have an easy game. From now on I will do everything I can to resist the government." She looked directly at David. "Please count me as supporter of your clandestine network."

David gasped. "There's not really a network. I've mostly been working alone."

"Well, I'd say then it's about time to start one," Julius suggested.

Together they would survive the Nazi regime and rescue as many others as possible.

A LETTER FROM MARION

Dear Reader,

Thank you so much for reading *The Berlin Wife's Resistance*. If you enjoyed it, and want to keep up to date with all my latest releases, just sign up at the following link. Your email address will never be shared and you can unsubscribe at any time.

www.bookouture.com/marion-kummerow

Thank you so much for accompanying me and my protagonists, the Falkensteins, the Goldmanns, the Lembergs, and the Gerbers on their journey through the Third Reich.

For now, most of them are safe, released from the Rosenstrasse holding camp by the courageous actions of their relatives. There will be one more book in the German Wives series, which will take us all the way to the end of the war.

When I first read about the Rosenstrasse protest, I was instantly intrigued. It was the only time that Germans publicly protested against the Nazi regime—and were successful. Of course, there had been other types of resistance: sabotage of war production, assassination attempts, resistance organizations spiriting endangered people out of Germany.

Yet, the Rosenstrasse protest was the only public, out-in-the-open, mass demonstration against Nazi policies. For an entire week around six hundred people, mostly women, protested in front of the building, day and night. In the end they were successful, and their loved ones were liberated.

Up to this day, historians disagree on whether Jews in mixed marriages were indeed destined for deportation or were going to be held indefinitely in the Rosenstrasse. In my opinion, it doesn't matter. Women like Helga and Edith didn't know and were, rightly, worried. It is a testament to their courage and determination to defy the Nazis, the SS soldiers, the machine guns, even the Allied bombs, to stand by their families.

Twenty-five Rosenstrasse inmates were sent to Monowitz, one of Auschwitz's sub-camps. In an unprecedented move, all of them—except for one who died during transport—were returned to Berlin after a few weeks. Due to the secrecy surrounding the extermination camps, they were not released but imprisoned near Berlin, where most of them survived the war.

If you're interested to learn more about the real event, I recommend Nathan Stoltzfus' non-fiction book *Resistance of the Heart*. Several of the anecdotes in *The Berlin Wife's Resistance* have been inspired by eyewitness interviews in his book and elsewhere.

Early in this novel, Julius and Edith are turned away at the border. I don't know whether this actually happened to anyone. The fact is, on October 23, 1941, the Nazis issued a decree prohibiting Jews from leaving the country. I couldn't find out whether this applied to people who'd already been issued a visa and a leaving permit, or just for new applicants.

One of the more devious laws, justified by the supposed threat to public hygiene, was the decree to kill all pets belonging to Jewish households. Heartbreaking scenes happened in the queues of the people lining up to give their beloved animals away.

The obvious choice for our protagonists would have been a cat or dog. I chose rabbits in honor of my grandmother, who kept angora rabbits in her garden during and after the war. She lived in a small agricultural town, spun fine wool from the rabbit's fur and then offered to knit baby clothing for the regional farmers in exchange for milk and food for her toddler.

Joseph's role in the book has diminished for the simple reason that he's become so appalling. I literally didn't want to write from his point of view anymore. The visit with Edith to convince her to stop protesting marks the moment when the very last shred of his humanity is stripped away and he has truly turned into a monster.

When Helga takes the Gerber children to the Lembergs, Silvana mentions a Swedish pastor. In reality, his name was Birger Forell and he was the pastor of the Swedish church in Berlin, where he ran a vast network of helpers to hide illegals and spirit them out of the country.

In April 1942, he was forced to leave Germany, having been declared an "undesirable person" by the Nazis. Forell appointed as his successor Erik Perwe, who expanded the underground network, tirelessly working to help Jews and other illegals. He died in November 1944 when his plane crashed into the Baltic Sea on a trip home to Malmö in Sweden. Rumors abound that his death wasn't an accident, which has never been proven.

Roxana, or Roxi, showed up out of nowhere, demanding to be part of the story. She came to my mind the same way as I describe her in the book: mysterious, stealthy and close-lipped. I still don't know very much about her and am looking forward to finding out what she and David are up to in the next book in the German Wives series.

Once again, thank you so much for reading *The Berlin Wife's Resistance*.

Marion Kummerow

KEEP IN TOUCH WITH MARION

www.kummerow.info

facebook.com/AutorinKummerow

x.com/MarionKummerow

instagram.com/MarionKummerow

goodreads.com/MarionKummerow

PUBLISHING TEAM

Turning a manuscript into a book requires the efforts of many people. The publishing team at Bookouture would like to acknowledge everyone who contributed to this publication.

Audio
Alba Proko
Sinead O'Connor
Melissa Tran

Commercial
Lauren Morrissette
Jil Thielen
Imogen Allport

Data and analysis
Mark Alder
Mohamed Bussuri

Cover design
Jo Thomson

Editorial
Jayne Osborne
Imogen Allport

Made in United States
Troutdale, OR
03/14/2024

18451321R00170